Penguin Books

OCTAGON

Fred Saberhagen has had some forty short stories and more than twenty books published since he began writing professionally in 1960. Before then he spent four years in the U.S. Air Force and worked as an electronics technician and at a variety of other jobs. In the late sixties and early seventies he wrote on scientific and technological subjects for the *Encyclopaedia Britannica*. He enjoys travel and does sporadic maintenance jobs on his own house. Once a serious student of karate, he now engages in nothing more violent than an occasional science-fiction convention or chess tournament.

Fred Saberhagen

OCTAGON

PENGUIN BOOKS

Penguin Books Ltd, Harmondsworth, Middlesex, England
Viking Penguin Inc., 40 West 23rd Street, New York, New York 10010, U.S.A.
Penguin Books Australia Ltd, Ringwood, Victoria, Australia
Penguin Books Canada Ltd, 2801 John Street, Markham, Ontario, Canada L3R 1B4
Penguin Books (N.Z.) Ltd, 182–190 Wairau Road, Auckland 10, New Zealand

First published in the U.S.A. by Ace Books 1981
Published in Penguin Books 1985

Made and printed in Great Britain by
Cox & Wyman Ltd, Reading

Typeset in Times

Author's Note

Starweb is a real game, played pretty much as described in the story. It is the property of Flying Buffalo, Inc., of Arizona. The company called Berserkers Inc. is fictional, as are all the people in this book. None are intended to resemble real persons, particularly not the people of the Flying Buffalo or any of the players in the games there moderated.

But, at this writing, the computers and most of the other hardware in this book are real, or very nearly so. Like it or not.

—Fred Saberhagen
Albuquerque, New Mexico

ONE

Next time, he might be a Pirate.

Or maybe the Mad Scientist.

Not a Berserker, Carl Tartaglia told himself thoughtfully. For him there was something repulsive in that dark concept, even if it was all in fun, only a game.

The Artifact Collector, maybe? But it seemed to him, novice that he was, that winning the game with that character type would be very difficult; a successful character needed some type of extra ability, which the Collector just didn't have. But maybe the time after next—Tartaglia already liked the game so well that he was sure he was going to play again and again—he'd try being a Collector, just to see what it was like.

This game he was in right now was twenty turns along with no end in sight, and it was Tartaglia's first experience with Starweb, and he was having a ball, being an Empire Builder, which other players had told him was a good choice for beginners. The EB gained points simply by owning worlds and factories and population units. It had seemed to Tartaglia after a determined study of the rules, that the Empire Builder must be one of the most likely character types to win. In fact the only thing that bothered him at all about Empire-Building was that maybe it was just a shade too much like selling housewares, a neat and orderly way to make a modest income, and God knew he got enough of that eight hours a day

1

anyway. That was why Tartaglia hadn't even considered taking the Merchant character in the game.

Delia's recent departure, with substantial baggage, had had both its bad points and its good, from Tartaglia's point of view. One of the positive aspects was that he could now let all his game paraphernalia sprawl and expand all over the apartment just as he pleased. The floor of the spare bedroom still had Diplomacy laid out on it, from last Friday when the guys were over. They meant to resume it one of these evenings when they could all get together again. And now Tartaglia's Starweb map, a home-made construction, dominated the center of the floor in the living-dining area, with the table nudged over by about a foot to give it room. Surrounding the map on the floor were stacks of papers, notes and folders and envelopes, all useful in keeping track of the game's complexities. Of course the moderators, who had to deal with all the players' moves simultaneously, used a computer in their office to calculate the result and print it out. Tartaglia was beginning to yearn for a little home computer of his own, which he supposed would offer a much neater and more efficient way of keeping track of what was going on. Maybe he would really try to get one, someday, when they had come down even more in price . . .

Tartaglia had hand-drawn the map himself, on a rather expensive sheet of special game paper. It was about four feet square and printed with hexagonal spaces. He had scrounged up a large scrap of smooth, thin plywood to put under the map to provide a surface for drawing and writing on. Colored hexes on the map represented the worlds in the game, or at least the ones that Tartaglia's enterprising space-fleets had occupied, or visited or probed. The explored area of a couple of dozen marked hexes, centered on his original homeworld, was surrounded by blank space. Out there were more worlds to be discovered—unknown territories, the domains of other players, some still unknown even by their code names to Tartaglia. Pirates, Berserkers, Mad Scientists, other Empire Builders, who knew what. Of the other players whose fleets and worlds he had encountered on the printouts, the code names were all he knew of most.

Near the upper right-hand corner of the map, Tartaglia's diplomatic envelopes awaited his attention in a neat stack—you had to have *some* organization about *some* part of your life. Each envelope was marked with one other player's code name, and contained all the messages that had come from that player to Tartaglia, as well as copies of whatever Tartaglia had sent out in return. He had realized from the start that to play this you would have to be methodical.

Not far from the small stack of diplomatic envelopes lay the rules booklet, forty well-thumbed, closely printed pages ready for consultation. Close to the booklet a pile of computer print-out sheets, one sheet for each past turn of the game, showed its progress from the viewpoint of Tartaglia's character.

And then there was the pile of Tartaglia's previous move-sheets, orders he had written to be fed by the moderators into their computer, and which were then returned to him by mail. And then the set of little plastic bins, used by Tartaglia to hold supplies of the various counters, bits of wood and plastic recruited from other games, that Tartaglia was using on the map to represent his fleets and industries and populations and sources of raw material.

All in all, Starweb was fun. Tartaglia considered it to be by a considerable margin the most fascinating game he had encountered yet. And now no one else was around to walk on it and grumble about its litter. Being able to let it expand across the apartment this way gave a sensation somewhat akin to that of loosening a too-tight belt: you were too fat, you were a slob whose wife had left him. But there was a certain comfort in being able to relax with the fact.

Immediately on getting home from work tonight Tartaglia had broiled himself a small steak, and had thawed out some french fries in the oven. When he had opened a can of Coors, and another of green peas, dinner was ready. Soon he had it out of the way, along with a few cleanup chores, necessary to keep the roaches from gaining too great a foothold in the apartment; in their own way, roaches were as aggressive as anyone, even OCTAGON, about Empire-Building. By a quarter after six, the few dishes and utensils that Tartaglia had used were soaking in the sink, and he was lighting up his pipe as he let himself take the first good look of the evening at his Starweb map.

A very few feet beyond the map's top edge, a sliding glass patio door gave access to the fraudulently small balcony, upon which Delia had used to try to get him to find room for two chairs so they would be able to sit together and watch the mountains. The Sandias, tall, barren-looking, about five miles away, were now starting to acquire a ruddy sunset pink, streaked with dark, rugged shadows. There was hardly a visible spot of snow remaining, even on the crest. Spring in New Mexico. Wishing to avoid a certain distraction, Tartaglia went over to the big window and drew the drapes shut. Having done that, he next had to turn on some lights.

This is the War Room now. Part of the Emperor's personal headquarters, maybe. Sort of like Hitler's bunker. The Imperial wall-to-wall carpeting shows some signs of wear, mostly from previous tenants. On this none-too-clean worn carpet there sprawls a man in his mid-thirties, a salesman in moderately mod clothes, suit coat and tie removed. His dark hair is just starting to go a little gray, his belly is feeling just a little paunchy. Time to loosen the belt. Tartaglia felt the sensation ease when he belched some Coors.

Amidst the half-orderly litter of papers on the floor he located the blank form he was going to have to fill out and mail in for his move. And now a ballpoint pen. A copy of a gaming magazine provided a good undersurface for writing; there was no room left on the plywood under the map. He would get the turn in the mail tonight or in the morning, and the game moderators should have it tomorrow or next day, which was the deadline. The fact that Berserkers Incorporated were right here in town was handy for Tartaglia, and something of a disadvantage, he supposed, for the players in New York or Seattle or Atlanta.

The empire ruled by AGRAVAN—that was Tartaglia's code name in the game—was in trouble. Under attack on two fronts. Chiefly by OCTAGON, who was supposed to be an Empire Builder too, but came on like a Berserker; but another player was shooting at Tartaglia/AGRAVAN as well. Somewhere he had read that it was usually a military mistake to split your forces, particularly when you were outnumbered. So what would Napoleon have done as AGRAVAN? How about Alexander the Great, or Patton? Undoubtedly the best thing, if you could do it, would be to knock out one of the attackers quickly, then turn quickly to face the other. But they both had hordes of ships . . .

AGRAVAN had a few moves ago concluded a mutual defense pact with LUCIFER, who ought now to be sending him some help. But however many times Tartaglia looked at his most recent printout, there was no sign of help on the way. Suppose LUCIFER had decided to remain neutral? Or, worse, was betraying him, in league with his enemies . . . probably the best thing to do would be to get someone else to attack OCTAGON in the rear . . .

By the time Tartaglia got up from the floor to make himself some instant coffee, the sunset was completely over. He closed more drapes, and turned on some more lights. On the busy street outside the multiple lanes of traffic were mumbling and hissing like faint surf. Year by year, almost month by month, Albuquerque was growing into a big city.

Tartaglia/AGRAVAN had already tried several times to open a diplomatic correspondence with OCTAGON, but the enemy had responded only briefly and grudgingly, communicating little more than his real name and address. Okay, if that was part of a plan to psych out Tartaglia, it wasn't going to work.

On the other hand, LUCIFER, even if he didn't help, always responded willingly enough. He lived in Atlanta. Tartaglia wondered how much it would cost him to phone LUCIFER now. He hadn't yet made any long-distance phone calls to confer with other players about the game, though he understood that it was quite a common thing to do, seldom were two players in the same game in the same city; Berserkers Incorporated organized it that way, to keep any two from having an easy time about getting together for conferences.

Now in his imagination Tartaglia could hear LUCIFER's wife, assuming he had one, answering when he had made the call. As soon as Tartaglia told her it was about Starweb, she would turn away from the phone, and call out in a patient, long-suffering voice: it's for you dear. Her tone would say: Another of your crazy game-playing friends.

And when he got LUCIFER on the line, what would he tell him? You bastard, you had really better send fleets to help me now, or you can forget about our alliance. Couched in politer terms than that, of course. Games like Starweb and Diplomacy were really a whole lot like real life. Rarely could you just speak your feelings. Everything depended on how good you were at manipulating other people, getting them to do what you wanted.

Somewhere not far down the street teenagers were racketing in a car. They yelled back and forth. Something funny had been done to the car's muffler, if it hadn't been taken off altogether. Tartaglia sipped his coffee, which tasted pretty bad, and set the cup down on the carpet near his papers.

Delia must have been present on some level in his thoughts. Because as soon as he heard someone trying very gently to open his back door, his interpretation of the knob-rattling was that his wife was back. His second thought was that she was probably here just to pick up something she had forgotten.

Getting up to let Delia in, Tartaglia had moved as far as depositing his coffee cup on the messy sink before it occurred to him to wonder why she hadn't simply used her key. He was positive that she had kept one. Or if she didn't have a key with her, why not knock, or for that matter come up to the front door and ring the bell.

Standing in the kitchen Tartaglia came to a halt, one extended hand still touching the cup that he had just set down. He called out sharply: "Delia?"

No answer came. No, worse, the wrong kind of answer—

the fumbling at the doorknob was repeated. The knob was turning back and forth, Tartaglia could see it moving, and there was a firm pull against the lock. Something wasn't right. Delia would have answered. A burglar ought to have run away at the sound of Tartaglia's voice. And a drunk at the wrong door would be cursing, breathing heavily, dropping his keys and banging things about—wouldn't he?

The kitchen's only window was on an adjoining wall. The only way to see who was standing outside the door was to open it.

Tartaglia called out again: "Who's there?" He was pleased by how confident and aggressive his voice came out. But no voice at all replied. Only something metallic sounding began to scrape against the door from the outside.

Without being aware of having thought out what to do next, Tartaglia found himself in his bedroom, opening the small drawer on the bedside table. *I wish you'd get rid of that thing,* said Delia's remembered voice. His hand was shaking just a little as it picked the .32 automatic out of the drawer, and held it up while his thumb pushed the safety catch off.

He was just re-entering the kitchen when something that sounded like a hammer or a baseball bat delivered a hard jolt to the outside of the back door. He thought he could feel the whole building, cheaply built, shudder with the blow.

And now came the methodical scraping again. And now Tartaglia thought he saw a flicker, as of a thrusting knife-blade, at the crack of the door near the cheap lock. He had told Delia he was going to put on a deadbolt lock but he never had.

Click from the lock, and click again. The door began to open, swinging slowly out into the night. Then it stopped, halfway open, with whoever had opened it remaining out of sight. Tartaglia, gun in hand, looking out into darkness, could see nothing but part of the dim backstairs landing, and the open-air wooden stairway going down.

Cautiously he stepped forward, trying to see more. Flood-lights showed him part of the parking area behind the build-ing. The space where Delia had usually parked was occupied, but not by her car. The machine in her space was a van that looked brand new, custom painted in yellow and gray. Tartaglia's concentrated thought dismissed the van; there was no particular reason to connect it with whoever was, had to be, waiting behind that motionless half-open door.

He didn't plan to yell at them again, whoever it was. He took another slow step, more or less aiming his gun. Where were all the neighbors now that they could be useful? Minding their own business, of course, inside their own apartments. But what was going on, who the hell could it be, what kind of a crazy man or joker would do a thing like this?

Whoever was behind the door was demonstrating an insane patience, simply continuing to wait there. Or else, Tartaglia realized abruptly, feeling something like the first break of relief, or else the intruder had already fled, upstairs or down. Once released from its lock, the door might have swung part way open by itself. It was hinged to a poorly constructed, slightly leaning wall.

Tartaglia stepped forward with increasing boldness, thinking: The crazy bastards! They don't know how lucky they are. How easily I could have put a bullet right through—

He was just about to touch the door, when it banged shut on him with incredible force. Struck on the right shoulder and on the side of the head Tartaglia started to fall right in the doorway. But before his fall could be completed he was caught, agonizingly, his head jammed in a wooden vise made by the door and frame.

He had one knee on the floor and couldn't get up. Could not push forward against what felt like a mountainous weight, could not pull back to get free either. In his desperation he tried to trigger the automatic, aiming it to fire through the door. But now his finger had somehow got outside the trigger guard.

Abruptly the terrible pressure eased, and Tartaglia dropped forward on his hands and knees, the weapon falling from his hand. All he could think of was his head, which felt like a great vacuum, about to suck all the pain of the world into itself. In a moment, he knew, the bones of his skull were going to explode.

Now he could see a part of what had been behind the door. The shape he beheld there was familiar, at least in its general outline, easily identified. But of all mad possibilities to be here on this small landing between stairways—

A wheelchair?

The door, blurring again toward his head, came much too fast for Tartaglia even to attempt to duck.

TWO

"This is Robert Gregory speaking."

"Hi, Uncle B—"

"But I am not at home. When this recorded message ends, you will have thirty seconds in which to leave a message for me. Please begin to speak immediately following the tone." Though he had lived for decades, most of his life, in various parts of the South, Uncle Bob's voice still sounded more like New York than anyplace else.

Standing in the ultramodern Atlanta airport terminal, Alex Barrow felt a little annoyed. He felt a little foolish for having started to deliver a warm greeting to a machine. He grimaced in the phone booth and made ready to start over, as soon as the damn thing gave him a chance. The moment the beeping tone in his ear had stopped, he said: "Hello, Uncle Bob. This is Alex. Alex Barrow. Remember I wrote you a little while ago that when I got discharged I might look you up on my way north? Well, I got out of the Air Force Tuesday, and—"

"Alex?" It was the same New York voice that had interrupted his before, but this time with a different quality in it, living and responsive. It was quick, and it somehow suggested the outdoors; maybe the voice of a sailor or a pilot.

"Yes, I got your letter. Are you here in Atlanta now?"

"Is that you, Uncle Bob? You're on live now? Yeah, I'm at the airport. Just changing planes, on my way—"

"Hop in a cab, come on over here. You have my address?"

Alex had checked, just out of curiosity, and it wasn't in the phone book, any more than Uncle Bob's number was. Alex's mother had sent him both. She was always a great one for looking in on family when traveling, which in her case was not often. "Yeah," said Alex. "Sure, I—"

"Good, see you soon." The voice sounded friendly, and mildly enthusiastic about meeting, but also very busy. And now there was no more connection.

Alex looked at the phone and hung it up. Maybe his wealthy uncle would reimburse him for the cab fare, maybe not. Anyway, what the hell. He had his mustering-out pay in his pocket. If he could afford to fly home, he could for once afford to take a cab, clear across town if need be.

The ride did turn out to be that far, though to Alex's relief the cab rates were cheaper than back home. Atlanta, which he saw now for the first time while riding a bisecting freeway through it from south to north, was more like one of the big northern cities than he would have expected. Still the redness of the earth, wherever the earth showed bare, meshed with Alex's developed mental image of the South. And so did the spring heat.

At what Alex took to be the northern edge of the city, where it appeared to be shading into upper-class suburbia, his cab left the freeway for a narrow concrete road that curved into a green tunnel of tall pines. The tunnel went on and on, crossed by similar roads at intervals. There were no sidewalks. This part of the city was an inhabited forest; elegant houses appeared irregularly among the million trees, never more than two or three houses in sight at once. The houses kept getting bigger, their driveways longer. All this was not exactly to Alex's surprise. If there was anything about Uncle Bob that the entire family always agreed on, it was that he had money.

The taxi driver was slightly built, sallow, and soft-voiced when he spoke at all. He found the right address in the green maze without discernable difficulty. The place was undoubtedly a mansion, at first glance from outside by far the most impressive residence that Alex had ever entered. The drive went into the grounds through iron gates in a tall stone wall; the wall itself disappeared into thick pine woods before it had gone very far to left and right, so it was hard to estimate just how big the whole layout was.

The house itself, judging by the incomplete first view of it available from outside the gate, did not look all that large considering its setting. No one had warned Alex what to expect; Uncle Bob had only been at this address for a few years, and as far as Alex knew none of the family had visited him here before.

The cab, motor idling, had halted on gravel outside the gates. The driver looked out of one side window and then the other. He started to say: "There oughta be a—"

With a sudden faint hum of well-maintained motors, the gates were rolling back. They ran in tracks, Alex noted now. And he watched them roll shut again behind the taxi as soon as it had driven in.

The long gravel drive curved toward the house through vast and well-kept grounds. Here and there on either side of the drive was evidence of recent digging and planting, garden projects in all stages of maturity. Greenhouses far and near, some with what looked like banks of active solar panels attached. One human being in view so far: a black man in faded khakis, kneeling, working patiently beside a distant flower bed. Even farther in the same direction, the apex of a metal pyramid rose tall as a man from behind some shrubbery, shining brightly in the sunlight. The pyramid appeared to be rotating slowly as Alex looked at it. Another solar something-or-other?

The cab stopped in a loop of drive at the front of the house. From a nearby wire enclosure that recent plantings had not yet grown up enough to camouflage entirely, three large dogs looked out in hard-eyed, still-legged silence. The house itself was mostly red brick, two stories high, with suggestions of Greek columns along its front. Seen from here it was obviously bigger than it had appeared to be when viewed from outside the grounds. From somewhere on the other side of it, a small internal combustion motor blatted; probably a riding lawn mower, Alex thought.

The driver eyed his one dollar tip for a few moments, his face expressionless. "Hope that-there gate lets me out," was all he said at last. "Iffn it don't, Ah'll be back."

Alex stood on the gravel alone, with his one bag. Summer insects, jumping the season, whined and droned among the trees. Inside an extra wide but otherwise commonplace front screen door, a great wooden portal stood ajar. He hoisted his B-4 bag and approached, while the caged dogs commented in low tones among themselves on what they would like to do to him.

Peering in through the screen, Alex saw a dim room, stretching away; and, just a few feet inside the door, another metal pyramid. This one was topped with a black thing the size of a rural mailbox—maybe it *was* a metal mailbox, for furled down along its flank was what looked like a small metal flag. Was Uncle Bob in his retirement going in for modern art? Or—

Uncle Bob came on stage, appearing halfway down the great dim hall inside the house. He was dressed in walking shorts, tennis shoes, and an open-necked sport shirt of gaudy colors.

"Come in, Alex," the white-haired figure called from fifteen yards or so away. "Need any help with the luggage?"

"No. I've just got the one bag." Alex opened the screen door and lugged the blue B-4 inside, where he dropped it with a thud. There was no squeaking from the screen door as it swung itself shut again behind him, but a faint multiple clicking just as it closed. Must be some kind of fancy latch, Alex thought vaguely. His uncle was coming forward, reaching to shake hands.

Long-term southerner though he now was, Uncle Bob's face and hands were not particularly tanned. Under the white hair with a crisp natural bend in it that made it look more steely, his face was craggy. Distinguished, enough so that you thought he probably could have done well in politics. He had to be somewhere around sixty years old now, Alex was thinking. But under the blazing shirt his belly was as flat as Alex's, and his hands looked stronger than his nephew's, as muscular as his grip felt. He and Alex were very nearly the same height, just about average.

"Alex, how are you? Last time I saw you, you were only about the size of . . . but I'd know you anywhere. Got carrotty hair like your father, and your mother's stick-out ears. How are they all at home, by the way?"

"Fine, as far as I know."

"Good." The strong handshake dropped. "Last time I saw you, must have been on the farm."

"Farm? Whose farm?"

"No, no, that's not right, of course." And Uncle Bob, amused at his own mistake—or something—grabbed Alex around the shoulders, and pulled him along deeper into the house, letting the blue bag lie where it was behind them on the floor. "I suppose I was thinking of someone else . . . how about a drink? You must be what, now, twenty-three?"

"Right."

"Or is it too early in the day for you?"

"It's afternoon, isn't it? I guess I'm safe."

"Had your lunch?"

"They fed me on the plane." He could see into more rooms of the house now. The place was—distracting. What you might expect from the house of a bachelor millionaire who had been around the world a lot, but who had probably never cared much one way or the other about interior decoration. Though Uncle Bob was evidently concerned about the appearance of the grounds, to judge from the amount of work Alex had seen going on out there.

Behind Alex came a sound, suggesting something heavy, rolling on firm wheels. He turned to discover that the metal pyramid that had been standing near the front door was now in motion. It was rolling in a straight line toward his B-4 bag.

As Alex watched, a wide lip of metal in the front of the machine dropped open, almost to floor level. As the machine proceeded forward smoothly the lip encountered the bulky bag, scooped it up and swallowed it. The pyramid, a closed unit again, moved on at a walking pace without a pause, now coming straight toward the two men watching. The machine bore down on them methodically; the flaglike thing on its mailbox had been erected now.

Alex started involuntarily to back out of the pyramid's way, but he found himself being held in place by his uncle's continued grip around his shoulders. Uncle Bob was laughing, mildly and silently.

Sure enough, the pyramid detoured neatly around them on its hidden wheels. It resumed its course down the middle of the hall, then made a sharp turn at right angles, going unhesitatingly down a side hall. Alex followed and looked. At the end of the side hall, an old-fashioned wooden stair wound upward. He watched and waited.

As the device reached the foot of the stair it eased to a stop. The rolling sound of its heavy wheels on uncarpeted wood died out, to be replaced a moment later by a faint mechanical shuffling. Small struts or poles with padded tips appeared under the skirt-like rim at the base of the device. Shuffling up and down with quick precision, they lifted the pyramid and walked it right up onto the narrow stairs. Without tilting it, then, they carried it upward in a smooth ascent. A normally agile human would probably have made the climb faster, though not by much. And it was made by the machine with perfect steadiness, and on an even keel.

His uncle had let go of Alex's shoulders now, and was no longer laughing. "I told it to take your baggage after you came in. Hope you don't mind."

"Yeah, sure," said Alex, still looking after the machine. "I mean, no." The climbing pyramid vanished around the curve of the stair. A moment later Alex could hear its wheels on a wooden floor again. "What *was* that thing?"

But his uncle was already a room away, standing beside a bar of dark wood and doing things with glasses. Alex followed, into a large room richly paneled and weirdly furnished. Things were a mixture of old and new, and of elegance and shabbiness. At the room's far side, low against the wall, an armored cable conduit as thick as a boa constrictor seemed to have bored its way in through one wall and out again through the wall opposite.

Uncle Bob, frowning at the pair of clean glasses he had set out on the bar, looked up as Alex approached. "Refresh me a little on what your job was in the service. Something technical?"

"Radar maintenance."

"Airborne or ground?"

"Airborne." Alex hoisted himself onto a chrome barstool. "Oh, once I finished tech school I never really got into the nitty-gritty of it all that much. Most of the time I was just installing equipment in aircraft, or taking it out and bringing it back into the shop. Changing units around depending on mission requirements."

"I suppose their gear has changed somewhat since I retired."

"How long ago was that, about five years?" Alex wasn't sure what retirement meant, in his uncle's case. That he had sold his business, probably. But he had the vague impression that Uncle Bob was supposed to have owned more than one. "I guess it's changed some. But we still had some of the stuff that you developed. That thing that reads railroad tracks from the air and estimates the weight of loaded trains. And one of the multichannel recorders."

Uncle Bob was nodding vaguely. He waved with an awkward gesture at a row of bottles behind the bar. "What do you like here? People tell me these are all pretty good."

"Chivas Regal." Alex noted that the bottle was still full, its seal unbroken. "Just on the rocks. Here, let me."

His uncle gave up fumbling at glassware and things and got out of his nephew's way as Alex came behind the bar. "Help yourself, Alex. Just get me a can of that diet ginger ale out of the cooler, will you?"

The small refrigerator attached to the bar looked older than the whiskey, but it was still working silently and with something of the same elegance. Alex handed Uncle Bob his ginger ale, then tonged ice cubes into a squat glass and poured a little brown liquid over them, sighing faintly to himself. This was a brand he'd long wanted to be able to try.

His uncle, sipping his cheap canned drink, asked thoughtfully: "Are you in any particular hurry to get on home?"

"No. Why?" As soon as he got home his parents would immediately resume nagging him not to waste his brains. He would be urged to pick out a college, preferably one they would have some reasonable hope of helping him to pay for, and start attending it. They might even be able to persuade him. But the longer he stayed out of school, the less he felt like going back.

"It's just that I might have a job available. Kind of a special thing. But very temporary, you understand. It would involve a little travel."

Alex drank. Suddenly, watching his uncle watching him, he was motivated to drink quite lightly. "I like to travel. Is this an electronics job? Technical?"

"No. I have people doing that. No, there's a certain company that I'm interested in, for business reasons. I'd like to have someone I can really trust just go and take a look at it for me. There are people who do this kind of thing professionally, of course. But I have my reasons for not wanting to hire them in this case."

Alex said: "I'm no engineer, or accountant. I assume this is probably some kind of electronics company. But I don't know how much I could learn about it."

"When I want an engineer, I can usually find one and plug him in without much trouble. And as for being an accountant, I don't suppose they're going to show you their books."

Uncle Bob spoke in an absent tone, though he continued to watch Alex carefully. Again he raised his can of soda. From somewhere outside the house there came a muffled, precise splash, as of an expert diver entering a pool. Something made Alex immediately glimpse bikini'd flesh in his mind's eye. Bob was the most determined bachelor in the older generation of the family, as well as its only millionaire and certified genius. But, from what Alex had heard, there was no record of his not having friends.

"Sounds interesting, then," said Alex, inhaling a rarefied haze of Chivas Regal.

Uncle Bob nodded slowly. He was silent for a little while, studying Alex, though not staring at him, with an intensity that soon began to strain the nerves just a little.

The next question, when it finally came, was a surprise. "Know anything about games?" the older man inquired. "I mean computer games, specifically."

"You mean like those things they play in the arcades?" Alex rejoined his uncle on the customers' side of the bar and sat on a stool again, rattling his ice cubes. "I've tried 'em once or twice. If you mean the home kind, or the ones that come in little boxes, whaddya call 'em, microgames, no, I haven't. I thought maybe you were going to ask me if I knew anything about robots."

"Do you?"

Alex chuckled. "No."

His uncle smiled too, and appeared to relax a bit. "Okay. Actually I didn't mean any of the kinds of computer games that you just mentioned. I was referring to what they call computer combat-simulation. Where the players are human beings opposing each other, and the computer is just used as a moderator, to keep track of things and show the results after it figures them out."

"Well, okay. I have seen war games something like that, but not played with a computer. A guy in my barracks was into these elaborate combat games, where you re-enact the battle of Waterloo, or whatever. The game would have this enormous folding board, and there were about five hundred little cardboard counters, representing military units, to set in place and then maneuver around. You rolled dice to deter-mine the results of combat. He talked me into starting a game with him once, but by the time we got everything set up it was almost time to quit."

"A computer's a lot faster to play with than five hundred

little cardboard pieces. Come along, Alex, I'll show you something I've lately become interested in."

Uncle Bob was a fast walker. Alex grabbed up what was left of his drink and followed. He was led into another large room, this one an engineering-workshop sort of place, brightly lighted and filled with tool-cluttered workbenches and equipment. His uncle turned on half a dozen switches here and there, and started to adjust the controls of a CRT the size of a large television screen. The screen came alive with a snowstorm of video noise, flaring with flakes and sparks of light in all colors.

Another key when pressed turned the noise at once into a pattern made up of a score of small green circles. "Suppose," said Uncle Bob, "that these are worlds, in our imaginary game-universe." Another switch. "And these, the connections between them." The circles were now mortared with green lines into a brickwork pattern. He paused. "Now understand that my computer here is not the one that moderates the game. That one's out in Albuquerque, in the office of a little company called Berserkers Incorporated. We players mail our moves to them. They feed everyone's move into the computer and then they mail us back the results, showing us the situation for the next move. I'm just using my computer here as a display aid, and sometimes as a help in calculation."

"You mean the other poor bastards in the game are pushing those five hundred pieces of cardboard around? Drawing their maps on old wrapping paper?"

Uncle Bob smiled faintly. "Probably something like that. Though for all I know, some of them have home computers too."

"Seems unfair. I bet I know who's going to win."

"I'm not so sure." The smile grew quirky. "I won't win just because I have a lot of glowing lights to play with. You know what the real secret in this game is? Diplomacy. It's more like poker than like chess. There are about fifteen players, more or less, in each game, and if fourteen of them could ever manage to gang up, the fifteenth wouldn't have a snowball's chance in hell. I don't care if he's using an IBM 7600 to calculate his moves instead of my little micro here."

Alex sucked an icecube, faintly flavorful, all that was left. "Okay. You say that these are worlds."

"Right." From near the base of the console Uncle Bob picked up what looked like a small wand, with an insulated wire attached to it at one end. With the wand's free end he pointed at one of the screen's green circles, which in obedience to this wizard's gesture at once swelled up to dominate the screen. Inside the circle appeared a neat set of letters and numbers, in assorted colors. FACTORIES was one heading; POPULATION another. RMS, whatever that might be, stood at 46.

"Just a little micro, huh?"

"Well, I have it fixed up with a few peripherals."

Behind Alex there sounded a genteel hissing of weight-bearing wheels, and he turned, determined that this time he would confront a rolling pyramid with something like a-plomb. Instead he beheld a slender girl with brown hair framing a pretty face, riding toward him in a wheelchair. Small, pale hands rested idle in her lap, on the white terry-cloth of her muffling robe. Only her head moved, her chin nudging delicately at a small control that jutted up before her face something like a helmet microphone. The chair changed course slightly, and after one more nudge, slowed to a stop.

Blue eyes examined Alex, from under dark hair slightly damp. He found it hard to take a guess at the girl's age; under twenty, certainly. The prettiness of her face, small-mouthed and high-cheekboned, was intense. Part of some kind of metal and plastic body brace was just visible close under her chin. Under her engulfing robe her body appeared to be intact, not twisted or deformed but certainly badly wasted.

Uncle Bob said it calmly and plainly: "Alex, this is my daughter, Caroline. How was your swim, Hon?"

Alex had heard an active diver, bouncing off a board. But then of course there would have to be at least one fully mobile companion. He started to reach out to shake hands, then remembered how still those small fingers were inside the ends of muffling sleeves, and aborted his reaching movement in confusion.

Caroline's hands did not move, but she continued to smile at him with fine self-possession. "Hello, Alex. You're the first of my cousins I've ever met."

At last he reached forward, pressed two small fingers as if they were a baby's, and murmured something. What brilliant dialogue. What a clod he was; there went his chances for Uncle Bob's sending him on any kind of a mission that required speech.

"Didn't know I had a daughter, did you?"

"No sir, I didn't."

"The swim was fine, Dad. Alex, you'll have to try out the pool. I hope you're staying?"

The wish sounded reasonably sincere. Alex looked at his uncle.

"He is, for a day or two at least. I may be about to offer him a job."

Caroline's eyes took in the display screen. "Not Starweb." Her tone seemed to imply that Alex ought to be worthy of better things than that. "*That's* the job?"

"What I have in mind is related to Starweb, certainly. But it isn't trivial."

The girl's eyes, turned cautiously thoughtful, searched her father's. At the far end of the room a black woman dressed in nurses' white put her head in through a doorway, then entered and stood smiling vaguely, still far enough distant that she had not really joined the group. Caroline said: "Well, I'm going to get my hair dried, and get into something just a touch more formal. See you both at dinner." Then she chinned the control and the chair spun away slowly, with a soft whining of electric motors. "Show him some of your fancies," she told her father, looking back at them once, and then with a gentle hiss of wheels she was gone. The nurse or helper went out with Caroline, walking beside the chair but not touching it.

"Didn't know I had one, did you?" Uncle Bob repeated, when he and Alex were alone again.

"No. Well, I had heard that you liked girls. What were the 'fancies' she was talking about?"

"I think she meant some of our graphics here. Computer-generated pictures. In the next few years computers are going to change our world so damn much . . . the graphics aren't really related to what I wanted to talk to you about, but we can take a look."

He shut off the game screen and moved across the room. There a solid, waist-high platform had been constructed, the size of a puppet stage. It was enclosed on almost three full sides by plywood walls painted black, shading the stage from the chief light sources in the room. "I suppose you've seen holograms, Alex?"

"Yeah, once or twice. In tech school they showed us that radar system that used a hologram presentation. I don't know if you had anything to do with . . ."

"I did work a little on that," said Uncle Bob absently, giving his attention to a new set of controls. A fog of pink light bloomed into being on the shadowed stage. A new space, or the illusion of one, had been created, and in this space a doll-sized figure, fully three-dimensional, came into view. The figure was that of a young woman, completely nude, trim and athletic-looking, with auburn hair cut short. At first she was standing perfectly still, hands at her sides, almost as if at military attention. But almost at once she began to move, as if following a rehearsed routine in dance or gymnastics. The movements were simple and easy, though; walking, turning, bending, straightening, walking some more.

It was obvious somehow from the start that this was not meant as porn. After a minute Alex had decided that neither was it intended to be Art; exactly what it was, he didn't know. Suddenly he was reminded of those very early photographic studies by—what had the man's name been?—Muybridge, something like that. The photographer who had examined human and animal motion as no one could possibly have done in the days before highspeed photography.

The girl's face was serious, businesslike. She sat down in

the image of a chair that somehow materialized when needed and vanished as soon as she got up again. Now, completely filling the space in which the girl moved, there appeared a three-dimensional grid of fine, straight lines of fiery white. The vivid lines defined precisely the moving outline of her body. Now numbers and other symbols, in crimson and bright blue, began to come and go around the edges of the display. The hologram image was completely solid looking, more real than the best two-dimensional photograph could be, except that Alex thought the skin tone did not look quite true.

"This was made in this house, last year," Uncle Bob informed him. "A live recording of a real model."

"Yeah, I can see she's live." The longer the staid graph-paper dance went on, the more it seemed to develop erotic possibilities.

"*Can* you?" asked his uncle, and touched some switches. The girl and her pink haze vanished, to be replaced by another model who moved against a clear blue background. This image too was quite sharp, and the colors were better now. This young woman wore a leotard, and her hair was shorter and darker than that of the first model had been, but she was going through the same almost formal movements. There was something familiar about this girl . . .

"Caroline's been crippled now for almost three years," said Uncle Bob.

Alex heard him, but at first did not connect the words with what he was watching. Then it hit him. This girl had Caroline's face, though a trifle fuller. He looked at his uncle, not understanding.

"We made this sequence just a few months ago," his uncle said. "I'm not sure this is what Caroline had in mind, when she suggested some fancy graphics, but here it is."

In the image, Caroline's limbs were round with health and strength, their movements ballet-smooth. Had an image of her somehow been electronically grafted to a gymnast's body? But these were certainly not the limbs and torso of the previous model, she had been more muscular.

"This, you see, Alex, is Caroline's body as it ought to be. We scanned a lot of old photographs of her, stored the information—a lot of information. Then extrapolated mathematically for normal growth and development, to see what her optimum condition should be now." Uncle Bob chuckled softly as the image girl suddenly sprang forward into a totally improbable handstand, ending with a perfectly balanced pose on one finger. "She likes it when I put in some little tricks here and there."

"This is—photography?" Alex asked, groping for understanding.

"Not at all. Every bit of this is graphics, a drawing done by the machine. Making it look real is largely a matter of how much information the machine can store, and increasing the resolution of the image to put in fine detail. And of course once we have Caroline in the memory we can change her in any way we like, make her do anything."

"This is . . . jeez, I just don't know what to say. I've never seen anything like it."

Now Caroline had sat down at a small, real-looking table. With graceful motions of arm and wrist she nibbled at a meal set before her.

"This is really . . ."

Uncle Bob was looking at him shrewdly. "You may be thinking about now that this is really a little sick on my part. Why generate a dream world in which she isn't crippled? But that, my dear Alex, is not at all what I have in mind. What I do have in mind is coming along, but it's going to take time, and money." He paused, then went on, seeming to choose words with great care. "I think that finding out more about the company that runs Starweb may just do me a lot of good financially."

"I would go out to Albuquerque and try to find out more about them? I guess I could do that."

"Good." With a sweep of Uncle Bob's hand Caroline and

her magic snack vanished back into her magnetic bubble, or whatever the hell kind of memory this thing used. The room contained a lot of equipment Alex couldn't begin to identify, though there was some he could. He recognized a phone terminal, what they called a modem, which would mean that his uncle could tie into almost any big computer in the country that would sell him time.

"Confidentially," said Uncle Bob, "I'm really intrigued by this Starweb game as an investment. The whole field of computer games has a simply tremendous potential, and the big companies are getting interested. This fella in New Mexico has a head start on the field. His name is Ike Jacobi. I've talked with him on the phone, but I can't seem to get a real handle on the man. He always impresses me as abstracted, maybe absent-minded. It could be he's just extremely busy, which I could understand, the way his operation is evidently growing. Or it could be that he's just not a very good manager. You understand that I'm telling you all this in the strictest confidence."

"I understand."

"This is an important job I'm talking about, Alex. It's not something I'm thinking up to do a favor for a nephew. You're going to have to apply your intelligence out there, and stay alert."

Alex smiled lightly, nodded.

"So. What I'd like you to do is to go out to Albuquerque and look over this Jacobi and his operation. Don't let him know you're working for me, of course. Don't even mention my name. You should be . . . just a young man, interested in games, who has some money from somewhere, and you're thinking of investing. I know Jacobi sells stock in his company, I know he pays high interest on loans."

"How am I supposed to have come by all my money that I'm going to invest?"

"You don't have to explain that. People who are really wealthy usually don't."

"I get it." Alex nodded, thought about it all, nodded

more. It sounded like fun. Serious fun, which would make it all the better.

Uncle Bob pulled two office-type swivel chairs from under a vast workbench. He scooted one of the chairs toward Alex, while seating himself in the other. "I want you to find out all you can in a few days about what Jacobi's operation is like; the more details the better. Who are the people close to him, what does his office look like, how many employees does he have. I recognize the fact that you're not a professional at this kind of thing. But I think that in some ways that fact could work to our advantage. Now don't take any chances of alarming him, whatever happens don't get caught going through his papers or anything like that. I'd rather have you come back without any information at all."

Alex found his interest and eagerness continuing to grow as he listened. "Maybe I should change my name."

"I've considered that, but, all in all, I don't think so. I don't think he'll know your relationship to me; it's not as if you were my son, or we had worked together in the past. Just approach him under your real name, as a possible investor. Don't mention me, of course, but basically the less deception the better. Gather what intelligence you legitimately can. Think you can handle it?"

"Sure," said Alex at once. Then he wondered if he should have appeared to give the question a little more serious consideration.

But Uncle Bob appeared to be satisfied. "Good. I want you to stay here a couple of days. You can study up on games and we'll go over some details of how you'll approach Jacobi. Then I'll pay your expenses while you're out there, plus five hundred dollars. You should be able to fly back here within a week after you leave."

"You don't have to pay me that much, Uncle Bob."

"No, it's not too much. I expect a reliable job."

From some distant room of the house, or more probably from outside, Alex could hear what sounded like workmen's voices calling back and forth. He couldn't make out the words but they sounded full of energy and enthusiasm. Great things were going on here, and people were well paid for taking part in them. It sounded like those men were on an urgent job of some kind, facing a problem, mobilizing energy and cleverness in trying to overcome it. Suddenly Alex experienced a pang almost of fright, when he thought of how close he had come to not stopping over in Atlanta at all.

Uncle Bob had fallen into frowning thought. "An old friend of mine lives out there, not too far from Albuquerque. In Los Alamos, Dr. Henry Brahmaguptra. We used to work together." Alex's uncle paused, looking at Alex. "If you should get a chance . . ." The sentence ended in a sigh.

"I should say hello to this Dr. Brahmaguptra if I get the chance?"

"I . . . don't know. Henry is one of the few people in the world that I'd trust completely. Personally, that is. If you saw him, you could tell him that I asked after him. That I'd like to know how he's doing." Uncle Bob's keen eyes appeared to be taking Alex's measure once again. "Oh, hell, never mind. It's probably best that you don't bother him at all."

The way it sounded to Alex, some proud and sensitive old friend had fallen on hard times in one way or another. "You mean you'd like to know how he's doing, but you don't want him to know you're trying to find out?"

"Something like that. I do hope he knows I'm interested in his welfare." Uncle Bob looked at the workbench before him as if in search of some precisely fitting tool or part; then he gave up the matter with another sigh. "But let it go, Alex. Ike Jacobi, and Berserkers Incorporated. These are what you should concentrate on."

"Jacobi, and—?"

"Berserkers Incorporated. The name of the little company he runs, and owns. He got the name from some science fiction stories, I understand, about some kind of killer robots."

That night's dinner was Alex's first outside a restaurant in which he was attended by servants; and there were a few distracted moments in which a part of his mind began to wonder who was going to pay the check. And it was the first time inside a restaurant or out that he had seen a robot working as a busboy. Everyone else was familiar with the thing and casual about it; it was obviously more than just a stunt. The machine, about the size and shape of an automatic dishwasher, followed one of the human help around the table silently and discreetly swallowed all the used plates and garbage that it was fed. When Alex asked how the thing worked, Uncle Bob answered only briefly; his mind was obviously elsewhere.

Caroline in her wheelchair sat between Alex and her father, and they took turns at helping her with food and drink. For dinner she was wearing a long-sleeved blue dress whose frilly folds gave some illusion of fullness to her limbs and body.

What, Alex wondered, were the older generation of the family in New York going to say when they heard that Bob had a teen-aged daughter living with him? But then he realized suddenly that it was probable the old folks already knew; most likely they had been keeping Caroline's existence a secret for years, that the youth of Alex's generation might not be scandalized. Oh, well.

There were two young men at the dinner table too, introduced to Alex as engineers working for, or with, Uncle Bob on projects that were never very clearly specified. They reminded Alex of the civilian engineers working at the airbase where he had served most of his enlistment, even to their shirts and ties. Albie Pearson was black, and about thirty, Alex judged. He spoke little during dinner, and that mainly cryptic shop-talk with his employer. Ronnie Fisher was white, younger—a recent graduate, maybe—and talked mostly about sports.

Alex kept wondering who Caroline's mother was or had been, what the story was. But no information along that line had been volunteered, and he wasn't going to ask any questions, not yet at least. Caroline kept the casual table talk going for a while, then started looking pale and speaking

less. Before the meal was over, she asked to be excused,
saying she felt tired. Uncle Bob gazed at her soberly and
nodded, but neither he nor the nurses who came to take her
away appeared to be surprised or alarmed.

Shortly after that, Uncle Bob excused himself, saying he
had some work to do, and went off with the two engineers.
Alex was shown to a telephone, which he used to call home,
telling the folks not to expect him for some days yet, as Uncle
Bob had persuaded him to a lengthy stopover.

Then one of the help showed Alex to another room and left
him to play for a while at a billiard table, large, well-lighted,
and apparently little used. Around the sides of the billiard
room were stacked unopened boxes of what looked like new
electronic gear. Somewhere in the middle distance, unknown
machinery was whining.

Later, one of the live servants showed Alex up to his room,
just like in the movies. His bag had been neatly unpacked for
him. Whether by human or robot there appeared to be no way
to tell.

From the window of his large and elegant guest room he
could see the swimming pool; still lighted, but deserted now
except for one of those automatic vacuum-cleaner things
crawling its random pathway on the bottom, humming
faintly. That was the only machinery now audible.

Along one side of the pool, what appeared to be a special
kind of diving platform had been constructed, wood painted
white. The side of the platform, like the sides of the pool
where Alex could see them, had been marked off with precisely painted black lines, meters and tenths of meters, Alex
guessed. The grid suggested reminded him of the finer grid in
the hologram of the gymnastic girl.

The sound of more machinery, this time rapidly growing
louder, a familiar noise but here surprising. A whistle gave
out a lonesome bellow, as what must be a fright train passed
somewhere nearby though remaining perfectly invisible. The
track, thought Alex, must be down out of sight in the bottom
of one of the pine-grown ravines that sliced up the region.

That night, between satiny sheets, he had a dream about trying to use a magic wand to erase an electronically drawn-on leotard.

THREE

There turned out to be direct Atlanta-Albuquerque flights available. The Sunbelt is booming, thought Alex, as he boarded the aircraft wearing a new business suit, with a newly purchased traveling bag, considerably smaller than his B-4, in hand. He had spend part of the last couple of days shopping, part being briefed for his mission by Uncle Bob. There had been time out for a couple of swims with Caroline. His cousin wasn't quite as helpless in the water as she was on land, but still at best only marginally able to take care of herself; and attendant had always been close by.

Looking at the other passengers now, he wondered what they thought, looking at him, what sort of mission they imagined he was on. But they were not thinking of him at all, as far as he could tell. Well, fine, so far. He hadn't been at all sure what kind of job he was going to look for on returning to civilian life, but industrial espionage hadn't been on the list. Still here he was. Working for one of the good guys, of course; the family relationship, at least in the traditions of Alex's family, made that true by definition. And maybe something permanent would come of it after all. It sounded like maybe his uncle was on the verge of buying out a

company, expanding operations into games in a big way.
And if so, he, Alex, might get in on the ground floor.

Electronic games were already a large industry, anybody
could see that. Thinking over the situation, he felt a slowly
maturing excitement about the prospects. Starweb, for
example. Imaginary battles over imaginary worlds were in-
trinsically no sillier than trying to knock a little white ball into
a hole with a stick, or running with an inflated leather bag to
cross a chalked line on artificial turf.

Alex had with him his five hundred dollar fee, paid in
advance, inside a new money belt. And more than five
hundred more, expense allowance, deposited in various
caches about his person. Travelers' checks were getting
harder to cash, Uncle Bob had said. And anyway he didn't
really expect to be waylaid by thugs.

A couple of hours west of Dallas, the first real bulk of
western mountain came into view. The range was green-
forested upon its relatively gentle eastern slopes, and fell
away on the west in steep and barren folds and canyons,
below which lay a city, insignificant. The city was traversed
from north to south by a winding brown river and its accompanying belt of green. The Rio Grande? Alex thought so.
Surrounding all this was a vast brown emptiness, notched
round the horizon by more mountains to the north and west
and south.

After the plane had landed Alex walked down a mobile
stair to an exposed ramp. Winds from far away blew at him a
little of the dust of the high plains. The air had no particular
smell. And yet the sunlight was like wine.

The advertised promise of a free limousine ride determined his choice of a motel. When he reached the place it
turned out to be a high-rise building, very new, nestled
almost in the corner of the intersection of two large highways. If you've got it, spend it; and he was supposed to be
making an impression of at least moderate wealth. He asked
for and was given the biggest ground-floor room available.
Instead of ordinary locks the rooms had numbered buttons on
the door; you punched out a four-digit combination that you

could pick yourself, and was programmed in from the front desk. Alex chose the last four digits of his Air Force serial number.

As soon as he had settled into the room, and had telephoned to arrange for a rented car, Alex gave Berserkers Inc. a ring.

A girl answered at once. For some reason, as he waited for her to see if Jacobi was available, Alex pictured her getting up from behind a battered desk and walking away barefoot, wearing jeans, her breasts loose under a dark sweater. Long, tangled hair, and under her eyes there were blue circles. Last night or this morning she had smoked pot. Hell, it was just that her voice reminded him of someone he had once known. And he was getting horny.

A few moments later Jacobi himself was on the phone, sounding harried but in control, as Alex supposed a busy executive ought to sound. Sure, he was interested in talking to a potential investor. Yep, it was certainly better to do it face to face. Sure, Alex could come over to the office right now. It was as good a time as any.

It was three in the afternoon. Alex asked some directions in the lobby, then bought a map of Albuquerque. The corporate credit card Uncle Bob had given him, an odd thing unlike other cards in Alex's limited experience, and titled with the name of some Dallas company he had never heard of, had perhaps struck the car rental people as odd also; they had called him back to say something about their central office still having to do some checking. His car was unfortunately not yet available.

He therefore took a cab, which involved some wait while one was dispatched to the hotel. Manhattan this was definitely not. Berserkers Inc. was right downtown, but it was evident on reaching the area that in Albuquerque downtown was no longer the high rent district. Jacobi's enterprise occupied a sort of storefront in what had once been a bank building, right on Central, the old Route 66. A couple of blocks to north and south, construction was noisily in progress on taller towers, or at least on what passed for towers this far west. Right here on Central, though, things were somewhat gritty, amid what had been brave new construction back around 1950.

The storefront windows of the former bank had been painted, up to about eye level, in a translucent white. BERSERKERS, INC, said a sign of at least semi-professional quality, a piece of white cardboard leaning in a small unpainted section of the window. Below the lettering on the sign an android robot, drawn in early Buck Rogers style, leered with heavy menace.

Alex went in. The girl he had talked to on the phone was nowhere in sight, unless she could possibly be this neat, chubby blonde with innocent face and pink-rimmed glasses who sat at a small front desk. The desk lacked a modesty panel and he could see that her legs were encased in wholesome business nylons. IRIS CARDANO said a small plastic nameplate standing on her desk beside the phone. Alex approached and stated his business. And in the voice of the imagined black-sweater girl Iris assured him that Ike would be with him in just a moment.

Beyond the receptionist's new-looking desk and chair, there appeared to be a certain shortage of furniture, though there was plenty of room. Papers were stacked here and there on the new carpet. Doorways led away to several other rooms. Everything smelled and looked new, or at least recently redecorated. A cork bulletin board lay on the floor, in what would be a convenient place for the help to read it if they came crawling in on hands and knees. There were new-looking ceiling lights, partitions, doors.

"What do people do for excitement around Albuquerque?" Alex asked, ignoring for a moment the two visitors' chairs not far from the desk.

"Play Starweb a lot," Iris assured him, straightlaced. "Try to pay the rent." She was one of those people, it was plain, about whom it was hard to tell at any given moment whether they were being serious or not. In general Alex liked the type. She asked him: "Are you going to be in town long?"

"I'm not sure. I tend to move around a fair amount." And here, from one of the inner rooms, came a man who must be Jacobi, looking not at all robotic. He was about Alex's height, lean and rather intense looking, dressed in jeans and loafers and a sport shirt. He, if not his receptionist, had long dark hair. Limping slightly, he approached and said hello to Alex and led him away.

The shortage of furniture seemed to extend throughout most of the establishment. There were three or four more rooms; unless there were more somewhere else, it could not be a very big operation in terms of personnel. Jacobi explained that until last month he had been running the business out of his house. Then he paused to exchange a few words in technical jargon with a clean-cut young man who was loading small rolls of tape sequentially into a machine. Each roll when loaded induced a burst of clattering noise from a nearby printer, after which the tape was pulled out of the machine again and tossed into a handy cardboard box. Many more boxes were stacked about. On all four walls of this room were pasted cryptic, hand-lettered plastic charts, showing God knew what.

In the next room, a very small private office, Ike settled himself behind a cluttered desk, gesturing for Alex to take the chair opposite. Vaguely Alex had been expecting to find here something like the wonderland of Uncle Bob. But again, unless there was a branch office, or a very different back room still undiscovered . . . besides the tape-reader and printer, Alex had seen nothing that looked to him very much like computer gear.

Talk about specific investment plans was slow to get under way, somewhat to Alex's relief. Jacobi stayed behind his desk most of the time, and seemed to be trying to give Alex the background of his business, but the two or three young aides in the office took turns popping in at his doorway to present him with problems, or bits of what must be useful information. Alex could not understand either very well. He made what mental notes he could, and tried to miss as little as possible of what was going on around him.

A few of the items were easy enough to grasp. A box of advertising pencils had just been delivered by the pencil-makers, and their proper distribution had to be decided on. Alex promptly sprouted two of them in his shirt pocket. BERSERKERS INC., said the lettering. *One-half die weapon when sharpened.* While trying to comprehend the joke evidently intended, and hoping no one would try to pin him down on his own game experience, he heard talk about the big games convention coming up in San Francisco soon, and who was going to represent the firm at that?

"Business must be pretty good," Alex remarked.

Jacobi made a face. "Business is very busy. Maybe some-day the time will come when we can start to clear some real money. When I can pay these people working for me more than three or four bucks an hour. When some money sticks in my pocket instead of just flowing through my hands."

A good opening. "How many people do you have working for you now?"

"Four full time. Three or four others part time. Most of them are students at the University. Eddie has a full time job elsewhere; he works here part time just because the games fascinate him."

"The others all manage on three or four bucks an hour?"

"Well, a couple are shacking up together, and I guess that helps. Two more have part time work at the Labs, that I guess pays them more than full time here. How else am I going to hire a decent programmer?"

"What Labs are those?" A capitalization had seemed audible.

"Big corporation in town here, doing government work. They've been here since the days of the first nuclear weapons development. About three-fourths of what they do is still weapons. But they're also into solar energy, all kinds of different things. New Mexico's heavy on research. We've got more Ph.D.'s per unit of population than New York or California, or almost any state."

"Is that why you set up your business here?"

"I set up here because it's cheaper living than in California. That's where I'm from originally. You sound like a New Yorker, sort of."

Iris Cardano was standing behind her pink-rimmed glasses in the doorway of Ike's small never-private room. Just behind Iris hovered a dark woman, thirtyish, well dressed but with the look of someone who really needed a good night's sleep.

"Ike? This is Mrs. Tartaglia," Iris announced, and then withdrew.

"Oh." Ike immediately knew Mrs. Tartaglia by name, though he hadn't seemed to recognize her face. He got up and limped around his desk, past Alex's chair, to meet her. "Very sorry to hear about your husband," he murmured flatly.

Mrs. Tartaglia acknowledged this condolence with a slight facial twitch. In one hand she was holding a small bundle of white, letter-sized envelopes, together with a few other folded papers. "I could have written or phoned," she answered in her own monotone. "But I work just down the street at the First National, and I thought I'd just drop in." She was looking at Alex now, though her mind seemed to be somewhere else. "I brought these over. They were Carl's. I thought you people might have some use for them. I understand Carl had some kind of an account here with you people? To pay for his games?"

"Yes, he did." Ike accepted the little bundle of papers, then extended a hand out of the doorway of his private office to hook a passing aide by the arm. "Eddie, get out Carl Tartaglia's account—it's in his folder, you know? I don't know just how his account stands at the moment."

"I hope you're not going to claim *he* owes *you* any more money."

"Let's just see. I don't think there could be a whole lot in question, one way or the other."

An awkward half-minute passed. Then Eddie, tall and dark-bearded, was back with a manila folder. He put it into Ike's hands and walked away.

Ike opened the folder, looked at figures, puffed his cheeks.

"He was overpaid by eleven dollars. I can give you the eleven bucks right now if you want it."

"Oh. Yes, if you wouldn't mind."

Ike came back to his desk, the lady following. Alex didn't know whether to stand up or not, finally did so. It didn't matter, he wasn't going to be introduced.

"Ten and one, there's eleven. I'd just like you to sign a receipt for that, if you don't mind."

"I don't mind, that's all right." The Widow Tartaglia smiled a little foolishly, apologetically almost. Perhaps she had been expecting more of a hassle from these strange people who preyed on vulnerable men who took peculiar games too seriously.

"You seem to have a procedure all worked out," she remarked, handing Ike the signed receipt.

"I went through something like this last month." Ike accepted the paper, didn't know where to file it, at last tossed it onto his desk amid the litter. "Woman in Arizona, her son was playing Starweb. He was killed, evidently by some intruder."

"I guess Carl just fell." Mrs. Tartaglia smoothed back dark hair. She probably won't be a widow long, thought Alex, once she stops looking so tired. She went on: "The police say there's no evidence that it was anything else. Fell and hit his head on the door. Well, it's possible, he was clumsy. I can't say I'm grieving a lot, I had already moved out on him."

"Oh," said Jacobi, neutrally.

"Only thing is, he kept a gun in the apartment, and now I can't find it. Nothing else is missing. I didn't even mention the gun to the police. I was afraid they'd be on me for not having a permit or something. Maybe Carl pawned it somewhere." She gave a nervous little laugh.

"I really don't know how that works, gun permits and so on."

"Well, I guess I've taken up enough of your time. Thanks for the refund."

When Mrs. Tartaglia was gone, Ike sat down behind his

desk again and looked at Alex as if trying to remember what Alex was there for. ''Now we need a standby,'' Ike said.

''How's that?''

''We should put a standby player into that game, to take over Tartaglia's position.''

''Can I volunteer?'' Alex asked, on impulse. As he and Uncle Bob had agreed, one good way to learn something about a business was by becoming a customer.

Ike thought it over. ''Well, we do have a list of people who've signed up to be standby players; they get into games at a reduced cost that way. But sometimes in special cases we use someone on our staff, or . . . just a minute. I'll be right back.''

Left alone, Alex sat studiously ignoring the papers on the desk. The chance seemed too easy. Though he had to admit that nothing he had seen so far suggested that any of these people were capable of craftiness.

In just about a minute, Jacobi came strolling back into the room, carrying another folder whose contents he was studying as he walked. ''I didn't realize that,'' Ike muttered, as if to himself.

''What's up?''

Jacobi looked at him a little strangely. ''This is the same game I had to make the replacement in before. The guy in Arizona. Well, it doesn't matter. Sign-up fee for a standby player is six dollars. You know the Starweb rules? Never mind, I'll give you a copy of the new edition. And I'll have to get your address.''

Alex pulled out six dollars, but before the fee could be accepted there was an interruption, Eddie back to consult on some new problem. When that was disposed of, Ike led Alex back to the computer room, where after some preliminaries Alex watched his name being typed into the small computer. Now he saw that there was a telephone modem here, too; Ike must buy time on a large unit somewhere just like Uncle Bob.

''And your address?''

''All I can give you right now is the hotel,'' said Alex after a moment's hesitation. ''When I leave Albuquerque I'm really not sure. I'll have to let you know later where to mail the moves.''

Ike shrugged indifferently. "Okay." The address of the hotel went in, type, type, type, with careful concentration. Then Ike said: "Oh, I almost forgot," and picked up something he had brought with him from his private office, and handed it over to Alex. It was the stack of envelopes and other papers that Mrs. Tartaglia had brought in.

Alex scanned the papers casually, or started to. Then he opened his mouth to say something, closed it again, and went on trying to look casual. The name lettered large on the top envelope was LUCIFER, and it was followed in smaller lettering by the name of Robert Gregory, and the familiar address in Atlanta.

Then this was the same game that Uncle Bob was playing in. Alex couldn't very well comment on the fact to Ike, but it struck him as an oddity. Hell, it was more than odd: Ike had said there were hundreds of games in progress simultaneously, and Alex was sure Uncle Bob had said that he was in only one. It didn't really make sense. But figuring it out would have to wait.

Alex was stopped again when he came to the third envelope down in the small stack. Henry Brahmaguptra, he read, followed by an address in Los Alamos, New Mexico.

OCTAGON.

"Good luck," Ike wished him, smiling.

FOUR

At Berserkers Incorporated, regular office hours seemed to peter out for the day gradually between five o'clock and six.

Ike looked at his watch and sighed. "I've got a real busy weekend coming up. Are you going to be in town Monday?"

Alex said: "Yeah, I expect I'll be around a few more days."

Ike appeared to be relieved. "Good. Monday and Tuesday I'll be around, we can talk some more. Then Wednesday I've got to leave for a big game con in Los Angeles. We're setting up a booth, and demonstrating some things."

"I'll see you Monday or Tuesday, then," said Alex. "I'm interested in your operation here. Will anyone be in the shop here over the weekend?"

Ike waved a hand in a vague gesture. "Some people will be working."

Alex got the impression that Ike would prefer he didn't come around when the boss wasn't present. "That's okay, I have some other things to keep me busy. I'll be back sometime Monday to see you, then. Or Tuesday, anyway."

"Good." Ike appeared to be pleased.

It was getting dark as Alex returned to his hotel, where he found a message stating that his rental car was ready at last. Having secured the car, he left it parked outside and went into his room. There he turned on some lights and settled down to look over the Starweb materials.

First, the garishly illustrated rules booklet; it contained more than twenty pages, mostly filled with fine print. Uncle Bob had given Alex a general idea of the game, but it was obvious that he was still going to have a lot to learn. The second item Ike had given Alex was a blank turn sheet. On it the orders for AGRAVAN's next move were to be printed, according to the code (provided in the rules) which the computer that moderated the game would accept.

Alex put turn sheet and rules aside for the moment, and looked more carefully into the small bundle of Mrs. Tartaglia's bequest. Each of the diplomatic envelopes was marked with the code name of one other player, lettered in black ballpoint, presumably by dead Tartaglia's hand. There were OCTAGON, VIKING, LUCIFER . . .

And LUCIFER, of course, as the small real-world name and address on the envelope testified, was Uncle Bob. Alex considered again the fact that he and his uncle had landed in the same game. It would be something of a strain to accept that as coincidence. And that the old friend from Los Alamos, Dr. Brahmaguptra, should wind up in the same game too . . . Either there were not nearly as many Starweb games in progress as Ike said there were, or there was some other explanation other than chance.

Inside the LUCIFER envelope Alex's questing fingers found a number of folded, typewritten pages. The paper was thin, canary-yellow stuff. Looking at them closely, Alex saw they were carbon copies, evidently of typed messages that Tartaglia/AGRAVAN had mailed off to Uncle Bob in Atlanta. Mainly they were pleas for help. LUCIFER, you must send fleets to my aid, OCTAGON is attacking. That was the main idea. You must help me against OCTAGON . . .

Also in the LUCIFER envelope were three incoming notes, evidently from Uncle Bob, though Alex wasn't familiar with his uncle's handwriting. One of these contained a couple of sentences that Alex found thought-provoking:

I don't have any common border with OCTAGON, and so can't attack him very well. I don't even know who he is.

But OCTAGON was supposed to be Uncle Bob's old

friend. That would seem to indicate they didn't know they
were in the same game; they had heard of each other's
characters in the game, but only by code names. And that
would seem to scratch the explanation that they were in the
same game because they had asked to be . . . the point
nagged at Alex. He would try raising it with Ike, as a
theoretical case, when he had a chance to talk with Ike again.

Alex put the LUCIFER envelope aside and took up the one
for OCTAGON. Maybe some explanation here. But there
was not much of anything at all. Only a couple of three-by-
five cards bearing brief, jargony game messages, badly typed
on a poor ribbon, with many misspellings and X-outs. There
was no handwriting on these message cards at all. But there
was one name, Brahmaguptra, and the address.

Alex told himself firmly that because the seeming coincidence was mysterious didn't mean it was important. There
was doubtless a trivial explanation to suit the trivial problem.
And if not, so what? He wasn't going to sit here in his room
and brood on it all weekend.

Since he had arrived in Albuquerque, a couple of people
had mentioned Old Town to him. It was some kind of a goal
to have for going out. He wished now that he had invited Iris
Cardano out on some kind of date when he had the chance; he
had seen no evidence that she was attached to someone else.
Well, he would doubtless see her again on Monday . . . that
didn't do him any good right now, of course.

Old Town proved to be no great distance from Alex's
hotel, and there was parking. The souvenirs on sale in Old
Town Alex judged to have a lot in common with those
available in New York and Florida, except for the Indian
jewelry, pottery, and rugs. He had no idea how much of this
stuff was real, how much junk; certainly he had never
guessed that this much existed.

Alex had a drink, something with tequila in it, thought it
over and decided that he didn't really want another. What he
really wanted was to grab that young waitress by one of her
large, rounded parts the next time she passed by. That would
be a no-no. Maybe he ought to have just one more drink. If

only he had asked Iris out, before she vanished from the office. There had been one other girl working in the office but Alex wasn't sure about her name. Was it she or Iris who was shacking up with someone? Maybe it was both.

Next morning Alex woke in his solitary motel bed to a fine view of sunlight against drapes, and the busy sounds of nearby highway traffic. Playboy magazine lay where he had tossed it on the floor. Ah, for the romantic life of a secret agent.

Alex sat up, rubbing his eyes. He had to decide if he was going to try to look in on the Berserkers office today. Maybe he shouldn't, Ike had indicated that Monday would be the time, and might be annoyed.

Besides, another idea seemed to have grown up overnight in the back of Alex's mind.

Squinting out into sunlight past the edge of the drapes, he had a view of sandy embankments studded with some desert weeds, and supporting swooping concrete ramps that led up to a highway. The urge was strong to simply hit the road, take a look at some of the country hereabouts. When he pulled the drapes a little farther back, Alex could see a white arrow on a green roadside sign, showing which was the way to get to Santa Fe.

He dressed and went into the hotel coffee shop, which surprised him with how busy it was. After breakfast, back to his room, where he considered for a few moments and then picked up the Starweb papers and carried them with him out to his car. The hotel swimming pool was filled with water, though no one was using it in the cool morning. In the distance mountains still wearing firm snowcaps notched the clear horizon.

Alex consulted his street map and then drove downtown. The place looked even deader than he had expected it would be on a Saturday morning. He parked across the street from Berserkers Incorporated, around which there were no signs of life at all. Still Alex got out of his car and crossed the street and tried the door, and then the button beside the door. The place was locked up, and there was no answer from inside.

Now would be the time for an expert secret agent to break in and rifle their safe. Ha ha and ho ho.

Last night in Old Town he had bought himself a pair of sunglasses. As if he'd known even then that he'd be doing some highway driving today.

At Santa Fe Alex left the Interstate, which here curved off to the east. The City Different, claimed the signs; he was curious about the place and took the opportunity to drive into it and look around. On the outskirts were large encampments of mobile homes, looking just about like the ones he'd seen elsewhere. None of the buildings in town were tall, not even by Albuquerque standards. This was a smaller city, but still gradually tightening streets brought Alex into a traffic jam worthy of Manhattan as he approached its center. Its center appeared to be a Plaza, which looked not all that different from the one in last night's Old Town. This Plaza was evidently famous for something, but Alex couldn't find out what. He couldn't read the signs very well for having to concentrate on traffic; there appeared to be absolutely no hope of finding any place to park. Gradually he maneuvered his way back out of the center of town, and stopped at a commonplace drive-in to grab a hamburger for an early lunch. He consulted his maps. Los Alamos, he noted, was now something less than fifty miles away.

As he drove out of town, there were mountains on every hand, some of them quite close. The country here, he thought, had to be considerably higher than Albuquerque's five thousand feet or so above sea level. Alex had the impression that he had been driving almost continuously uphill since leaving Albuquerque, and now evergreens of one kind or another were taking up more and more of the landscape. He could see patches of snow now, at elevations not much greater than the highway he was traveling.

The highway now went up and down, but up was still predominant. At last the two narrow lanes of it scaled one more minor mountainside and delivered him to Los Alamos. On the outskirts of town he drove past a radar-equipped landing strip overlooked by an elegant new control tower, and decorated with a parked rank of expensive private planes. Just beyond the landing strip, Alex beheld a concentric cluster of thin metal towers, all bearing solar mirrors. The mirrors were focussing the midday sun upon something encased in dark metal atop one more tower that was central to the group.

Downtown, smalltown Los Alamos. This place was smaller than Santa Fe, but had a lot less adobe and was a lot less crowded. Outside a small drive-in bank, Alex found a public phone booth with an intact book. Sure enough, there was Brahmaguptra, H. He drew a deep breath and dialed.

The voice that answered on the first ring was high-pitched, yet still somehow obviously male. And it sounded ready, in a fatalistic way, for anything. At least that was what Alex read into the single drawn-out *helllooo*.

"Hello. I'd like to speak to Dr. Brahmaguptra."

"Speaking. Who is this?"

"Sir, my name is Alex Barrow, I'm a nephew of Robert Gregory's. I'm in New Mexico on some business." Here Alex paused, but got no immediate reply. "I was passing through Los Alamos today." A longer pause, long enough to nourish Alex's doubt that this visit was really a good idea.

"Not many people just pass through Los Alamos," the friendly voice in his ear remarked at last. "It doesn't really lie on the route from anywhere to anywhere, as you might say. However. How is Dr. Gregory these days?"

"Why, he's just fine, sir. At least he was when I saw him a couple of days ago. He suggested to me that I might look you up when I got to New Mexico."

"Indeed." The thin voice seemed to take this seriously. "Yes, then I think we should get together. Yes, it will be pleasant to see you. Where are you now?"

Directions to the Brahmaguptra house were moderately complicated because it seemed there was only one road bridging a large ravine that divided practically everything. But still Alex had no real trouble.

The house on 20th Street, when he reached it, was moderately large, built of timber and stone, with a shingled roof peaked sharply enough to give it an alpine look. Nothing like the mad scientist's castle in Georgia, but it certainly looked comfortable and prosperous enough. Uncle Bob's old friend had evidently not had to go on welfare. Walking across the winter-dry grass of the front yard, Alex could look into the distance in almost every direction and see mountains. Several sizable Douglas fir were growing in the yard, and snow persisted on the north sides of trees and house alike.

A woman in her thirties, wearing faded blue jeans and a checked shirt, answered the door; she was as dark-haired as Mrs. Tartaglia, but infinitely more cheerful-looking. She lacked the dark skin coloring that the name of Brahmaguptra had led Alex vaguely to expect. "Hi," she greeted Alex, in friendly Middle-western tones.

"Hello. I'm Alex Barrow. I just called—"

"I know. Come in. I'm Jennifer, Dr. Brahmaguptra's my father-in-law."

"Thank you."

The inside of the house was snugly warm, and appeared at first to be heavily and confusingly over-furnished. But Alex, as he was led from one room to another, quickly got the impression of powerful though subtle organizing forces at work. The place was not as chaotic as it had seemed at first glance.

Green chalkboards must have been on sale somewhere at a discount, for there appeared to be a dozen of them scattered about the house. They were mounted on walls, standing on draftsman's tables, leaning against other furniture. Some of them were covered with scrawled mathematical formulas; Alex could recognize calculus, if not understand much of it; and there was much beyond what he could recognize. One board bore a grocery list, another what looked like an attempt to solve a cipher. Others had been erased to dusty obscurity. In every room at least one table held papers and books, many of the books with improvised page markers protruding. The

top of the piano was similarly laden, and at its feet one of
those East Indian instruments with many strings was snugly
bedded down on cushions. Half of the walls seemed to have
been built over with bookcases, and most of the shelves were
full.

On a small cleared space of pine floor before a color
television console, two boys about twelve years old were
playing a TV game. They held small wired boxes in their
hands, and pushed at levers; on the screen two little basketball players, mere sketched stick-figures instead of Uncle
Bob's vital dancers, slid from left to right and back again as if
stuck in electronic grooves. A small light-spot of a ball was
bouncing noisily, for the moment eluding the players' symbolic arms. The score was 26 to 12, with 3:28 to play and
counting down. One of the boys was blond, but the other
looked as if his family name might well be Brahmaguptra.

Jennifer threaded a graceful path through all of this; and
Alex, following, watched how her hips moved in her tight
jeans. From this angle she looked a little younger than he had
thought at first.

"Dad?" she called ahead.

In a door frame of dark wood, beside what looked like a
real suit of medieval armor, there came into view a stocky old
man muffled in a great sweater. His dark hair had little gray
in it, and there were few wrinkles on his olive face, but he
was old. Probably, thought Alex, older than Uncle Bob.
Dark eyes studied Alex from above Ted Kennedy-style reading glasses. "So, come in, young man," the old man said in
his light voice, and turned to lead the way.

They went through a narrow hallway, walls decorated with
small rugs that looked like the ones the Old Town merchants
had advertised as Navajo. Now Alex was led into a room that
looked even more like a mathematician's study than the rest
of the house did, where he was offered a comfortable chair.
He was hardly surprised to see a modem near the phone.
There was no computer in view, however, only a fancy
calculator on the desk near the old manual typewriter. Had
OCTAGON's diplomatic messages been typed on that? It

somehow seemed improbable, this did not strike Alex as the
room for games.

Jennifer stayed hovering near until all the expectable re-
marks about weather and roads and such had been got out of
the way. Then the old man and the younger woman exchanged what Alex took as a possibly meaningful glance,
and she went out, shutting the study door softly behind her.
The thud of the bouncing electronic basketball had already
ceased.

"Now." Brahmaguptra leaned forward in his chair, elbows braced widely on his desk. "Had your uncle any
particular message for me?"

"No sir. There was no message in particular."

The lightly seamed brown face changed subtly.
Brahmaguptra leaned back in his chair again. When next he
spoke it was in the same friendly voice, yet something had
been altered. "Did your uncle ever tell you how he and I
became acquainted?"

"He said you had worked together, off and on."

"Yes . . . we did. Let's see, Bob has two brothers and a
sister, as I recall?"

"No sir, two sisters and a brother." Something about this
conversation reminded Alex of the first words he'd exchanged with his uncle in Atlanta. Uncle Bob, too, had got
something about the family history wrong at the start, some
kind of nonsense about a farm. It suddenly occurred to Alex
that this was as if he himself were being tested, made to prove
by knowledge that he was who he claimed to be. Now he
said: "My mother's name is Emma. She's the one who
stayed in New York."

The old man nodded pleasantly at this. Then he chatted on
a little longer, reminiscing about the old days when he had
met and visited with some of the Gregory-Barrow clan. Alex
got a chance to answer a few more questions. Brahmaguptra
appeared to have met many of the older generation of Alex's
family in the past, and to remember them with real interest.

"So, I am really glad that your uncle suggested that you
call on me. He and I have had our differences, but . . . one

feels isolated here, sometimes, though in fact there are many good people to talk to. You must stay and have dinner with us, certainly.''

''Uh, if you're sure it wouldn't be too much trouble.''

The old man dismissed the objection. ''Would you like some coffee now, maybe, Alex? Hot chocolate? Hold us over until dinner time.''

''Thanks, hot chocolate sounds great. I haven't had any for years.''

Brahmaguptra heaved himself up from behind his desk. It was plainly a strain on his corpulent old frame to do so, yet he made the effort with a flare; his aging flesh embodied the spirit of a dancer, or a triumphant athlete. He stumped his way to the study door and opened it and exchanged mild shouts with Jennifer. Somewhere out there the two boys were arguing about something. A door slammed. In the distance, a dog barked.

Leaving the study door open, the old man came back behind his desk where with a heartfelt grunt he collapsed into his chair. ''So. Yes. It would seem desirable that your Uncle Bob and I should have a talk.'' He raised his eyebrows inquiringly at Alex, as if he sought agreement.

''Yes,'' said Alex. He didn't know what else to say.

The old man nodded. ''There are things, though, about telephone conversations that are unsatisfactory.''

''You mean somebody listening in. Yes, I suppose there's a lot of industrial espionage, things like that, going on. When you play in the league Uncle Bob does.''

''What league is that?''

''Well . . . I meant big business and all.''

''Yes, big business,'' said the old man, as he might have said: ''Yes, Satan and all his minions.'' He went on: ''Your uncle *did* express a wish to talk to me?''

''I certainly got the impression that he would like to.'' That was true. But Alex was having a hard time remembering exactly what Uncle Bob had said and what he hadn't.

Uncle Bob's old friend had turned his chair partially away, and was enjoying the view from his study window. In this at

least his house had the edge on Robert Gregory's. "Yes,"
Brahmaguptra said, "I should like to talk to your Uncle Bob
again—like very much to see him face to face." He swiveled
back to face Alex directly. "Did he perhaps hint at any way
that such a meeting might be arranged?"

Alex found that his own hands were clenched together in
his lap, his palms sweating slightly, he didn't quite know
why. He was getting into something, and he didn't quite
know what. "No," he finally confessed. "I can't remember
that he had any arrangements for a meeting to propose."

"He would be welcome here. To visit me. Surely he
knows that."

"He did say you were one of the few people in the world he
felt he could still trust."

"Ah." Slowly, and with satisfaction. "He said that."

"But as for the two of you getting together, well, I don't
think Uncle Bob travels much any more. I mean, he sent me
out here rather than come himself."

"Yes, I see. With what instructions did he send you, if you
don't mind my asking?"

There was a deep worry in this old man, who Uncle Bob
had said he trusted. Alex took a plunge. "It's supposed to be
confidential, but he's getting interested in computer games.
In particular, the company in Albuquerque that runs Starweb."

"Starweb?" The keen old eyes for once were unrespon-
sive. Brahmaguptra might never have heard of the game.

"The computer game; you know, the space war thing.
You and Uncle Bob are both playing in it. You're in the same
game, actually."

"The space war . . . ah, of course." Brahmaguptra demonstrated recognition, if not understanding. "But that is
Hank, you see. Not me."

"Hank?"

"My grandson, Jennifer's boy. You probably saw him on
the way in. He is Henry Brahmaguptra the third, you see, and
he does not always make the distinction clear when he uses
the name. Yes, now I recall the computer game you mention,

played by mail. Hank wanted me to try it. I looked over the rules, and the game, I thought, is not bad. At least it is not entirely violence; it seemed possible to sometimes win by peaceful means. But I don't care much for games. Hank did join, he needed a raise in his allowance . . . but you say your uncle is interested in this game. And playing.''

"Yessir. And having a hard time winning, too, I gather. Young Hank must be pretty bright. Anyway, Uncle Bob's main interest is in the way the game company is being run.''

"He's thinking of investing?''

"It's a good thing you're an old friend, I'm letting you in on all his secrets. This is all confidential, of course, as I said.''

Brahmaguptra, with something of the air of a hopeful child about him, studied Alex in silence for a time. Then he asked: "Bob said, he really said, that I am one of the few people in the world he can still trust?''

"Yessir. He did.''

"Did he say that recently?''

"Yessir, just before I left to come out here.''

"Is he in good health?''

"Oh yeah, he looked fine.''

Brahmaguptra was still regarding Alex in silence when the hot chocolate arrived, borne on a tray by Jennifer, who hovered for a moment beside the desk. "Everything all right, Dad?''

Her father-in-law smiled at her, very briefly. "Alex has not told me of any disasters, anyway.''

Jennifer gave him back an intent, concerned look. Not really surprised that disasters were on the old man's mind. She perhaps knew more than Alex did of why meetings between two old friends should be carefully arranged, why there was reason for worry in the air.

The old man told his daughter-in-law, seriously: "Bob Gregory and Hank are in the same Starweb game.''

She received news of Starweb with the same utter blank-ness that the old man himself had shown the first time the game was mentioned. "Whatever does *that* mean?" she asked finally.

"The game, Jen. The computer thing—"

"Yes. But does it *mean* anything, that the two of them are in the same one?"

Brahmaguptra relaxed suddenly, with a rueful little laugh. He sounded definitely non-paranoid. "I don't know. Perhaps it means only that there are not so many Starweb games in progress as the company claims in their advertising."

Alex sipped at his cup of hot chocolate; yes, it was good. He watched the other two carefully.

Now something had started Jennifer thinking seriously. "Eddie might know—but how *could* it mean anything?"

The old man sighed. "Is Hank around, still? Ask him to step in here for just a moment, would you, Jen?"

The dark boy, brought to the study by his mother, stood in the doorway a few moments later, looking thoughtful at his grandfather's question. "How many games? There's about four hundred Starweb games in progress right now. That's what the newsletter says, anyway."

"Doesn't your game have a number?"

"Yeah. X-430. But they don't assign the numbers sequentially, Eddie says, so you can't tell by that."

Alex asked: "How did you happen to get into the particular game that you're in, Hank?"

The boy shrugged. He looked a little worried, Alex thought, probably because the adults were being so serious about this. "I guess it just happened to be the game that was forming when I signed up. Why?"

"I'm in it too," Alex told him, smiling. From the corner of his eye he saw both adult faces turn to him in silence. "I just signed up yesterday, as a replacement player for AG-RAVAN. He—had to drop out."

Hank was delighted. "That guy in Albuquerque had to drop out? You're AGRAVAN now? Boy, you got a bad deal coming in as standby into that mess. I'm gonna cream you in about two more moves."

"Oh yeah? We'll see."

Hank took thought, then came to what appeared to be a decision of some importance. "I can show you my setup if you want to see it. You'll be able to tell where my homeworld is and all, but there's nothing you're gonna be able to do about it anyway."

"Yeah, I'd like to see."

Grandpa too was interested enough to come along, and they brought their hot chocolate with them. Jennifer, after confirming Alex as a dinner guest, went to the kitchen.

Following Hank through a hallway narrowed by more bookshelves, Alex passed what was obviously a woman's bedroom, containing a single bed, more books, and a wall photograph of a dark-faced young man in white clothes with tennis racket in hand. The next room down the hallway was a boy's. Here the walls were mad with posters, there were still more books, and two more of the green chalkboards. Along one wall a long, somewhat crude wooden table had been built in, as if to support an elaborate model railroad layout. But instead of tracks the table was loaded with wires, a parts cabinet, soldering gun, black boxes and wired breadboards, along with assorted other electronic gear. There was a picture tube scavenged from some color television, and what had to be a small homemade power supply, from which wires spread out everywhere. Half-disassembled among the rest were components Alex thought he could recognize as belonging to a home computer system, a Radio Shack TRS-80.

"Let me show you the worlds I have in my control," Hank was murmuring. Already half gone in abstraction as he bent over the equipment, he sounded like a pre-pubescent, unconscious parody of a C-movie villain. Primitive and laborious as his activity at the workbench was, Alex was reminded inescapably of the wizardry in Atlanta. Alex moved closer, watching.

Hank said: "Look out for the back of that CRT, there's thirty thousand volts."

"I know," said Alex, and got a quick glance of approval.

In a couple of minutes, the nineteen-inch screen was

displaying a green network comprising circular worlds and their connecting pathways. A talented child, Alex thought, working from memory, might have made a sketch that looked like this of Uncle Bob's display.

Hank was scowling. "I gotta buy more memory," he muttered to himself. "This isn't gonna be good enough much longer. Only twenty-four K of RAM, what can you do?"

"All the goodies you would like are not always on surplus sale," remarked his grandfather, who had been waiting and watching patiently. "Maybe for your birthday you'll get some new toy. Maybe when you can show me that you've learned a little more mathematics."

"Maybe Eddie can pick some up for me," Hank muttered vaguely, engrossed with wires. Presumably he meant the goodies and not the math. He had pulled a battered chair up near the workbench now, and knelt sideways on the chair with his hands still working at connections, using spring clips. His fingers were agile. On the screen the picture jittered, went away, came back.

Alex set down his cup on a clear end of the long bench and turned around, stretching. In a far corner of the room lay a Nerf football that had seen some heavy use. Under the rumpled bed, a pair of spiked track shoes. And on the wall, just above the bed, a framed drawing of a castle, done with loving attention to realistic detail in the fortifications. Brave banners blew, atop a crennelated tower. There was one small armed figure on the tower, and two mounted knights outside, evidently craving admittance, or whatever it was you did to get them to let the drawbridge down.

"Did you draw this yourself, Hank?" It was somehow just immature enough to let Alex believe that might be possible.

The boy looked up briefly. "Yep."

"What is it? I mean, is it some particular . . ."

"Sir Lancelot's castle. You know, from Malory's version."

"Oh. It looks great."

"Thanks. Now, these are my worlds." Hank had at last managed to achieve the color differential he had been trying for, and some of the circles were now transformed to red or blue. "It looks like I don't have many fleets, but a lot of them are off invading your worlds. You want to see your worlds? I'll have 'em on in a minute. The ones I know about, anyway."

"You know who LUCIFER is?" asked Alex.

"His real name? I forget. I got it written down somewhere." Hank did not seem anxious to discuss diplomacy. "I think he's your ally, or at least he was allies with the guy who was AGRAVAN before you. Anyway I didn't like his code name much, or yours. AGRAVAN, that's a real loser's name."

"Hank," deplored his grandfather.

"Well, it is. I wish I knew some more people around here who like this game. Ted doesn't."

"Ted?" Alex asked.

"The kid I was playing basketball with. He lives next door. He just likes the regular video games—they're pretty simple, like that basketball. Here's your AGRAVAN worlds, colored white. I think your homeworld is over this way somewhere. No, I know it is, it's gotta be. I'd propose some kind of a deal but I think I'm gonna wipe you out soon anyway." But Hank sounded more worried than triumphant this time.

"Well, thanks for the warning." Alex had to smile. He'd had a sudden imaginative vision of Uncle Bob, surrounded by his small fortune in computing power, frowning over his calculations; from what Alex had seen of the game, LUCIFER too was in danger of going down before this twelve-year-old opponent.

"If we got into another game together," Hank said, wistfully changing tone, "we could be allies."

"I guess we could. I'd like that. But you never have any choice about which game you're put into, do you? Who the other players are?"

"No, I guess not." Hank became interested in adjusting the vertical hold on his display.

Alex turned and said something to Hank's grandfather

about how well and cleverly the kid had his electronics organized.

"Yes," admitted the old man. "He has some brains, I think, if he learns how to use them. Of course he had a lot of help with this construction here . . . Jen?" he called suddenly down the hall. "Is Eddie coming for dinner tonight too? I didn't realize . . ."

"He has to work late," Jen's answer floated back. "He said he'd pick me up about seven."

Dinner was pork chops, mashed potatoes, and some fancy spiced mixed vegetable dish reputedly from a recipe generations old when the Brahmaguptra family had been Hindu vegetarians. Dessert, a Sara Lee cake thawed for the occasion. There were no servants, robot or otherwise. Everyone took a hand at cleaning up, except Jen, who was getting ready to go out.

"Maybe you've met Eddie," Brahmaguptra remarked suddenly to Alex, above the gurgle of water in the sink. The old man had rolled up his sweater sleeves on his plump, hairless arms, and was washing dishes like an expert. "He works part-time for those computer-game people in Albuquerque. Or he did. Hank, does—?"

"Yeah, he still does," said Hank, who was busy wiping the plastic tablecloth with a paper towel. "Eddie's another game freak."

"Eddie," Alex pondered, gathering garbage. "Yeah, I think I did meet him. Tall guy, with a beard? He's the one who's coming?"

"Yes, that's Eddie. Oh, it isn't so great a coincidence as it might seem. The total population of northern New Mexico is not great, to begin with. And of that total only a part is Anglo—oh, even I am an Anglo here, you see, being neither Spanish nor Indian nor black. And the class of educated, professional people of whatever race is smaller still, you see. So in Albuquerque, or Santa Fe, or here, one keeps encountering the same people, same faces, at work, at social events, political rallies, everywhere."

Alex pictured this man with dark-bearded Eddie at a politi-

cal rally. Somehow he didn't think he'd be likely to spot
Uncle Bob at the same gathering. "Oh," Alex said. "Well,
do you suppose we could not tell Eddie who I am? I mean,
that Robert Gregory's my uncle? See, Berserkers Incorporated is not supposed to know yet that he's the one who's
thinking of investing."

Brahmaguptra frowned mildy. "Ah, I suppose secrecy in
these things is routine. Business. But let me speak to Jen."
He walked out of the kitchen drying his hands on a towel, to
return a couple of minutes later. "How about this, Alex?
We'll just say you're a nephew of an old friend of mine. I
don't suppose Eddie will feel any need to probe beyond
that."

"Fine, thanks."

A little later, Alex met Eddie MacLaurin for the second
time. This time the introduction was a shade more formal
than before. Away from Berserkers Inc., and better dressed,
Eddie looked older than he had before; probably he was just
about Jen's age. It came out in conversation that he and Jen
had met about a year ago. Tonight they had tickets for some
special preview of the summer opera in Santa Fe. Alex
gathered that Eddie's full time job was with the Labs, the
installations in Los Alamos rather than those down in Albuquerque.

When the couple had departed, the old man invited Alex
out into the fast-chilling night to look through the family
telescope at some lunar craters and whatever other celestial
objects could be found. Alex put on a heavy coat borrowed
from the old man. Somehow, without there having been any
apparent strain, it had worked out that Alex was going to stay
overnight, and drive back to Albuquerque in the morning
when, as his hosts put it, his chances of staying on the
winding, unfamiliar roads would be much better. Also he
would have an opportunity of seeing some real scenery.
There was a much more scenic route, they all assured him,
than the one he had driven coming up.

Placed at a vantage point above the densest, dirtiest, wet-
test eight thousand feet of earthly atmosphere, the small

telescope on its tripod showed the craters of the moon with merciless clarity. Then the old man went after other targets. He pointed out what he called an interesting eclipsing binary, a kind of double star. He explained what they were looking at lucidly, so Alex understood at once, or anyway was confident he did. He was shown a few more wonders of the galaxy, before the images began to get too twinkly to see much. The night still appeared perfectly clear, but there were currents in the air, the old man said.

Telescope viewing was over. Hank was sent to bed, to read until he got sleepy. Alex and his host returned to the study, where a cabinet was made to disgorge a bottle of something called Inca Pisco. It was fine brandy; like everything else about this household, different from anything Alex was used to, and at the same time very good and pleasing. He and the old man talked for a time about Peru, where the brandy came from, where the old man had visited and worked at one time, helping to set up a radio observatory.

At eleven o'clock Brahmaguptra yawned and shook his head. "It's ridiculous, I suppose, but I still wait up for Jen when she goes out. She'll be thirty-four this summer, and I still do it." He paused. "I don't suppose your uncle has ever married?"

"Not that I know of." The brandy was marvelously relaxing and mellowing stuff. "Well, there was a girl staying with him when I was there. Caroline. They said she was his daughter." Might as well, he thought, make a clean sweep of all his employer's secrets.

"I know about Caroline." The old man paused again. "She is still crippled, I suppose? Of course, she must be. That was a terrible thing."

"What happened to her? I never heard the . . ."

"Just senseless violence. They were in New York city at the time. One of those terrible pointless street attacks. It must be a couple of years ago, now."

"Longer than that, I think. But . . . I don't know that anyone in our family ever heard about it at the time."

The old man shrugged. "Bob . . . doesn't seek publicity.

He isn't very communicative about personal things. And these things come and go in the news all the time, like wars. Nothing much is made of them, usually.''

"Yes sir, I guess you're right.''

Ed brought Jen home at a little after midnight, and came in with her to have some coffee. Eddie had to go to work again tomorrow, he said, even if it was Sunday. From the additional terse sentence or two that he spoke about his job, Alex now got the idea that he was somehow involved with security at one or more of the laboratories; he had to travel down to Albuquerque and back; maybe the different Labs shared some kind of blanket security force. And one or more recent developments, unspecified, had the people in Eddie's section working overtime. No details were given, and Alex didn't ask.

They talked briefly about Starweb. Yeah, said Eddie, there were about four hundred games in progress now—he didn't know what the exact number was. No, there was no way ordinarily to tell who was going to be in the same game with you when you signed up. Ike used a program for assigning people that randomized, after it had first made sure that no two players in the same game were from the same locality. If there were two from the same city, it might be unfairly easy for them to get together as allies and make plans. Alex nodded. It all sounded logical. He didn't bring up the situation of the game that he was in—he couldn't, without getting into who his uncle was.

Alex slept in the guest room that night, under a heavy quilt. Once or twice he thought he could hear Jen breathing, right next door. Somewhere down the hallway, the old man snored, a trusting sound. Once during the night Hank, gripped by some fearful dream, cried out in his childish voice.

FIVE

In the morning Alex enjoyed a relaxed breakfast alone with the old man; they had cereal and toast, orange juice and coffee. Hank was up and out already, taking part in some bicycle event, and Jen was sleeping late. It was Sunday, no one in the household had to go to work, and a thick Denver newspaper had just been delivered. The old man pressed sections of the paper upon him, but Alex was growing restless and anxious to be off. He felt glad, though, that he'd come. He was making progress, he thought, at least around the edges of Uncle Bob's business problem. And he'd be able to reassure Uncle Bob that his old friend was doing all right.

Brahmaguptra looked at Alex over his section of the paper. "You're driving back through the Jemez, aren't you? You'll see some beautiful country that way."

"If that's the way you mapped out for me last night. Sure."

The old man put his newspaper aside. "When you see your uncle again," he said, and stopped. He let out a sigh, and rubbed his upper lip as if hoping for a mustache. "Tell him I agree that he and I should have a talk. Face to face. Actually I don't see any other way. And . . . tell him that I always wish him well. Personally."

"Yes sir. Personally, you say."

"He has been involved in other matters, political and so on, that I cannot support or go along with. He'll know what I mean." The old man's eyes were wary. Almost frightened, Alex thought.

"I'll tell him what you say, sir."

Uncle Bob, he supposed, would understand, and would perhaps explain. Alex left Los Alamos on a winding, two-lane highway, much like the one upon which he had entered. The town vanished at once, and the road was engulfed on both sides by a recently burned-over forest. At intervals, small, neat signs warned without explanation against stopping in the burned area. Now and then somewhat larger signs cautioned DANGER EXPLOSIVES and commanded that there be NO TRESPASSING.

Alex had heard that the world's first nuclear bombs had been designed in Los Alamos, back in the days of World War II. Maybe the mathematician Brahmaguptra had been living in the same house then, and working then on bombs . . . though with his present professed abhorrence of war and violence, he didn't seem at all the type. Alex had got the idea that the old man was working for the Labs in some capacity now, but had heard no details. Well, he supposed the laboratories now had their peaceful projects too.

Security, that kept Eddie MacLaurin so busy working overtime, was obviously of great importance hereabouts. The burned area was behind Alex now, and everything on both sides of the highway was healthy woods, lightly fenced off. Small enclosures of high, chain-link fence were visible at some distance from the road. Here and there a drive went back into the woods through a closed gate and past a military-style gatehouse, apparently unmanned. These entrances were marked only with neatly painted letters and numbers in cryptic groupings. All this went on for miles. The Labs. Los Alamos. Security. And Brahmaguptra was still here.

With no formal announcement of any boundary, the military indications abruptly ceased to be. Now there were no warning signs, nothing to be seen but unfenced mountain wilderness, and the highway, almost devoid of traffic, making its way through. Probably, Alex thought, this was still government land of some kind. Maybe national forest. He was a little vague about what national forest meant. The sun was bright and already warm, and he was driving now with the window on his side open. He forgot about business for a while, and games, and watched the scenery.

Certain questions, though, and problems, not all of them business matters, kept nagging at him. Back in Albuquerque before noon, he headed not straight for his motel but for downtown, where once more he drove past Berserkers Incorporated, checking for any signs of activity. Sure enough, there was one old car parked right in front of the office, on a street otherwise as dead as Pompeii on Sunday morning. Alex parked his own vehicle alongside and went up to the office door.

As before, the door was locked, but this time the doorbell got results. Iris Cardano appeared inside the heavy glass; today she was wearing jeans and an old shirt, evidently not having expected to be doing much in the way of receptionist's duties. She recognized Alex, answered his smile tentatively, and then turned a latch to let him in.

The moment he saw her, Alex had felt something turn on inside him, subtly.

"Ike's not around," Iris greeted him. "He's off on a weekend trip."

She hadn't exactly invited Alex in, but she wasn't blocking the doorway, either, so in he went. "Well, I just took a chance that someone would be here. I find this operation pretty fascinating. I was kind of hoping it would be okay if I just sat around and watched and listened for a while? Whatever kind of work you're doing. I wouldn't try to get any game secrets or anything like that."

The front room was illuminated only by daylight coming

through the storefront windows. But lights were on in one of
the back rooms, and now someone coughed back there, a
firmly masculine sound.

"Well . . ." Iris didn't appear unhappy to see Alex. But
she was plainly undecided.

Alex pressed a little. "I'm thinking of investing, you
know. I'm sure Ike wants me to have a good idea of how the
business is run."

"Well . . ."

The young man from the back room, who turned out to be
not Eddie but the clean-shaven one who had been loading
tapes during Alex's last visit to the office, emerged into the
front room now and stood looking at them. "I'm going to
take off now, Iris," he announced.

She looked back at him. "Oh. Okay, Paul."

Paul smiled his way past them and went out. He closed the
street door behind him, and Alex saw him get into his old car
in front of the building and drive away.

Nothing had been settled yet. "I've really got quite a lot of
work to do," said Iris. But there was no finality in her voice
as she said it.

Alex waved his hands accommodatingly. "I won't get in
your way. Promise. It's just that I've got a sizable chunk of
money that I'm thinking of investing, and I want to check
things out thoroughly before I do." He paused. "Take you
out to eat when you're through? Your choice of places. I've
got this expense account."

"Well . . . I think you've just made me an offer I can't
refuse."

Iris meant it about having work to do; it kept her busy until
mid-afternoon. Paperwork, mostly, jargony accounts and
records of transactions that Alex didn't try too hard to inter-
pret. They talked a little. He tried hard to avoid giving the
impression that he was a spy or snoop, but still he looked
around.

In the middle of the afternoon Iris locked up the place, and
got into Alex's car and directed him to a place that didn't look
expensive but turned out to be, where they ate Mexican. The

food was hot enough to bring tears to gringo eyes, though Iris guided him to the milder types. The Mexican beer was just the antidote.

And, one thing led to another. It was the way of the world for that to happen, Alex had observed. And sometimes—not often enough by far, but sometimes—the consequences were delightful. In this case, they were way way far ahead of Playboy magazine.

It was after dark now, but all the lights were still out in the biggest and best ground floor room of the motel. Iris's old shirt and jeans, with her bra and panties on top of them, were heaped in a chair at bedside. Alex's garments were even more recklessly strewn about the floor. And Iris's plump young body, which if not exactly beautiful was beyond doubt actively and hungrily female, lay beside him in the king-size bed.

"Wow," he said, rolling a few inches away from her to relax with a great sigh. "How you doing?" he added, considering it gentlemanly to inquire.

"Fine." Iris's voice in the gathering darkness was thoughtful. "Alex. How much money are you thinking of investing in the company? If it's any of my business."

"Aha. Oho. Ike has assigned you to try to seduce me, and learn my secrets. It's an old tactic." When there was no answer, Alex added in a different tone: "Why? Is there any reason I shouldn't?"

"Oh, I don't know. If *I* had a bundle of money I think I'd buy stock in something else. Exxon Corporation. Something safe." Iris's voice acquired a drawl. "You know what I think? I think *you* seduced *me*, to try to learn the Starweb programming. That's what a lot of people are after. But you're wasting your time, I don't know it. Ike never reveals it to anyone."

"I bet he would to you, if you got him into bed."

"I have. He won't."

"Oh." Alex rose on one elbow. In the darkness he couldn't see Iris's face well enough to determine anything from it. "Who's after the Starweb program?"

"All kinds of people. Guys who like to pirate games and sell them. Or even just players looking for a good way to cheat."

Alex puffed out his breath. "I can never tell when you're serious and when you're not."

"Oh no?" Iris maneuvered her soft body a little closer. Her hand reached out.

"Oh, wow. I can tell you're in a serious mood."

"Hm. So are you. You're going to be very firm about this."

"Yeah. Except first I've really got to go to the john." Alex disengaged himself, gently and reluctantly, and sat up, swinging his feet over the edge of the bed. "Don't go away, I'll be right back."

"I'll be here."

He closed the bathroom door behind him before turning on the light. More gentlemanly not to blind her. Then, squinting and shading his eyes against the brightness, he relieved himself. Even now Starweb was nagging at the back of his mind. It seemed to be tangled into everything. There had to be some commonsense kind of reason why it was. Probably it would all come clear to him sometime, sometime when he was neither too horny nor too sleepy to think straight . . . the way things looked, that wasn't going to be tonight. Alex smiled at himself in the mirror.

He heard a vague, soft sound as of movement out in the room, Iris up and doing something evidently, though the sound could possibly have come from the room next door or even out in the hall. Maybe she was looking for a cigarette. But no, he didn't think she smoked.

Anticipating her body, Alex rinsed his hands and dried them on a towel. He turned off the light and then opened the bathroom door.

His eyes were now unused to the darkness. But there was still enough light in the room, coming in around the edges of the imperfectly closed drapes, for Alex to see something of what was going on. The whitish blur of the girl's naked body was lying sideways now across the wide bed. She was on her back, her head toward Alex, her face tilted toward him upside down as her head lay back over the edge of the bed. What appeared to be a wheelchair was parked at bedside. Instead of a person it held some kind of a mechanical device, almost man-sized. The device was reaching out with two odd, thin arms, and doing something to Iris's throat.

Her legs and hips were moving, as if in slow passion. Her hands were locked on one of the thin, metallic-looking arms, and a sound, very low and peculiar, came from her open mouth. Alex, struck dumb, struck paralyzed, realized that she was being strangled, and came out of his paralysis enough to approach the bed. Had he been looking at some human attacker, he would have hurled himself upon the man and fought. But it went against all instinct and all training for a man to simply hurl himself upon machinery. When machinery menaced, you tried to see what was wrong with it, you tried to turn it off. When you saw another human had got caught in a machine, you gently tried to somehow work them loose . . .

Alex laid hands upon one of the metal arms. In his grip it felt cool and hard, dangerously powerful. It was vibrating with an overwhelming force, like some component of a lathe, a power saw, an engine. The limb scarcely moved with his first tug at it, and a moment later he had let go, a frightened reflexive pulling back. There was a smell of chemicals near the bed, and a very faint electric buzz, as of smoothly working motors. One of Iris's arms suddenly began to lash wildly about, and her nails caught and dug with sharp pain at the bare flesh of Alex's left forearm. He tried to pull away, just as something with overwhelming strength seized his right wrist.

He was off balance, falling toward the bed. His own neck was caught, from behind, in a crushing grip. The pillowed, rumpled surface of the bed was flying up to strike him in the face.

Coming awake was a slow process. And it was utterly

horrible, because it was not really like coming awake at all. It was only entering a new phase of nightmare, a different and more terribly distinct chapter. When Alex first awakened, he continued to lie still for what seemed like a long time. He was still dazed, and he was fighting for breath through a constricted throat. He had the feeling that the muscles in his neck had been physically paralyzed.

At last he managed to raise his head. All the muscles of his neck were aching, but now it was certain that he could breathe. He was lying sprawled face downward on the bed, with Iris's naked body an awkward lump caught partially beneath his own. He could feel with every touch of her that she was dead. There was something sticky, blood, a little blood on them both, and Alex thought that he could feel the chill blood congealing, and that her dead flesh was already turning cool.

Somehow he succeeded in getting his arms and legs to move. He pushed himself up on his hands, free of her body, and then got to his feet beside the bed. His breathing made strange noises in his throat. The open eyes of Iris, upside down, regarded him in the light that filtered round the drapes. His forearm stung where her nails had torn his skin. The unimaginable intruder was gone, and the room door was shut. It was still night, everything but Iris and himself was still intact, the room and the motel around were quiet.

Alex's clothes were still scattered about on the floor, just as he had dropped them. His breath moaned as he reached out to begin to pick them up. But there was blood on his arm, blood drying on his fingers . . . he must wash first.

In the lighted bathroom mirror he gazed into the eyes of a madman, a stranger who noted carefully that there was, after all, only a little blood. Apparently it had all come from the wound in his left forearm, where Iris's nails had scraped in what must have been one of the last moments of her life. The bleeding had now stopped. The wound when he washed it was quite small.

The mirrored madman washed and dried himself, throwing down a slightly bloody towel. Then he walked back into the bedroom and got dressed. He looked into the eyes of the figure draped on the bed, but he wasn't thinking about a thing, not a thing in this world except the details of getting dressed and getting ready to go out. He had to make sure that the clothes were on straight, that everything important had been picked up and put into the pockets. Here was the money belt, with money still intact. The wheelchair's motive had certainly not been robbery. Here were the car keys. All the essentials. Where was the room key? Alex stood rubbing his chin thoughtfully, trying to think carefully . . . but some time had passed before he remembered that there was no room key here, only the four-digit combination.

Later Alex could remember that moment. The next thing that he could remember was himself driving his rented car, at moderate speed and carefully, up the highway ramp that led to Interstate 40 going east. He was driving away without ever having paused consciously to formulate a plan. But now that he was in motion he did not even consider turning back. Flight once begun seemed to produce its own justification and its own momentum.

His first stop was under a sky full of indifferent stars, in a New Mexico highway town called Tucumcari. His car was low on fuel, and his bowels demanded to be emptied. Slowly, though, his guts were quieting, his body readjusting, his mind regaining something like its normal capacity for thought.

When Alex came out of the gas station and back to his car, he stood beside it for a moment frozen, watching a State Police car cruising slowly past. The police went right on by, ignoring him. Gradually, not yet moving, he reasoned out that the alarm could hardly have been broadcast yet. Iris's body would not yet have been discovered. He had closed the door of the motel room behind him, he was sure. By the time some maid came in and found her body he would be far from Albuquerque, certainly out of the state. In Atlanta, family alliance waited, there were understanding and money and power that could be arrayed in his support. He understood now that he was heading for Atlanta. Once he got there, he thought now, he would be able to tell Uncle Bob the mad truth. Uncle Bob could believe in a murderous machine if anyone could. Once he had Uncle Bob's support, Alex thought now, he would be able to give himself up.

The mad truth . . . it certainly felt like madness. In the bones of Alex's right wrist, when he pressed them with the fingers of his other hand, he could still feel the ache where that first overpowering mechanical claw had seized him—he could feel the ache, but the claw must have been somehow padded, for in the garish light outside the gas station he could see no marks. And the muscles of Alex's neck still ached, though inside the service station washroom the dirty mirror had shown him no marks there either.

The wound on his arm was hidden under his shirtsleeve now but he could feel its reality. It had bled a little since he left the motel, and the sleeve was stuck to it now. If the police car stopped, it would gush blood. He was going out of his mind.

No. He had been out of his mind there for a little while. Now he was coming back.

Alex got into his car and drove.

"Uncle Bob? I'm calling from Amarillo."

"Amarillo?" The quick voice sounded surprised, but alert. The sun was definitely up in Texas, and it must be getting toward midday in Atlanta.

Alex demanded: "Can we talk?"

"Talk? Yes, essentials anyway. What's going on?"

"Someone was trying to get me in New Mexico. I was set up. Framed for a murder. I'm on the run."

For a little time there was only a faint, soft static on the phone. Alex had just drawn breath to say it over again, when Uncle Bob's voice came back, much slower than before. "Alex, I'm sorry I got you into this. Very sorry. It appears that this thing is already much worse than I thought."

Alex began to laugh. There was nothing he could do about it. People going past the phone booth and into the nearby restaurant were going to take note of him, but there was no way he could stop. And the tears, he couldn't stop them either.

"Alex," his uncle's patient voice kept repeating in his ear. "Alex. Alex."

At last he managed some kind of control. Then a few more breaths, and he could talk again. "What kind of a thing are we talking about, Uncle Bob?"

A sigh of relief came with the static. "It's going to be a long story to tell you. First things first. Can you get back here?"

"I think so."

"Good. Do so, then. Don't tell me on the phone when you're coming, what route or time. But make it as quick as you can."

Alex swallowed. He felt a relief of his own, so huge his hands were shaking with it. "I will."

"Then do it." *Click* and the line went dead.

Heading east out of Amarillo, he did his best to stick close to the speed limit. Sometimes the traffic flow was moving too fast for that, but he tried. He had never seen so many police cars in his life, but none of them took any interest in him.

His first idea was that he was not going to stop anywhere for food until he reached Atlanta. Gas stops would be necessary, and maybe some stop for rest. Yes, he was going to need sleep, sometime, someplace, somehow. Once he jerked awake to behold aching sunlight off a crooked highway, a concrete bridge abutment hurtling at him. His waking thought was that Iris had just screamed at him in rage. He wrenched the wheel, got back into traffic. After that he was fully awake, his heart pounding, for long minutes as he drove.

But within an hour sleep was starting to come out of its cage again. Coming on soft cat-feet, smiling and beckoning. Anger turned the tide. He was not going to accommodate his nameless enemies by killing himself for them.

Near Little Rock he pulled into a motel, signed some phony name on the register and put a phony license plate number after it, and paid cash in advance for a bed. He had considered just pulling over and trying to get some rest at roadside, but had decided that the cops were more likely to spot him doing that than at a motel; and the motel should at least offer him a couple of hours of oblivion between soft sheets before he was arrested.

He was awakened by a jolt, murderous in intensity though it was completely psychic and non-physical. He sat up in bed with a gasp. It took him a while to feel confident that no one was knocking on the door. His room was perfectly quiet and he was quite alone.

Alex dressed and went out, leaving his key in the room. No buttons to punch this time. He went out into a light rain from a sky that showed no hint of dawn, drove a little way, stopped for gas, and found an all-night eatery where two cups of coffee and two grilled cheese sandwiches fortified him for the road.

SIX

It was getting dark again when Alex pulled into Atlanta. This must be Tuesday night, he thought. He was again half-blind with fatigue, but he had sworn to himself that he was not going to stop again until he had driven through those tall iron gates. He was lured into several minor false turns by the elegantly curving streets of Atlanta's northwest side, but he persevered and in the end he found his way. The tall iron gates were closed when he pulled up in front of them, and the grounds behind looked dark and deserted, but the gates opened promptly at his voice.

At first, as he moved along the drive, it was illuminated only by his own headlights. But before he had traveled half the winding, graveled driveway that led to the house, he was blinded by dazzling lamps that sprang to life from concealed positions close beside the drive to right and left.

"Alex! Please hold it right there for a minute." The voice was his uncle's, sharply amplified. The command was hardly necessary. Alex had already hit the brake because he could no longer see where he was going.

The moment he stopped, more lights, mercifully smaller, came to life on the drive ahead and trundled slowly in his

direction. These were too small to be automobile headlights.
A moment later Alex, squinting through aching eyes, could
see that these smaller lights were mounted one apiece atop
two of the rolling pyramids. And now a pair of similar lights
appeared in his rear-view mirror.

One of the pyramids approaching from the front rolled
right up to the car on the driver's side. Alex had been driving
with the window down, and there was nothing to interfere
with the robot's putting forth a slender metal and plastic
stalk, extending it right into the car. Alex, thinking of metal
arms, shrank back. The stalk held something that he realized
must be a small television camera, which it aimed right into
Alex's face, and then, methodically, into every corner of the
car's interior.

When this inspection had been accomplished, the lights all
around at once dimmed to gentleness. Now, just beyond the
pyramid that had stopped directly in front of his car, Alex
could see a vehicle that made him think of an armored
golf cart, drawn up just at the edge of the drive. A door in the
side of the golf cart was opening now, and a human figure,
helmeted as a policeman might be, was getting out. I hope,
thought Alex, that they let me sleep a while before they take
me back to New Mexico. No matter what, they're going to
have to let me sleep.

The figure as it approached the car turned into Alex's
uncle, not really in police uniform but wearing pieces of
protective gear. Alex couldn't tell if he was armed or not.

Smiling in at Alex, Uncle Bob opened the car door. Alex
hadn't yet felt up to doing that for himself. Now Alex got out
of the car, moving slowly, bent and cramped.

"You made it," his uncle was saying happily, holding
him by the arm and looking close into his face. His uncle
wearing the police-type helmet appeared to Alex to be
dressed up for a play. Albie Pearson, the engineer, also
costumed to take part, had got out of the golf cart too and was
standing by uncertainly.

"Yeah," said Alex.

"Give me your car keys," Uncle Bob ordered. "I'm

going to drive it into the garage until we can decide what to do with it. Did you have any further problems on the way?''

''No.'' Alex handed over the keys, then watched numbly as his uncle passed them on to Pearson, who after a moment's discussion with his employer got into the rental car and drove it on into concealment. The pyramids stood around Alex as if they were watching too. He couldn't help thinking that if he just fell asleep here standing up, the pyramids were going to pick him up and take him away. This thought helped him to keep his eyes from closing.

The headlights of the car, as Albie Pearson drove it slowly to the garage, shone in the middle distance upon yet another rolling pyramid; and this one, unless Alex was starting to hallucinate, was holding the leashes of two guard dogs. German shepherds. With Uncle Bob holding his arm, Alex began to stumble along the drive toward the house. Some pyramids fell in smoothly around them as an escort.

Presently Alex was inside the house, sitting in a comfortable chair in a comfortable, well-lighted room. He felt better, especially as there were no robots around at the moment. A tall, elegant blonde woman was there, wearing a fancy robe as if perhaps she had just got out of bed. She appeared to be about the same age as Jen Brahmaguptra, and she was handing Alex something in a glass—yes, he remembered, he'd just asked for a drink. On a table at his elbow was a sandwich on a plate.

He took a sip from the glass and put it down. Somehow he hadn't caught the woman's name, or what she was doing here. But he could rectify that later.

Uncle Bob, helmeted no longer, came nto the room. He pulled up a footstool and squatted on it before Alex, rather like a student at the feet of the master. He began asking Alex questions. Alex ran quickly through the story of the horror show at the hotel, and what he had been doing since.

His uncle asked him: ''You're sure this girl was dead?''

''Positive. My God. There was no doubt.''

''Was there a lot of blood around? You said there was some blood.''

"Only a little. Just from my arm, I think. From where she scratched me. I told you about that." He pulled up his sleeve now and showed them. It was only a scratch, and the shirt hadn't really stuck to it.

"How long were you asleep, unconscious, whatever, after this struggle, this attack?"

"I don't know. A few hours. It was still night when I woke up, and when I left the hotel, I didn't check the time. I wasn't just asleep, I tell you, that thing was choking me."

Uncle Bob looked at the lady, who looked back. "Well," said Uncle Bob, "I can see that you're just about asleep right now. You need some rest, before we can do any serious talking about what ought to be done next." He stood up from his footstool, and held out a hand which Alex gratefully accepted as an aid to getting back on his own feet. "Alex, I am sorry. I never thought when I sent you out there . . ."

Through a haze of fatigue Alex peered at him. "We're all in the same game," he muttered.

"What's that?"

"You and me. And Dr. Brahmaguptra's grandson. And Mrs. Tartaglia's late husband, too."

"Finish your drink, Alex, if you want it. Then you're going to hit the sack."

"I will." He gulped the drink, and wondered what it was. "You sent me out there to check out Starweb."

"Yes?"

"You didn't tell me everything about it."

The woman in the robe was standing nearby with folded arms. "Bob, I assume you're going to want me to be your legal adviser on this."

"Of course, Georgie."

"But you haven't told me everything, either. You're going to have to level with me completely on everything that's going on. Everything, Bob, or I'll drop it. I mean that."

Robert Gregory looked at her for a time. "I know you do, Georgina," he said at last. Then he looked at Alex. "You too. All right. A few people are going to have to know almost everything.''

"Everything, Bob. Or I drop it."

"Almost everything, Georgina. You'll see what I mean, in the morning."

Alex emerged from deathlike sleep in broad daylight, in the same guest room that he had occupied on his previous stay. He awoke amid soft sheets and pillows, in luxury and solitary silence. He raised himself on one elbow, listening to the silence. Obviously he was not yet under arrest. He looked at the small wound on his arm. In his neck muscles he could still feel that strangling clamp.

He lay for several minutes propped on his elbow, trying to organize his thoughts, before he even looked at the bedside clock. When he looked at last he saw that it was almost ten.

He was still looking at the clock when there came a discreet tapping at the bedroom door. "Who is it?" He pulled the covers up a little higher. As was his usual habit, he had been sleeping in the raw.

The door opened, and Alex sat bolt upright with a freezing fist clamped on his heart. A machine came rolling into the room toward him. Then he recognized it, and sagged back onto the pillows, feeling faint. It was only one of the mechanical table-servants, and this time it was bearing on its table-like upper surface a breakfast tray.

The thing glided right up to bedside and waited there patiently while Alex's heart and lungs resumed something like their normal pace. At last he reached over to the innocent object and gingerly picked up the tray, from which ingenious wire legs immediately sprang out; now the tray could be set down in a stable position across his knees.

A voice inside the robot spoke as soon as it had been relieved of its burden. "Clap your hands twice when you are finished," it said. Its tones were small and feminine, and sounded perfectly human. As it rolled away from the bed, it extended one thin metal arm, which in itself evoked grim memories. Catching the doorknob, it neatly pulled the door shut behind it as it left the room.

On the tray's covered dishes Alex found scrambled eggs, toast, and ham, all appetizingly hot. Coffee was in an insulated bottle topped by an inverted cup. There was even cold grapefruit juice . . . this was harboring a fugitive in style.

As Alex began to eat, he realized that he was very hungry. He finished the meal quickly, and got up. Some of the clothes he had hung in the closet on his first visit were still there; old stuff he hadn't bothered to take to Albuquerque with him. As he dressed, he thought of all the things he had left behind in that motel out there. The police would have no doubt about who they were looking for. So much evidence. There was no way he could have got rid of it all if he had made the attempt.

And to top it all, he'd run away. Well, he'd certainly be in jail right now if he hadn't, in jail and far from help. This way, he was at least going to have a good lawyer at his side when he faced the cops.

He showered, and dressed himself as well as possible with what was available. He'd left his razor back in Albuquerque with the other stuff, and couldn't shave. In the mirror it now looked like he had the start of a beard for a disguise . . . but no, there was no way around it, he was going to have to face the cops. He put on his money belt, and went through the clothes that he'd dropped on the floor the night before, transferring things to the pockets he was wearing.

He fully believed that if he clapped his hands twice the waiter machine, wherever it was, would hear him and would come back for the tray. Maybe he would clap his hands when he got downstairs. He'd developed a definite dislike for robots.

Before leaving his room, Alex squinted out of its window into sunlight. The swimming pool with its cryptic border markings was there, an unused mirror.

He was halfway down the main stairs when Caroline's wheelchair came rolling along below and stopped at their foot, in position for her to greet him; as if she might have been waiting somewhere nearby, wanting to intercept him as soon as he appeared.

Dressed today in frilly yellow, his cousin looked somehow prettier than he had remembered her. She started to ask one question, called it back and put forth another: "Did you sleep well?"

"Like the dead." Alex managed a kind of grin, feeling faintly pleased that he could now manage to be that cocky. He wondered how much Caroline knew; he couldn't recall seeing her around last night.

She looked at him gravely. "Dad's told me—what you told him last night, about what happened to you out west. I'm sure he never intended to get you involved in anything like that."

Alex nodded. "But he did know more than he ever told me. He knew that something more than computer games was going on out there. Because when I phoned him from Amarillo with my crazy story, he bought it right away. And when I told him all the even crazier details last night, he didn't think that I was off my rocker, or lying. He—" Alex broke off, raising his eyes from Caroline's solemn blue ones. Here came the man himself.

"Alex, come this way please." It appeared that this morning no time was going to be wasted on sympathy or regrets. "Caroline, you come along too. You already know some things that Alex doesn't, but it's time you were told more. Both of you. You're both deeply involved now, like it or not."

"Involved in what?" asked Alex. His uncle didn't answer that one immediately, but led both of them into a private office that Alex hadn't seen before. The blonde woman he remembered from last night was there already, looking serious. There was a legal-pad clipboard on the desk before her, and she was dressed in a businesslike pantsuit, as if she might be leaving for the courtroom at any moment. She was, Alex seemed to recall, a legal adviser of some kind.

She stood up and extended a hand to greet him. "Alex, I'm

Georgina Hoyle. I'm your uncle's lawyer as well as his friend. I don't think we had any proper introduction last night. You were naturally exhausted.''

"I sure was. Glad to meet you.''

Everyone took a seat somewhere around the desk, Uncle Bob naturally in the central chair behind it. But he was content to let Georgia proceed.

She asked Alex: "How do things look to you this morning? I mean, has a night's sleep changed at all your— perception about your experience in Albuquerque?''

"Has it changed my—oh, the girl was dead all right, if that's what you mean.'' He looked round at the three faces; all of them were neutral, waiting. "Yes, what I told you last night is how it happened. While I was in the bathroom, some kind of damned machine sitting in what looked like a wheelchair came into the hotel room and started strangling her. When I grabbed it, it damn near killed me too. When I woke up, she was very dead.'' His voice fell to a whisper and almost failed on the last words. Yes, it still sounded crazy, even to himself. If he hadn't been standing in a house full of robots it would have sounded even worse.

Uncle Bob said: "Georgina, I told Alex last night that I believe his story. I wasn't just soothing or humoring him. I do believe it, at least until I see some good evidence to the contrary. When you've heard what I'm going to tell you this morning, I'm inclined to think that you'll believe it too.'' He leaned back in his chair behind his desk, with his fingers laced over his flat belly under another bright sport shirt.

Georgina looked at both men, shrugged a tiny shrug at Caroline, then sat back in her own chair. "All right, Bob. Give us the background. It had better be good.''

"Oh, it is good. It is good.'' Uncle Bob spoke quietly. He took a few moments of thoughtful silence then, apparently deciding how best to begin. Behind him, a sunny window looked out on flower beds.

When he did start to speak his voice was slow. "Alex, Caroline. Neither of you was born in 1946, not by a good many years. Georgina—in your case I won't ask. But have you, Alex, Georgina, ever heard of ENIAC? I know that my daughter has heard me mention it once or twice.''

Georgina shook her head minimally. She was watching Bob with the air on one withholding judgment, waiting for the point.

Alex responded. ''It sounds like one of those early computers.''

''Right. The grandaddy of 'em all. It was built using vacuum tubes, of course. It was very big, very clumsy, not at all reliable by the standards of today. It was not very powerful, either, by those same standards. But it did prove in 1946 that the electronic computer could be built on a large scale. That was the year that Henry Brahmaguptra and I met for the first time. We were both young guys called in to work on ENIAC.

''You know, as I look back on it now, that seems to me to have been a very good time to be alive. Partly, I suppose, just because I was young then. But there were other reasons. Hitler was gone, almost everyone in the world felt good about that. Nuclear power in the form of nuclear weapons had just arrived, and everyone who was able to think at all was awed by it. The thing to do, if you were young and had ability, was to pitch in and build the brave new world that everyone had been saying for years we could have when the war was over. At that time Henry and I shared a lot of the same ideas.''

Restlessly, as if distracted, Uncle Bob stood up and sat on his desk with his back to the others, looking out the window over his flower gardens. It was not as grand a view as Henry Brahmaguptra had from behind his desk, but it was good.

''I hope, Bob,'' said Georgina, ''that all this preamble is necessary.''

Still looking out, he shook his head a trifle. Maybe he was irritated by the question; maybe he was trying to see what had become of that brave new world that he and others set out to build. ''I'll omit a lot of details. But in the 'fifties, problems started coming up between Henry and myself. Some were personal disagreements, some philosophical. I continued to work for the government, mainly for Defense. When I started my own company it did a lot of Defense business. Henry . . . well, he went pretty far the other way politically. At one point in the late 'sixties he was arrested, I think for pouring blood on draft records, some nonsense like that.''

Alex put in: ''You told me, though, that you still trusted him.''

Uncle Bob turned. ''Oh, I did. I do, as far as his having good intentions. Henry's a pacifist, he wouldn't personally hurt a fly. But people like that can sometimes wreak havoc.''

Alex said: ''He's still living in Los Alamos, just like you told me. I told you last night that I went to see him. And he's still working for the government, the Labs—some kind of a consulting job, I think he said. I didn't ask for any details.''

Uncle Bob was nodding fatalistically. ''Exactly why did you go to see him? I seem to remember telling you that it wouldn't be a good idea.''

''I thought I tried to explain that last night. Maybe I didn't. I went to see him mainly because he turned out to be in the same Starweb game that you're in. And I was supposed to be investigating Starweb.''

Alex's uncle got off his desk and sat back in his chair. His gaze was alert but without understanding. ''Run that by me again?''

''I thought that your old friend was in the same game that you are. Actually it's his grandson who's in it, but when I saw the name I thought it was the old man himself. And since I was supposed to be investigating Starweb and Berserkers Incorporated, I thought that maybe he could tell me something.''

''Starweb.'' Uncle Bob was looking as blank as Brahmaguptra had at the first mention of the game. ''You were raving a little about Starweb last night, Alex, but I assumed it was because you were out on your feet. Now you say Henry's grandson . . . yes, there was a kid. I don't suppose Henry told you that his only son was killed in Viet Nam.''

''No. He didn't tell me anything about that.''

"But now you say Henry's grandson's in the same game I'm in . . . that does sound like it ought to mean something. But I'm damned if I know what."

Caroline's pale face seemed to Alex to be trying to offer him wordless encouragement. He said to his uncle: "The kid is in it. He's OCTAGON. And I'm in it myself now. I'm AGRAVAN."

"He's OCTAGON? But he can't be more than ten years old."

"Maybe twelve."

"And I have AGRAVAN's name and address. He's some man who lives in Albuquerque."

"Tartaglia. But he's dead now. Violently, a few days before I got out there, apparently. I got in as his replacement."

"Bob." It was Georgina's controlled voice. "Are we going to play games all morning? I haven't heard anything yet that sounds in the least relevant to our immediate problem. Which is this young man's legal position with regard to what he reports to have been a very serious crime."

Alex turned to her. "What I report? What else could you call it?"

The woman lawyer was watching him carefully. "Alex. How long is it now since you left the hotel room with this girl's supposedly dead body in it?"

"Supposedly—" He controlled himself. He stopped to calculate. "I left there early Monday morning, before dawn. I was careful, I didn't speed. Monday night . . . Monday night I had to stop and rest. In Little Rock. It was getting dark on Tuesday before I drove in here. This is Wednesday morning . . ."

Georgina was nodding at him, in calm encouragement. "So by now her body must have been discovered. Surely by now a maid's been in."

"I would say so. Yesterday sometime, if not the day before."

"So by now this young woman has been found murdered in the room you rented under your own name, with your belongings in it. You're missing and so is the car that you rented. Obviously by this morning the police all across the country have to be searching for you.''

"Well, yeah. Obviously.''

"Except they're not.''

Alex's mouth moved. But he couldn't get out a word.

Georgina's gently probing eyes were puzzled. "Alex, the Georgia state police, at least, are *not* looking for you, or for your car. They never heard of you, nor of any recent mysterious killing in New Mexico. I have connections that allow me to find out such things, without being too specific as to what I'm looking for. I used my connections just this morning.''

"I . . .'' Looking from one face to another in search of aid, Alex could do no more than gesture helplessly.

Georgina pressed him: "Alex, if someone told you such a story, wouldn't you be skeptical? Wouldn't you think it sounded—''

"I saw her dead, I tell you. I know what—''

"Alex.'' His uncle's voice cut in. A tired judge in a bright sport shirt, requiring and getting order in the court. "Alex, it's all right. I don't think that you were dreaming. Georgina—you have a nice mind, imagining lies, dreams, hallucinations. I wish you were right. I wish to God I thought this was just a nice, simple, old-fashioned drug-and-blackmail plot, something like that. That's a nice, benevolent, unthreatening kind of explanation. It would be manageable, by one means or another.''

They were all staring at him in silence.

He sighed. "Right after you talked to Henry, Alex, this happened to you. I don't suppose it can be coincidence. I'm sure he's not involved directly, but now I'm afraid he had to be involved, somehow, with the people who did this to you.''

"Who were they? What did they do?''

"They were, I expect, some of Henry's political associates. What they did was send that machine into your room.''

Alex found that he was on his feet. He made himself sit

down. "It sounds," he said, "like you know more about what happened to me than I do."

"In a way," said his uncle, "maybe I do." He sat behind his desk running his hands through his crisp hair. "Sometimes I wish I smoked," he interjected to the world at large. "Anyway, we come now to the early 'sixties—God, how long ago that seems. Henry and I were reconciled for a time, working together again, building the walls of Camelot. People tend to forget that Camelot depended on swords. Our nation was going to bear any burden, pay any price, to defend freedom in the world, remember? Sure we were. Like hell we were, but I guess Kennedy believed it. For one shining moment. God, that one bullet seemed to go through all our brains, shattered our collective national head. I can't say I liked the man personally, but he did have some guts.

"However, at that time Henry and I were working together again for the federal government. Computers had come a long way since ENIAC. They were already starting to take over a lot of government work, and if you looked ahead you could see how things were going to be, technologically anyway, in ten or twenty years. A master plan was wanted, for all the data processing that the government did. The idea was that if some kind of central control on programming could be established, maybe the task could be kept manageable, the costs under control. The project was kept very quiet, for various social and economic reasons. When even a few hints of it got out there was a tremendous fuss, perhaps rightly, about personal rights and privacy and so on. Eventually the original project was abandoned, as quietly as it had been started. But there for a little while, when we were planning and testing, a few of us had all the reins in our hands."

"I'm not sure I understand," said Georgina. "The reins controlling what?"

"Listen and learn, Georgie. Henry and I worked well together. We always did, when it was just a matter of getting the job done, not of deciding on ultimate purposes. But as the long job went on, both of us were growing more and more concerned, in our somewhat divergent ways, about the changes that we saw coming in the world. Primarily about all the computer power, which means power of knowledge and control, that our work was going to put into the hands of some unknown future government. In those days I was beginning to fear that by 1980 we might be under a puppet regime controlled from Moscow. And Henry . . . well, if Henry ever visualized Nixon or Reagan as president, I'm sure it was only in his nightmares.''

Here Uncle Bob paused for a time. When he resumed he was choosing his words with extreme care. ''So . . . the two of us, acting secretly and on our own, did something. Something that I've never told another human being about until this day. There were hundreds of other people working on the project, of course, but they didn't know about it. Henry and I created . . . call it a secret pathway. A door. An entrance. I'm talking about programming, now.''

He looked steadily at each of his audience in turn. ''A programming entrance. A door that leads right to the center of control, at least partial control of just about every large computer system in the country. The systems were beginning to interlock in the 'sixties, and by now they're interconnected like a mat of vines. I'm talking specifically about two code phrases, both of which are probably quite simple.''

''Oh, Daddy.'' Caroline was almost whispering. It was as if she had just been struck by some overwhelming realization.

Her father looked at her and nodded gently. ''I've spoken you sometimes about a secret, that you were probably going to have to cope with one day. But until now I've never told you what it was.

''Only Henry knew one of the code phrases. I was the only one who knew the other. We decided that if a situation ever came up where we two could agree on using it, there would be no doubt that it should be used.''

''Used for what?'' Georgina demanded.

''Used in defense of the United States of America. Used

on behalf of human freedom. Against a government, perhaps, that truly cried out to be demolished."

His lawyer was growing increasingly unsettled. "Bob, if it was anyone else telling me this . . ."

"It's not. It's me."

"Codes, opening a pathway, you say? To the control of all the computers in the country?"

"Of most of the large, interconnected computer systems. Which is enough. Using the code, you could put in orders that will override any ordinary programming. You can extract information from supposedly secret, protected files. You can do other things, things we didn't even dream of when we played our little trick twenty years ago. Henry and I were wrong when we guessed how big the megasystem of interconnected systems was going to be in twenty years, when we guessed how far it would spread to things outside of government as well as in; we underestimated it all, by about an order of magnitude. Thank God, not all the big military systems are accessible—at least I pray they still aren't. So you can't use the code to order a missile launch, for example. But anyone having both halves of the code could certainly tie everything in knots—industry, railroads, airlines, banks, you name it." He looked at Alex. "You could, for example, screw up the system that connects various police departments across the country, with the FBI and with each other. That's the system that would ordinarily pass along any bulletins about you being wanted in New Mexico."

Alex couldn't accept it. Not even from Uncle Bob. Not quite yet, anyway. "But in twenty years all the hardware's changed, changed a hell of a lot. You couldn't find anyone who has the same computer now that they had then."

"Of course not," said his uncle patiently. "But the master programming tends to perpetuate itself in the system as the hardware is renewed."

He looked at his hearers, a teacher judging that the lesson had not yet sunk home. "Look here. What people don't realize is that in the typical large computer system, no one of the individuals who works on it any longer knows what the hell is going on. Will you buy that?''

Georgina, at a loss, shook her head.

"I . . . don't know," said Alex doubtfully.

Uncle Bob concentrated on him. "It generally takes years for such a system to be established. By the time it's fully established, at least some of the original programmers have moved on, or died, or retired. All along the way, unknown numbers of unknown people add or subtract something in the way of programming. And as long as the system works, or works most of the time, or seems to work, nobody is going to put in the great amount of time and trouble that would be necessary to understand it fully.''

"I guess I'll buy that.''

"So it's a good bet that no one has rooted out our secret pathway. But I have more positive evidence than that, that it still exists.'' He paused. "Somebody's been using it.''

Georgina objected: "I thought you said that both halves of this secret code were necessary.''

"If you want it to be really effective, for something like bringing down the government, I would presume they still are. But I can't really be sure of that any more, not without trying; things have changed a lot. I'm positive you can get in with either half of the code, and raise all kinds of hell. Because someone's been using Henry's half to do just that.''

"How do you know?''

Bob gestured. "The code's been used; there's no other explanation for some strange things that have been happening. *My* half hasn't been; because I've never revealed it to anyone, and I certainly haven't been using it myself. Therefore it's Henry's half that someone is using to do the damage. I suppose he trusted his part of the secret to someone who turned out not to be trustworthy. Or else some of his leftist friends got him to turn it over, to help them in their fight against Fascism. But I have trouble believing that Henry would be that dumb deliberately.''

"And these people,'' asked Georgina skeptically, "the ones you call Henry's leftist friends, they've used their power to call off or delay the police search for Alex? After they went to the trouble of framing him for murder in the first place, by somehow sending a machine to his hotel room?''

''Yes.'' Uncle Bob's fingers drummed his desktop. He could certainly be authoritative and convincing when he tried. ''I know it sounds inconsistent. But that's the best explanation I can come up with that fits the facts.''

His lawyer was getting back on her home ground. ''Have you any idea,'' she pressed him, ''*why* they would do these inconsistent things?''

''I keep coming back to that same question,'' put in Alex. ''What was I doing in New Mexico that was so important to anyone that they'd want me dead? Was I somehow close to discovering the existence of this secret code? I was investigating Berserkers Incorporated, that's all. It keeps coming back to Starweb. Why *did* you want me to investigate Starweb? There was more to it than you told me.''

''All right, yes. Though I hope you believe me when I say I had no idea it could blow up on you as it did. First, I began by being genuinely interested in the game as a business proposition, just as I said I was. Second, it's a small community out there, as perhaps you noticed. All of northern New Mexico. I was hoping you'd find some connection to Henry from the games company; or that if I got a foothold in the company as owner or partner, it'd let me put people there who could keep an eye on the people around Henry. People who'd be in the computer field in one way or another . . . maybe it wasn't a good plan. Anyhow it blew up.''

''They somehow knew who I was.''

''And that you were working for me. Maybe they didn't know exactly what you were working on, but you offered them a way of getting at me. And the point is, Alex, I don't think that they really wanted you dead; if they had, you'd be dead now. The attack machine that they sent was choking you, and you passed out. Then it must have stopped choking you, though it made sure of the girl.''

Georgina was not yet convinced. She appeared unable to take the whole idea seriously. But she was being forced to try. ''I suppose one of your machines here, for example, could be programmed to do something like that?''

"Yes, it could. Though it would be easier if a human was running it by remote control. It could seek out a particular room in a particular building. It could identify objects within the room as human beings, and, within limits, discriminate between them. Kill one, silence another. Of course . . .''

"What?''

"If I were out to kill someone, I don't think I'd send a machine to do the job. Maybe in ten years . . . but human agents still have a great advantage in flexibility. And they're a lot less conspicuous in hotel corridors.''

There was a troubled silence in the room. Then Georgina asked: "Just who are these enemies you say we're facing, Bob? Exactly what are they trying to do?''

"They might be actual Communist party members. Some kind of radical leftists, certainly. Friends of Henry's, or friends of friends, who've managed to get his code. As to exactly what they want from me . . . there've been no demands. Just things going wrong here and there. Computer-controlled things, all of them. My bank accounts, my business, even my utility bills—just enough so that I know they're working on me. Don't tell me it sounds paranoid, Georgie, I know it does, but I can document it all.''

He looked at his nephew. "Now the plan seems to be, Alex, for you to be in prison charged with murder. Or else—or else for you to be here, just where you are. Maybe that's it. I'm to be implicated for harboring a fugitive, or whatever the exact charge is that Georgina keeps warning me against.''

The lawyer drew a deep breath. "I would have been warning you a lot more strongly, Bob, if I were totally convinced that there was a killing in Alex's motel room at all. I can't say that I'm fully convinced of that yet.''

Alex started a protest, then kept silent. He looked hopelessly into the eyes of Caroline, who still watched in silent sympathy. However he tried to explain to himself what had happened in that Albuquerque motel, it still seemed unreal. Maybe he *had* been drugged, and induced to hallucinate a murder. Maybe, as in dreams, bits and pieces of impressive reality such as Uncle Bob's robots had been incorporated in the vision; there never had been a thing in a wheelchair.

But Iris Cardano no doubt had been a real person—*and maybe she still was*. She could have been with Alex in that room, and maybe in that bed. And maybe she was back at work, this minute, in the office of Berserkers Incorporated . . .

"We could pick up the phone and call the Starweb people," he suggested. "Ask for Iris Cardano."

"Let's think first," said Uncle Bob. Then he blew out his breath in a sound that would have been a sigh if it were not so forceful. "They seem to be *daring* me to bring the whole thing out into the open. To force me to go to the government with the story about the code. Maybe I ought to do just that."

"Maybe you ought," agreed Georgina. "Provided you can prove that it's not as insane as it all sounds."

"That's it," said Uncle Bob, very quietly, gazing at her. Then he slammed the flat of his hand down on the desk, making three other people jump. "That's it! They want to force the entry of my half of the code into the system. Once I start telling people about the code, that'll be inevitable; someone will try it, to confirm my story. They must have used Henry's half of the code to concoct some kind of booby trap in the system, so that when my half is entered too, the thing goes off."

"Goes off?"

"Oh, I don't mean a bomb, Georgina." He turned on her impatiently. "But the whole megasystem, or a large part of it, could go down. I mean collapse in programming terms, become inoperative. Can you imagine what a sudden, nationwide data processing failure would be like?"

"Tell me."

"No worse than taking apart everyone's house, barn, and apartment building, and leaving them in piles of pieces. Our whole economy absolutely depends on interlocked computers now. Knock out the megasystem and attacking us with missiles would hardly be necessary. Though if some kind of aggressive military move were made against us at the same time . . . I tell you, people, I'm scared.''

"I've been scared for several days," said Alex.

His uncle turned to him. "Alex. How much did you see of Henry's friends and associates when you were visiting him?''

"Not much. One man, Eddie MacLaurin—I talked to him for about five minutes. He works in Security at the Labs, he told me, and he's dating Jen; that's Brahmaguptra's daughter-in-law.''

His uncle nodded. "Eddie MacLaurin," he repeated thoughtfully. "The name doesn't ring any bells for me.''

"Also," said Alex, "Eddie is the one who programs Starweb, for Ike Jacobi. That's his part-time job. And Iris told me that Jacobi keeps the Starweb program a secret. A lot of people are after it, she said.''

Uncle Bob was staring at him blankly.

Georgina was looking at her watch. "We're going to have to make some decisions, people," she announced. "If we really believe in this killing in Albuquerque, we're going to have to get in touch with the authorities about it. Just because there's been some mixup in police communications doesn't alter our responsibility along that line. Now I think we can all swear to it in court that Alex arrived here last night in a confused, exhausted state, and had to have some rest before he could talk sense. But now he's rested, and he's told us the same story over again, calmly. And if we think there's any truth in his story at all, it's our legal duty to report it; he's talking about a murder.''

Uncle Bob looked grim. "Is he going to be held, do you think?''

"I'd say that if the murder he described is confirmed, then his chances of *not* being held are very small. Especially since he's already run away once to avoid arrest. I'm sorry, Alex.''

"I was dazed when I ran, like you said. I was in shock.''

"Fine, I'm sure a court will take that into consideration,

especially as you'll be coming forward voluntarily now. But you did run.''

Uncle Bob was grimmer still. ''I don't like it, Georgina. I don't like it at all. I have the feeling that we're playing right along with what they want if we turn in Alex now. In effect he will become a hostage, once he's in jail somewhere.''

''You're crediting this mysterious 'they' with a lot of power.''

''I am indeed. I'll bet my life on that.''

Georgina made a gesture. It was the first time that Alex had seen her looking helpless. She asked: ''Are you suggesting that we try to help him escape? You should realize that's out of the question.''

''I know you can't sit still for anything like that, Georgie. I wouldn't ask you to. I think you've given us all you can, for the moment, in the way of legal advice. Now if you and Caroline would run along for a little while, I'd like to talk to my nephew alone.''

Without another word the lawyer pushed back her chair, picked up her legal pad, and went out, pausing in the doorway for one long cautionary glance back at the two men. Caroline, looking troubled, rolled her chair quietly after her. Georgina reached back in to shut the door.

There was a silence, with uncle and nephew looking at each other.

''Alex,'' said Uncle Bob at last, ''if this were some ordinary crime we were dealing with, or even some ordinary frame-up, I'd advise you to go and face the charges. I don't have to tell you how strongly we'd back you up. The best in legal help. Private investigators . . .''

''I know,'' said Alex, suddenly feeling a little dazed. He could hardly believe he was going to hear what it now seemed he was about to hear.

''But,'' his uncle pressed on inexorably, ''this business is far from ordinary. I'm sure you realize that, but Georgina doesn't seem able to grasp the fact. I'll work on her, but it's going to take time, and I may even wind up having to get myself a new lawyer. This is so far from ordinary, so vital, yes, to the whole country, that we as individuals have to take chances and make sacrifices. Damn it, even break the law and risk prison if we have to. Are you with me, Alex?''

''I think I'm even a little ahead of you.'' Alex got to his feet. ''I think you're telling me that I've got to get the hell out of here, hide out somewhere, stay out of sight.''

''And you will? Georgina's right about one thing, hiding out will make it rougher on you if you're caught.''

''I know that. But . . .'' In his guts Alex felt that doing something, anything, active and positive would be better than meekly letting himself be taken off to jail, however good the lawyers at his side. ''I'll disappear. If there's some hope of getting this whole mess straightened out that way.''

His uncle stood up, making sounds of deep relief, and gripped his hand. ''Good boy. I'll help. Now the two of us are going to have to make some arrangements in a hell of a hurry. And carry them out fast. I have about a dozen people working in and around the house today, and the fewer of them find out you're here, the better.''

SEVEN

Outside the office and five paces down the hall, Georgina stopped and turned. The girl following stopped her chair, and met Georgina's eyes.

"Caroline. Your father's talked to you before about this, this secret code?"

"Daddy's talked about important secrets that I might have to deal with. He's never spelled it out this directly before."

"How long have you been here with him now?" Georgina was not very well informed on the girl's early history; she knew who Caroline's mother was, but not a great deal more.

"Three years now. Since my accident." That was the term Caroline generally used to describe what had happened to her in New York.

"I see. Well. As you know, I've only been associated with him about half that length of time. But I like him very much and I hope he doesn't get himself into deep trouble."

"You mean about Alex," said Caroline. Her blue eyes were troubled. "Well, if he does, I guess I'd still trust him to know what's best. You're a good lawyer and all, I'm sure, but . . ."

"I understand. And I wonder sometimes how good I am."

The chair rolled forward, slowly, as if its occupant would like to be accompanied. "You haven't seen my office yet, have you, Georgina?"

Georgina followed. They passed a couple of men in work clothes, Albie Pearson and some temporary employee she didn't recognize, going the other way along the corridor. The two men were avidly talking shop about the new emergency generating system. They returned Georgina's nod and smile with glazed eyes and walked on quickly, talking still.

"No, I haven't seen it, Caroline. But I'd like to."

Caroline led her into a newer wing of the house, an area where Georgina hadn't been for several months. In that time the place had been extensively transformed. Caroline had said 'office', but to the lawyer that word meant something other than what she now saw here. These were more work-rooms, rather, with wide benches filled with tools and parts.

The girl rolled her chair to a stop in one of the new rooms. "Decorating isn't finished yet," she murmured, rather unnecessarily. A start had been made, with a few plants placed here and there. On a bench before Georgina were metal and plastic ribs and rods, still unassembled but bringing to mind the idea of a life-sized model skeleton, maybe something that the gift shop of a museum would have on sale.

Actually Georgina could have made a better guess than that of what these were; but right now Caroline seemed to be eager to show her something else. She had brought her wheelchair to a stop before a narrow bench that held an impressive assortment of electronic equipment, stacked in a tall array on a rack. There were several television-type screens, and one screen, flat as a picture, hanging on a nearby wall. Georgina seemed to recall hearing Bob once call such a device a liquid crystal display panel. It was dark and inactive now.

It came to Georgina, as it did almost every time she explored these regions of the house, that the man she worked for and sometimes slept with was a rare man indeed. Bob Gregory had a lot to offer the world, a lot that he must be prevented from foolishly throwing away.

In this house Georgina had seen a lot of odd electronic hookups. This one, though, had something especially odd about it—what, exactly? Only after Caroline had finished maneuvering her chair carefully into the exact place she wanted it, before the bench, did Georgina realize just what the peculiarity was: on this setup there appeared to be very few manual controls of any kind.

She waited for Caroline to appeal for some kind of assistance in operating the whatever-it-was. But the request did not materialize. Instead Georgina only had to watch as the girl used the chin-control on her chair to work it into a place where its weight, wheels now resting on two metal plates just before the bench, evidently activated a switch. Only now did Georgina notice the metallic, crown-like device that had been suspended near the ceiling, over the same spot. This thing was now descending on wires, slowly and gently, to come softly to rest a moment later on Caroline's dark hair.

A moment later the CRT's and the liquid panel all came to life, displaying various glowing symbols and traces.

"Alpha waves, Georgie." Caroline could turn her head far enough under the crown to be able to smile back at the older woman.

"Alpha . . . ?"

"My brain waves. See, there, on the screen?"

"I . . . those are signals from your brain?"

"Just the ordinary electrical activity. Daddy says it shows there's something inside my head after all. With the right gear it's easy to pick up and amplify. People have been doing it for years. Learning to modify it at will, though, so I can use it as a control signal, is tricky. Right now I work best in eyeball mode."

"Eyeball . . ."

"Watch, Georgina, what happens when I look back toward the panel in front of me. See the tiny thing that sticks down in front of the crown, almost like a microphone?" That, in fact, was what Georgina had taken it to be. "It has a little laser on it that continually probes my right eye with a faint beam of light. According to how that beam is reflected, it can tell precisely what point on the panel I'm looking at. And then when I blink just right—''

On the equipment before Caroline more lights appeared. These were within an area suggestive of a chessboard, whose squares and rectangles were marked with symbols. The symbols included, Georgina noted now, all the letters of the alphabet and the numbers zero through nine, as well as some punctuation and math signs. The color of a few squares of the board now changed, in rapid sequence, as if some short code were being entered.

A few seconds later, a door at the other end of the room swung open, and one of the flat-topped general purpose serving machines entered.

"Go kitchen," Caroline enunciated, using a loud clear voice. "Bring back. Two. Iced teas."

The machine in its soothing feminine voice repeated the instructions once. Then it rolled backwards, on its way.

In the ensuing silence, Caroline requested: "Georgie, would you rub the bridge of my nose just a tiny bit? There's this maddening little itch, and I'm not hooked up to my arms right now . . . ah, that's better. Thanks.''

"Those things over on the other bench are what you call your arms, I take it.''

"And legs. But it looks like it'll be some time before they're anything like what Daddy will consider ready. I can swim a little, now. I can stand up with them, but likely as not I topple over when I try to walk. There are servomotor problems and battery problems and all kinds of problems. The engineers are happy with the control programming from the holograph tapes, though. They say once they get the hardware working I'll be able to jump up and dance—waltz at least—and it won't look grotesque. Just like a dancer wearing a costume, with all those plastic supports on. I'm not holding my breath, though. Daddy keeps telling me not to get my hopes too high. Anyway, my office here is functional now, wouldn't you say? I can be a real working secretary. I can operate a typewriter from the panel here. And the computers, of course. And the phones.''

Caroline was still explaining her command of the household machines from this position, and the robot had just come back with two iced teas, when there sounded a subdued and regular chiming.

"Incoming call," said Caroline. "Excuse me." Without moving a muscle except in her eyes and lids, she answered it. "Gregory residence." Somehow, Georgina noted, the girl had already managed to learn how to sound like a pro secretary.

It was a thin voice incoming. Georgina wasn't sure at first if it was that of a man or woman, but it struck her as elderly, and strained. "I would like to speak to Robert Gregory, please."

"Who shall I say is calling?"

"Tell him Henry Brah-ma-gup-tra." The last name was enunciated with special care, as if to forestall any request that it be spelled out.

No one was about to make any such request. "One moment, please," said Caroline, and with swiftly directed blinks she put the call on hold, while activating some in-house intercom. "Dad? Something important."

Bob's voice came in from somewhere. "What is it, Hon?"

"Dr. Brahmaguptra's on the phone. I'm in my office. Want to take it in here?"

A pause. "Is Georgie there too?"

"Yes."

"Tell him to hang on. Tell him one minute at the most. I'll be there."

Caroline passed along the message. Georgina looked at her watch. It actually took Bob about a minute and a half, which was something of a surprise.

He stood a little breathlessly before the panel. "Henry, is that you? What's up?"

"Bob?" Georgina had never seen the caller, but from his voice she pictured him as a thin, distraught old man, his hands a-tremble. "We just heard it on the news out here, a terrible thing. About that young man who was here visiting me? Do you know who I mean?"

Bob paused before answering. Georgina, watching, thought that the pause was calm and calculated. And she had begun to think that she knew Bob Gregory well . . .

"My nephew Alex was out there recently, Henry, if that's who you mean. What's happened?"

The thin voice quavered: "Some young woman was found murdered, in his hotel room, in Albuquerque. And he's disappeared." Georgina, listening, felt a twinge of professional, intellectual disappointment: scratch one beautiful if still incomplete theory about drugs and blackmail . . .

"When was this, Henry?"

"A few days ago. Sunday night, they just said on the news. None of us here listen to the news much, we didn't hear about it until just now. But now we'll have to report that he was here, of course. The news reporters usually get things garbled, I know, but there's no doubt it's Alex that the police are looking for. Did you send him out here, Bob?"

"I did, Henry. Henry, whatever the situation looks like now, you can rest assured that he didn't murder anyone."

"I know, Bob, I couldn't believe it of him either. Do you know where the young man is now?"

"Are you concerned about his welfare? Who else have you discussed this with?" Bob made a swift gesture to his daughter. She evidently took his meaning at once, for new lights appeared on the panel, silent switches closed. He's recording this, thought Georgina. But the beeping tone that the law required for the legal recording of phone conversations was not in evidence. I'm going to have to walk out on Bob soon, probably today, she told herself, at least as his lawyer. I don't see any way around it. But still I wonder if I can.

"I have talked to no one," Brahmaguptra was saying. By the excitement and worry in his voice, you would have thought it was his own nephew that the police were after, if not his son. "I wanted to speak to you first. Bob, Bob, why must you always be difficult? Of course I'm concerned."

"I shouldn't have to tell you this, Henry. But I suppose it's possible you don't already realize it. There may well be much more at stake here than your newscasts have ever mentioned. In fact I'm damn well sure there is."

"What do you mean?"

"Henry. There's a road that you and I once built. A pathway, call it. It leads to important places. I think it pretty obvious that pathway's connected with what happened to Alex in Albuquerque."

There was a considerable pause.

"Henry, are you still there?"

"Bob, listen to me. I have to tell you something. I lied to you, years ago, about my part of that project. I never completed my part in the way that we had planned. Your half of the code is the only effective part. It always has been. My half does nothing."

Georgina, listening, felt quietly stunned. She could feel her lower jaw beginning to sag, her lips parting; she had not, until this moment, been really ready to believe in the story of the code.

Bob, irritated but not perturbed, was shaking his head. "No, Henry. My half has not been used. Yours has."

"That's impossible. I tell you, Bob, the thing as we planned it never existed. I had second thoughts back in 1964. But I didn't want to argue it all out with you again. So . . . my half of the code accesses nothing but a blind loop. A gigantic, elaborate loop, but that's all. So now if anyone is going to a great deal of trouble to learn what my code phrase is, well, they're wasting their time."

"No, Henry." Bob was still patient, as if he were dealing with a child. "The truth is that you're lying to me *now*. I know that you weren't lying then."

The thin voice stammered. "It's true that we had many earnest discussions. But as I just told you, I had second thoughts."

"All right, Henry. Have it your way. Whatever you say. So tell me, what was your code phrase?"

A pause. "On the phone?"

"Henry, you ancient klutz. You've just told me that it's

utterly useless. So why not give it on the phone?''

A little soft crackling, nothing more, was coming along the wires from Los Alamos.

"You're a rotten liar, Henry, always have been. You weren't cut out for intrigue, and I hope you stay out of it if still can. Now, you can tell me some false phrase if you like, and it'll take me only a little while to check it and see that it doesn't lead to anything at all, not even a blind loop—so save us both the trouble. I know the real phrase exists, and I know perfectly well you're not going to tell it to me on the phone. You're transparent but not dumb. And, Henry, what's this about Starweb?''

When Henry answered he sounded stalled by the apparent irrelevance, much as Bob himself had sounded earlier. "Starweb?''

"Yes. What do you suppose I ought to make of the fact that your grandson and I are in a game of Starweb together? That people who are in that game are getting killed, or violently attacked, in real life? What is Ike Jacobi up to, anyway?'' Georgina noted that Bob now seemed to be taking that idea a lot more seriously than he had when he was talking to Alex. Watching his face, she couldn't tell how serious he really was.

"Bob.'' The distant voice was no longer simply strained; now there was something new it it, something that Georgina could not certainly identify as fear, or rage, or sorrow, but certainly it was not good. "Bob, I think I'd better see you, face to face.''

Bob looked round at the women with him, his eyebrows giving a formal signal of surprise. "Fine, I agree, in principle.'' He added dryly: "But conditions aren't right just now for me to travel.''

He's afraid, Georgina thought, with new amazement. Robert Gregory is afraid to leave his fortress here. That's why he hasn't wanted to travel lately, anywhere at all . . .

"I'll come there,'' Henry volunteered, and sounded not afraid at all, but as if he were immediately becoming preoccupied with details. "I suppose I can get a plane out of Albuquerque . . . probably tomorrow . . ."

Bob leaned forward toward the speakers in the panel. His hands were on the back of his daughter's wheelchair. "How about this, Henry? There's a plane belonging to me sitting on the ground in Dallas right now. I can send it to pick you up tonight. No, make that by this afternoon sometime."

"All right. I'll come. I'll be ready."

"See you this evening, then." He stepped up beside his daughter's chair, and made a gentle throat-cutting gesture with one finger. A moment later the connection had been broken. He looked at the women with quiet elation. "I believe he's going to do it. I believe he's going to come and talk to me."

Georgina consulted her watch. Time was pressing. "We're going to have to arrange to have Alex turn himself in before this evening, I'm afraid. The sooner the better."

Bob's voice was slow. "I don't think we have to do anything of the kind, Georgie."

She looked at him with a sinking feeling. "What do you mean?" But Georgina knew the answer, even before she asked the question.

Bob's look of grim determination was as strong as she had ever seen it. "If you think Alex is presently in my house or on my grounds, you're welcome to search for him. At this moment I couldn't locate him if I wanted to."

EIGHT

Henry Brahmaguptra, left to stand by himself for a few minutes on the dry brown earth at one side of the high Los Alamos airfield, while the pilot who had identified himself as Scotty ducked into operations to file his flight plan, found he had a lot to think about.

First in Brahmaguptra's thoughts, as usual, was Jen. When she had learned that he was off to Atlanta today, she had offered to drive him to the airport. But Brahmaguptra had declined; in the first place, he didn't know exactly when Bob's plane would be arriving. In the second place, knowing Bob, he expected that complete door-to-door service would somehow be provided. So when Jen had gone back to work after lunch as usual, Brahmaguptra had simply said goodbye to her, casually, as he did customarily.

He hadn't been able to entirely kill the question in his own mind, though, as to whether he was ever going to see her again.

And Hank. Hank had gone off to school today, as usual. There had been no special goodbye there, either.

He was not particularly worried about the welfare of Jen and Hank. If anyone should try to bother them . . . well, Brahmaguptra had made provision for that. He meant to make sure, as soon as he reached Atlanta, that Bob (and therefore the people around Bob) understood clearly what kind of provision had been made.

So Dr. Henry Brahmaguptra had spent the early part of the afternoon at home alone, first getting ready the few things he needed for the trip, and then just waiting and thinking, until Scotty's arrival in a taxi at the door. Actually Brahmaguptra spent a lot of time these days at home alone, just thinking. As he got older he found himself thinking more and more about humanity and its future, and less and less strictly in terms of science or mathematics. Though he was still on the Labs' payroll as a consultant, and still did valuable work for them in magnetohydrodynamics and solar power, he no longer showed up at office or laboratory more than once or twice a week. He still earned his pay, handling most of the jobs at home. After debating with himself for a while this afternoon, he had phoned in to let them know he was going to be out of town for perhaps a couple of days. He had not told them where.

Personally, he admitted to himself now as he stood beside the airstrip, he was a little scared, though he thought he had been successful in concealing the fact from Jen. That horrible killing down in Albuquerque . . . he still couldn't believe that the nice boy who had visited in his house was really guilty of that. Somebody was, though. And Bob said it was connected with their programming trick of twenty years ago—and Bob should know.

Somehow, Brahmaguptra over the decades had almost managed to convince himself that neither of the code phrases would ever have really worked, that it had all been some kind of sophomoric stunt, though they were both a long way from being sophomores when they worked it . . . but underneath he had known all along how real it was. He should never have tried, on the spur of the moment, on the telephone, to concoct that clumsy lie about his half of the code being ineffective. Would that it were so in fact . . . but Bob of course had seen through the lie at once.

He would know better than to try to lie to Bob when the

two of them were face to face. He would tell the truth, and trust that Bob still had left in him enough humanity to listen, and be swayed. Then the two of them would come to some good agreement that would end the growing terror. Or else . . . or else the other men would come out from behind the curtain that Brahmaguptra tended to visualize as hanging behind Bob's chair. The Reaganites, the hard-core men of Nixon, unreformed. Brahmaguptra always involuntarily pictured them as white, Teutonic Anglo, clean-shaven, fleshy men with close-cropped hair. Perhaps in uniform, or more probably just out of it . . .

Brahmaguptra had thought about the possibility that they would take over the coming meeting openly. At last they would confront him face to face, and would try first to bribe and then to coerce from him his portion of the code. If they were to try using physical force on him, well, his heart wouldn't take much and then they would be out of luck. If they had ideas of getting at him by threatening Jen or Hank—that was why he had to make sure at the outset that they understood what provision he had made.

"Dr. Brahmaguptra? We're all set now, sir." It was Scotty, coming out of Operations. The pilot was indubitably Anglo-Saxon, a little fleshy, close-cropped and clean-shaven, more or less in uniform . . . castigating himself for being unable to stop thinking in physical stereotypes, Brahmaguptra smiled almost apologetically at the courteous pilot, and with a shake of his head indicated firmly that he was still capable of carrying his own bag.

Then, suitcase in hand, he followed the man across the ramp to where a Lear jet waited, magnesium skin shimmering silver in the high brilliant sunshine.

It was a long time since Brahmaguptra had ridden in a private plane, and the prospect of doing so now inevitably brought forth memories. Had Bob Gregory actually been with him on his last such flight, and had it actually been Bob's plane that time too? Brahmaguptra honestly couldn't recall. There had been stretches when they had spent a lot of time together. They had been close friends. Was it utterly

hopeless, even now, to dream that perhaps, one day, once
again . . .?

His mind was elsewhere now as he went through the
mechanics of getting himself settled into the aircraft, his one
piece of luggage stowed away. All these empty seats around,
he thought mechanically, I should be sharing the ride with
half a dozen other passengers . . . but of course if his
mission succeeded it would be anything but wasteful of
energy. In fact it would be one of the best energy investments
that could possibly be made.

"Didn't you have a briefcase, sir?"

"No, just the one bag." It occurred to Brahmaguptra to
wonder whether Scotty might never before have carried on
this plane a passenger who was not playing the role of busy
executive. *Executive,* deriving from Latin words meaning 'to
follow out from.' One English meaning of *execute* was to do
something; therefore, and the fact had long amused
Brahmaguptra, an executive is someone who tells other
people to do things.

But the question is, he thought, who or what are all those
men with briefcases following out? And to where? The men
who ride this particular plane, especially?

Brahmaguptra smiled to himself. When he got home
again, he would try out his briefcase thoughts on Hank. Hank
was extremely bright, almost frighteningly so sometimes,
and maybe not too young to appreciate the point . . . my
pills, he remembered suddenly. Did I bring all my pills? He
couldn't recall with any certainty whether he had packed
them all or not, his mind had been on other things . . . the
doctor had said it would be bad to suddenly stop taking the
ones for hypertension, there could be a dangerous rebound
effect . . . the window by his seat needed washing . . . he
wondered suddenly if he might be airsick . . .

Stop it, he told himself sharply, just as the aircraft suddenly began to move, taxiing toward takeoff position.
You're starting to sound senile and panicky. Maybe you were
never dashing and adventurous but in the old days you had
some guts at least. If you weren't afraid of being arrested in

the draft office why should you be afraid now? You know perfectly well that Bob Gregory doesn't mean you any harm personally; he's Bob; remember Bob? And the invitation had come from Bob in person. Whoever is with him when you get there, whoever his present friends turn out to be, he's going to see to it that you get back home safe again.

Oh, but it was childish to have such worries. With one good talk, they ought to be able to straighten out—a lot.

The trouble was that years had gone by, too many years, almost unnoticed as it now seemed to Brahmaguptra. The discussion they were going to have now should have taken place long years ago. It had happened through some inertia, some timidity (on his own part, at least), the easy tendency in crowded lives to put things off.

They were two old men now, and if either one of them died, which could easily enough happen at any time, the problem they had created would be dropped in others' laps. Brahmaguptra of course had made provision for his half of the code to be passed along, with a letter of explanation, if something should happen to him suddenly, and he had to assume that Bob had also done at least that much with his. But two sharp worries followed at once from this: first, who had Bob chosen to be his heir? And second, had he, Henry, really any right to inflict such a burden upon Jen? Was she, could she be, prepared? How could you prepare a person for it without giving it to them?

He had dropped vague hints to Jen for some years now; she knew that some kind of extra responsibility would attend upon his death. But . . .

But if not Jen, who?

Maybe, Brahmaguptra thought, as the jet taxied toward takeoff position, I should after all just let it die with me. But what a horrible mess that was certain to leave, for others to someday face. If he really believed it was good for the secret code to die, then he ought to have killed himself some time ago, and not left Jen any letters. There had been one or two days in his life when the thought had seriously crossed his mind.

Had the secret, there at the very start, been Bob's idea or his own? With so much time and thought and work gone by between that time and this, Brahmaguptra now found it impossible to say. Certainly they had both worked together on it there at the inception, worked closely and well.

The aircraft was at one end of the runway now, turning in its tracks, a bird slow-walking on the ground. Inside the cabin the whine of the jets was thoroughly subdued by good acoustic insulation. With the turning motion the new control tower passed before Brahmaguptra's gaze. Flying in and out of Los Alamos was certainly no longer what it had used to be, in those old days of bad and good, the war days, in the DC-3's that the army people had refused to ever call anything but gooney birds.

In and out of here young Henry B. had gone, to and from Washington, White Sands, Oak Ridge, you name it, riding with Teller, with Oppenheimer, with how many others whose names had begun to grow into legend now.

Yes, General, we know it's taking longer than we once thought, but we are making progress. And then the wargod hatched here forty years ago had made two stamping steps of his great taloned feet, permanently flattening the militarists of Japan, and extinguishing a few score thousand innocent human lives in the process as if by accident. Those who take up the sword shall perish by the sword, and so shall a lot of others who have never handled anything but plowshares. More would have died, if we'd had to invade Japan. Many more . . . for a while Brahmaguptra had been able to find some comfort, some justification, in the Truman argument.

And before his smudged window, as the aircraft lined up with the runway, there appeared what Hank liked to call the metal-petalled power-flower. A many-trunked mangrove tree of metal, its hundred mirrors groping cleanly, electronically, safely for the sun. We *can* build safely, reasonably sometimes, Brahmaguptra thought with pride, we can devise with other things in mind than profit and destruction. Always, for the sake of the children, a brave new world must be attempted. And always there must be a readiness to fight, with courage if not with nuclear threats.

Earth's sun was very bright.

The aircraft had stopped turning and stood still. It was lined up with the runway, poised for its takeoff run. Scotty, the back of his head visible through a glass panel forward, must be exchanging some last preflight words with the control tower.

The Lear jet leaped forward, quickly gathering speed.

A great, blinding light filled the cabin from the left side. Brahmaguptra twisting away from the window with seared eyes could feel the fatal swerve, of wheels not yet free of runway but still too nearly airborne to have controlling contact with the ground. In a moment, he thought reflexively, the sound of the great nuclear blast will come. The Soviets have launched, war has begun. The aircraft was tipping, twisting, crashing, bursting into flame.

NINE

Grandpa was dead. And the fact hurt worse than any other grief that Hank could remember.

When word of his father's death had come, Hank had been much too young for him to now retain any memory of how that knowledge had been imparted to him, or how the first awareness of a loss had felt. Nor could he now remember clearly anything about his living father. There were a few images, growing more and more confused with those of still-existing photographs. There was, sometimes, the sound of a laugh, a voice. But sometimes Hank thought those were purely imaginary.

Hank doubted that he could have felt worse than this over his father, even if he had been old enough at the time to understand.

Today a policeman he knew by sight though not by name had come for Hank at school and had brought him home, assuring him several times along the way that his mother was all right, but she was going to need some help from her big son. And still, when he got home, the way his mother looked had been something of a shock; Hank had never seen her so really knocked out by anything before. Or if he had, he was too small then to be able to recall it now.

Right now, late in the afternoon, Hank's mother was on the telephone. She had been on the phone a lot since the police had brought her home after identifying Grandpa's body. On coming home after that horrible duty she had looked even worse, more shocked, than she had before.

For his own part, Hank had mainly just been wandering about the house, feeling more than a little dazed, and sickly empty deep inside. A neighbor woman had stayed with him for the little time his mother was gone with the police. Now and then he would walk to where his mother sat in the kitchen, the phone usually in her hand, and they would hug each other fiercely.

Hank hadn't cried over Grandpa yet. In a way he wanted to cry, but he didn't feel that he ever would. It seemed too serious, too fundamental a disaster for tears to have any bearing on it.

A couple of times he answered the door, letting in one or another of the neighborhood women who had just heard the news and came round to offer condolences and such help as they could think of. Everyone of the women who came in made some comment to the effect of how grownup Hank was getting to be.

Well, he didn't feel much like wanting to be grownup right now. Today it would have felt better just being a child. Still, there was no getting away from the fact that today was not the day for childishness in any form.

Wandering into the kitchen once again, he got the impression that it was full of sympathetic women surrounding his mother, and retreated unnoticed to his own room. There he stood over the workbench, playing listlessly with the switches for this and that. When he looked out through the open door of his bedroom and across the hallway at an angle, he could just see, through the open door of Grandpa's room, how Grandpa's old bulky sweater was just hanging there as usual on its hook. It was almost frightening to Hank how an inanimate object could dare to behave like that, when its owner, the body that had given it shape, was dead. Grandpa's fingers that had put it on the hook were dead, but still it just hung there as if he was expected back . . .

Grief came in a great wave. But still Hank did not cry, or struggle against tears.

He turned from the doorway. In the framed drawing on the wall of his own room, Lancelot's castle was unchanged also. But that was as it should be, though the sight brought back all the stories that Grandpa had used to tell. A king who fought for justice and mercy for all, the brave knights who came to his support. In that world death was bearable, and could even be expected . . .

The workbench claimed Hank. He looked down at things, turned this, connected that and switched it on. Presently, under his controlling fingers, a crude electronic sketch of the empire ruled by OCTAGON came into view on the old television screen. But at first, this time, even Starweb was not much help. The lines and circles were only marks, areas where chemicals on the screen gave off light, energized by a flickering beam of electrons under elaborate control. It took an effort today to even start to get interested in the game.

But once he had made the effort, the game was ready and waiting, as always, to absorb him.

He wasn't going to be able to call for any help today. But when the wizards weren't available, the hero-king defended the kingdom, the empire, as best he could without them. Hank reviewed strategies, deciding as best he could what TAURUS was going to do on the next turn, and ARCH-ANGEL and MAIDEN and AGRAVAN . . . yeah, AGRAVAN.

Grandpa, taking enormous trouble with his choice of words, had told Hank something of the trouble that their recent visitor had been afflicted with, or had got himself into somehow, in the hotel down in Albuquerque. Listening sort of between the words, it hadn't been hard to tell that Grandpa thought Alex was really innocent, at least of anything as bad as murder. Then later Hank had listened to a few news broadcasts on his own and had heard how the Albuquerque police were still seeking Alex Barrow for questioning and were not getting anywhere with finding him. Hank had liked Alex, and he was ready to take Grandpa's implied word for it that the search, the accusation, was all some horrible mistake. Or maybe even a plot.

Hank was glad now that he had switched the other night, and declared AGRAVAN/Alex his ally in the game. Alex, in serious real-world trouble, obviously wasn't going to have time to concern himself with Starweb, or be able to send in moves. But Hank would feel terrible about continuing to attack him, even in a game; from now on, OCTAGON/Hank would consider it a duty to defend AGRAVAN/Alex to the last planet and the last ship . . .

Hank pulled up a chair to the workbench and settled down to work on the game a little, to decide as well as he could without help what the next move for OCTAGON ought to be. He would probably call for help on the move later, before he sent it in. Sometime when his mother was out . . .

When Hank at last came out of his room again, it was dark outside and lights had been turned on. The sound of voices from the kitchen had taken on a different quality, he noticed. When he looked into the kitchen again there were only two people there. His mother was seated at one side of the table. A florid, plump man in a business suit, who looked halfway familiar but whom Hank could not at once identify, was sitting opposite her with a half-filled coffee cup before him. In the middle of the table was an unfamiliar china plate, holding a coffee cake of unknown but evidently homemade origin, covered with plastic wrap.

Hank was glad that there was still at least one visitor. His mother, he thought, looked at least a little brighter than she would have if there had been no one else around.

The man seated at the table looked up as Hank came in, smiled at him somewhat vacantly, and went on with what he had been saying.

"As I say, Jennifer, all I really know is that Henry left it with me nine years ago last month. I think it must have been right after we had word of young Henry being killed. Ever since then we've had it in the vault.'' And with this last word, the man's identity if not his name suddenly came clear in Hank's mind; now he could associate the florid face and business suit with the lobby of the small downtown bank.

Hank's mother was smiling wanly at him now. ''Hi, honey. Were you asleep?'' She held out her arms to her son without getting up, and Hank went to her and accepted a hug, and gave one back.

''No,'' he said. ''Just working on the game.''

His mother, her mind already back on what the banker was saying, patted Hank and let him go.

The banker said: ''Henry was very careful in how he arranged this. In contrast, I'm sorry to have to say, to most of his financial affairs.''

''Is this a financial affair too?''

''I really have no idea what it is. Just that your father-in-law was very insistent, in his written and oral instructions both, that there must be no delay in getting this envelope into your hands once his death had been confirmed. There was to be no waiting until the next day, was how he expressed it to me once.''

''I see,'' said Hank's mother. She looked down at the table, where beside the cake on its plate there lay an ordinary white envelope that must be what they were talking about. It lay as if the banker had put it down there, but she had not yet made up her mind to pick it up. ''I see. Well, thank you, Frank.''

''Whenever Henry happened to be talking to me privately, on some other matter, he would usually say something about the envelope, as if to remind me. The last time was on the phone, just a few days ago, almost as if he'd had some premonition . . .''

''What did he say?'' Hank's mother asked.

''If something should happen to him and you weren't available, I was to take this to someone at the Labs.''

For a moment Hank's mother seemed about to ask another question. But then she only said again : ''Well, thank you, Frank. You've done your job.''

"Don't mention it." The visitor delayed a moment longer, as if he might be hoping to find out at last what was in the envelope. Or maybe he had some theory or comment to put forth, if anyone asked him what he thought. But no one asked him, and he stood up, brushing invisible crumbs from his gray-suited lap. "There are some routine financial things, regarding the estate, that I'll have to go over with you sometime soon, Jennifer. But there's no big rush on that. I'll be in touch with you in a couple of days."

"Yes, of course. Thank you for coming by."

When the banker was out of the house, Hank and his mother both sat down at the kitchen table again. They looked at the envelope. Still she hadn't picked it up.

"You know what's in it, Mom?"

"Not really. Something Grandpa wants me to look after. Something that he thought was quite important."

"Aren't you gonna open it?"

She sighed. "Yes, I suppose I'd better." Without getting up Hank's mother extended an arm to a drawer and pulled out a paring knife. When she picked up the envelope to slit it open Hank could see that on the side that had been turned down her name was typed, along with the words PRIVATE AND PERSONAL. Under that was what looked like Grandpa's signature. He had sure wanted to make the whole thing official.

As she used the knife, Hank's mother stood up from her chair, at the same time turning her back on the table so that the envelope vanished from his sight. Hank was curious and he stood up too and tried to peer over his mother's shoulder, but she put out an arm and fended him away with gentle firmness. "This is just for me, Hon. I'll let you know if it's anything you have to be concerned about."

Hank had been able to see only that there had been a couple of sheets of paper in the envelope, pretty well covered with close typing, like a fairly long letter. He didn't try to push the matter now, but sat down at the table again, watching his mother's face in profile and trying to get what information he could from that. He could tell that she read through the first sheet of the letter several times before she even glanced at the second. Then she read that a couple of times, too. Meanwhile the grief in her face was gradually obscured by worry. In a way, Hank was glad to see the change, even though it might mean fresh trouble coming. Because worry meant that something still could be done, things might somehow be made to come out right, and it was taking his mother's mind off that about which nothing could be done, ever again.

After reading both sheets of the message so carefully, his mother folded them both and stuffed them fumblingly back into the envelope. She was freshly upset, all right. She sat down, in the kitchen chair nearest the telephone, and looked at the instrument hanging on the wall.

"Who're you gonna call, Mom?"

"I was thinking of calling Eddie," his mother answered, abstractedly. But she made no move.

"This time of day he'll probably be at work." Most of the time Hank liked having Eddie around, working on things with him. Sometimes he wasn't so sure.

"I know," Hank's mother said. Still she just sat there.

A moment later, the phone rang. She sighed, and picked it up. "Oh, Ed. I was just debating with myself whether I ought to call you." She paused. "Yes. Yes, it was Dad, no doubt about it. I've just come from identifying him. And, oh."

Here came a fresh, small outbreak of tears. Hank found himself with hot and aching eyes, wishing he could join as he patted his mother on the back and tried to comfort her. But relief for him, he knew, was not going to be so simple.

"Maybe there is something you can do," his mother said into the phone, when she was back in control again. "I don't know." She looked at the envelope, which was still in her hand, and rubbed it between her fingers as if trying to read braille. "I don't know," she said again. "No. When you get off work will be time enough. I'm sure, yes. Thanks, Ed."

When the phone call was over Hank's mother hung up and just sat there looking at him for what seemed to him a long time. "Oh, honey," she said at last. "I wish you were a grown-up man."

TEN

Alex had read and heard the legends about Chicago gangsters. But on this sunny morning on a leafy street on the north side of the city, near the lake, as he sat in the car he had borrowed from Uncle Bob and watched the college kids walk by, murders of any kind seemed just about as remote and impossible as parking spaces.

God, but the students walking by looked young. He himself must be getting old.

Murder was doubtless possible here after all, for he had at last been able to demonstrate to himself the possibility of parking. He had even, on his fourth or fifth go-round of the neighborhood, come upon a vacant curbside place within sight of St. Thomas More University, and had succeeded on the third attempt at wedging the Grand Prix into it.

Parked at last—he would have taken a cab over here from his hotel if he had guessed how difficult it was going to be—Alex had turned the ignition off, and then settled back in the seat for what he told himself would be just a moment's rest. But the moment he closed his eyes the rest threatened to develop into a doze.

Eyes open, then. But the sun-dappled street of houses and clean apartment buildings was seductively peaceful, and he was tired. The scene even suggested movies about university towns, and he supposed that university towns in the real world probably looked much the same. One unique note here: in the distance, between gray Gothic-looking buildings, one white and fluffy cloud appeared to be just balancing on a line that had to be the lake's horizon.

The tiredness that Alex knew now was nothing like as bad as the utter exhaustion of his arrival in Atlanta after that last mad cross-country dash from New Mexico. But he hadn't even been given time to recover fully from that before starting on the run again, beginning the long drive to Chicago. Last night he had slept well, or at least dreamlessly, in his Chicago hotel. But it was all adding up in terms of tiredness, he could feel it. He needed a minute to rest now before he got out of the car, to run over things again in his own mind before he talked to anyone about anything important.

Guess what the first leg of this trip to Chicago had been? A short ride inside a robot, from Uncle Bob's office out to Uncle Bob's garage. Why his uncle had at least one of those pyramidal servant-guardians fitted with an interior passenger space, man-sized, comfortably lined and ventilated—Alex didn't want to take the time to think about possible reasons right now, and he wasn't sure he'd like the right reason if he knew it. But it had made his ride to the garage comfortable as well as secret.

Once they were in the garage, Uncle Bob had swung open a panel in the cone-slope of the robot's belly, and had given Alex a hand out. They were standing in the big garage with no one else around. Then his uncle had pressed into his hands a large manila envelope, holding it open first so that Alex could catch a glimpse of what it contained.

"Fifteen thousand dollars, Alex, cash. Mostly in fifties. Spend whatever you need to keep out of sight for a while, until I can figure out a way to get control of this situation. Now run our phone code back past me again."

They had devised a code, of sorts, during their last ten minutes alone in the office after the women left.

"Okay," said Alex, in the garage. "If I make a wrong

number call, that means I'm just checking in to let you know I'm okay. The more annoyed you sound when you hear my voice, the less closely you think the house is being watched. If you ask me what number I'm trying to reach, that means I should get to somewhere close to Atlanta, and call again soon.

"If I ask for some woman's name when I call, that'll mean there's serious trouble where I am. I need help, and we have to decide on the spot whether we should go to open conversation right away."

There was a little more to the code. Sitting in the borrowed automobile in Chicago with his eyelids sagging closed again, Alex thought that he had it still all straight in his mind.

"I think you have a real, unsuspected talent for this kind of thing," his uncle had observed dryly, meanwhile holding open for Alex the door of the new Grand Prix, which was of course far from the most expensive of the four or five cars in the garage. Among these was the orphaned rental that Alex had driven in from Albuquerque.

Uncle Bob thumped the top of the Pontiac whose door he held. "This one has Texas plates on it, you see. That may help us to confuse things a little. Less conspicuous, if you feel like heading for Texas."

Alex had his own ideas about confusion and its value, and also ideas about where he ought to head, ideas he hadn't yet discussed with Uncle Bob. "One minute," he said now to his uncle. Then Alex stepped quickly away to the side of the rental orphan, opened its door and reached in to quickly rifle the glove compartment. He came back to the Pontiac waving a handful of papers. "Starweb. I want to study it some more."

Uncle Bob hesitated, but only for half a beat. "All right. I'm not convinced that the game is really a key to anything. I don't see how it could be or why it should. But you're going to need something to do in hotel rooms."

When Alex was in the car and ready to go, his uncle bent down to the window with more advice. "You've got a full tank there, I think . . . Alex, whatever else you do, don't go anywhere near your parents, or even phone them.''

"I know that much.''

"Sorry, of course you do. I'm going to call them, and explain things as best I can. It would look strange if I didn't, now that I've been informed more or less officially that the police somewhere are looking for you.''

"Thanks. What're you going to tell the folks?'' Not that Alex even wanted to think about that attempted explanation.

"Leave it to me. I'll be as reassuring as I can. You just concentrate on remembering our signals.''

And Uncle Bob had stood back, and waved, and pushed a button to open the garage door.

If any of the human help were around in the grounds at the time to see him leave, Alex didn't notice them. He thought he was unobserved except for one robot sentry in the bushes near the front gates, that aimed lenses at him as he passed. And the big gates had opened smoothly, with perfect timing, as he approached.

Without hesitation, having the seeds of a plan already in mind, he had driven straight north out of Altanta. He stopped that first night at a motel near Mammoth Cave, Kentucky, where he spread out the Starweb materials on a table and one bed, and settled down to give the game some hours of concentrated attention, something he had never done before. By the small hours of the following morning, when he had to give up the effort to sleepiness, he knew very little more in terms of fact than he had known before. But he had found nothing to cast doubt on a certain wild-seeming theory that had begun to suggest itself.

The theory was that those who opposed OCTAGON in the game were in for a hard time in the real world. It seemed to make no sense, but such evidence as was available did tend to support it. AGRAVAN and LUCIFER were two examples. A third player, also an OCTAGON opponent, had been killed in Arizona, supposedly by intruders, according to what Alex remembered from his talks with Ike Jacobi. What that victim's code name in the game had been, Alex didn't know; there might be fifteen people, he had learned, in any particular game, and you might play through a whole game without learning the names of all your opponents if their domains in the Starweb world were far from yours.

That the game was connected somehow with his great problems Alex no longer doubted at all. That opposing OCTAGON in the game got you into real-world trouble was a much chancier theory. Alex thought that another player, ARCHANGEL, who lived in Chicago, might well provide a test for it. ARCHANGEL'S territory bordered OCTAGON's.

When Alex awoke in the morning in his motel near Mammoth Cave, he looked at his highway maps, and after some breakfast set his course firmly for Chicago, which he planned to reach before nightfall. He had never been there before, except for changing planes a couple of times when he was in the service.

The real-world name on the ARCHANGEL diplomatic envelope was Fred Riemann, and in front of it Tartaglia had lettered an "Fr." The address was in care of St. Thomas More University, and so Alex supposed that the fellow was a priest. At first that struck Alex as somewhat odd in a war-simulation game, but it would not be the oddest thing in this particular game by far. He couldn't remember ever talking to a priest about anything, but the ministers at home hadn't been hard to get along with. And if he spoke to a clergyman he ought at least to be told the truth.

Feeling as ready as he was likely to get, Alex got out of the car and carefully locked it up. A good share of his money was stashed inside, folded into a newspaper in the bottom of a trash bag under a few orange peels and crumpled Kleenexes. Another part of the money was hidden in the hotel room, and he was carrying still more in various pockets. When he had the chance, he meant to buy a money belt.

Alex started walking among students, heading toward the gray buildings, taking deep breaths of the northern spring. It was nostalgic. Everyone at home had always wanted him to go to college. Maybe he would give it a try when this was over.

Apart from some details such as street signs, this might almost be New York, and he knew a wave of homesickness. The leaves here were younger than in Georgia, the spring still fresh. Alex entered the university grounds, where students were scattered about in random movement. On a broad paved walk between spring lawns, he passed a girl who looked frighteningly like Iris Cardano. *What the hell am I doing here?* He had the sensation that for a long time he had been asleep, or dreaming, and that now he was awakening. He was back in the normal world, but in a part of it unknown to him. He was in public, being watched by a thousand people.

The sensation gradually passed. He stopped people and asked questions, about how he might locate Father Riemann. Directions given by well-meaning would-be helpers shuttled him this way and that, from one building to another. The boundless spring-blue lake came more fully into view, dotted with distant sailboats. The shoreline to north and south of the university campus was lined with apartment towers.

The lake vanished again as Alex turned away from it, walking through one gray stone arch after another. A final turn brought him into an enclosure of grass and spring flowers, surrounded by gray Gothic stone; for a moment he had the feeling that he might have been swallowed by some earlier century.

He pushed a button beside a carved wooden door that had one modern glass panel in its center. In a moment a gray-haired woman, wearing an apron, answered.

Alex recognized her from the movies: the priest's housekeeper. "Father Riemann, please."

"Are you one of his students?" The words came very quickly, a triggered response; it sounded to Alex like he was going to be dismissed instantly, or maybe shot, if he said yes.

"No, I'm not. I've come a long way to see him. Tell him my name is Agravan."

"Mr. Agravan," said the housekeeper, giving Alex a

wary reappraisal. It didn't take long. "Wait in here, I'll see if he can see you."

He was left standing in a small room, a parlor, looking out through neat lace curtains. This was not much like the houses of married ministers that Alex remembered visiting in his childhood. More like some old doctor's waiting room. Would an experienced old priest be able to tell by looking that the cops were after you?

But Father Riemann when he at last appeared, bouncing downstairs from somewhere, with both hands outstretched to shake, did not look to Alex old enough or calm enough for such penetrating insights. Alex for some reason had been expecting a large man, but Father Riemann was compact and energetic. His hair looked prematurely gray, and was cut short around a bald spot that Alex supposed had natural causes but which nevertheless gave the priest a tonsured look. He was wearing a long-sleeved Levi's sport shirt with both breast pockets stuffed full of writing implements. His general appearance and bustling manner, particularly after the waiting room, reminded Alex of the family doctor in New York.

"You're AGRAVAN. Come on upstairs, we can talk in the study. You picked a good time to drop by."

Alex, who had had his mouth open ready with an amplification of his identity, closed it again and came along.

Soon he was going to be some kind of an authority on book-lined offices. Here at least, for a change, nothing looked mathematical. *Computer Power and Human Reason,* read one title, about the closest of any Alex could see to being scientific. There was *Being and Nothingness,* which he had seen somewhere before. A spot check of authors' names on other books came up with Aquinas, Kant, and Plato. Almost blocking some of the shelves with its pedestal was a largish statue of some robed man, presumably a saint, whom Alex had no hope whatever of identifying.

"Uh, would you prefer if I called you Father, or—"

"No, no, Fred is fine. Whatever you're comfortable with. And you're Carl. Have a seat."

Alex sat. "Well, no, actually I'm Carl Tartaglia's replacement in the game." He was glad now that he had made some effort to rehearse this part. "He was killed, you know."

"Oh, I didn't know. I'm sorry." The priest, obviously concerned, stood blinking, waiting to hear more.

"His widow out in Albuquerque told me that the police called it an accident. My name's Henry Briggs." It had been put together from a couple of signs glimpsed during yesterday's drive into Chicago.

"Henry, glad to meet you." Alex half-rose from his chair to shake hands. No lie-detector alarms appeared to have gone off. "Do you play Starweb a lot?" the priest asked, dropping into his own chair behind the desk.

"No I don't. This is my first game, actually."

"Well, is it exciting enough for you?" Father Fred's fingers brushed at things on his desk, setting them aside. "What brings you to Chicago? You say you're from Albuquerque?"

"Really it's the game that brings me here."

The priest's hand stopped, holding a bundle of papers six inches off the desk. Then he let the papers drop. "Oh?"

"Father . . . Fred . . . don't you think there's something strange about this particular game? I take it you've been in others."

Father Fred looked back at Alex for several seconds before answering. "You know, it strikes me as odd that you should ask that."

"So. Funny things have been happening to you since you've been in it. Is that what you mean?"

"Well." The priest was looking at Alex now as if he didn't quite know what to make of him. "Fortune has certainly been playing odd pranks here and there. But if you come right down to it, I don't see how they could be connected with the game. It's just that they began when I got into it."

"Odd pranks such as what? If you don't mind my asking."

"Well. A certain bank loan for which I was responsible suddenly appeared in the bank's records as having been paid off. I knew perfectly well that it wasn't, that it couldn't have been paid. But the bank's computer said that it had. You wouldn't believe how much effort it took to convince them that something had to be wrong with what the computer was doing.''

''Was that all?''

''Oh, no, there were several other things. For a while I was playing with the idea that these things happened shortly after I sent in my game moves. But . . .'' A gesture of contemptuous dismissal. ''For example, the diocesan records began to list me as a monsignor, when I'm not.'' In response to Alex's blank look, the priest amplified: ''That would have amounted to a promotion.''

''So all the odd things that happened to you were good.''

''Well, they were. Or I should say they would have been, if they had been true.'' Father Fred had a nice, rueful smile.

''You haven't been attacked physically, then, anything like that?''

''Good heavens, no. Have you?''

Alex nodded.

''And you say that your predecessor as AGRAVAN—I never actually met him, but I know his name was Carl Tartaglia . . .''

''He was killed. In what was officially called an accidental fall. I doubt that it was accidental.''

Father Fred considered. ''And you think that the Starweb game is somehow connected with these attacks?''

''I know it sounds strange.'' Alex tried out his own rueful smile. ''But really I'm not a nut.''

''Did you take your suspicions to the police?''

''Not enough evidence.''

The man across the desk was squinting at Alex with empathic worry. ''I've been in other Starweb games . . . is it your idea that there's something wrong with the company that runs them?''

''I don't know.''

''I would doubt that,'' said Father Fred. ''Of course some of the players, a few, do tend to go overboard at times. Some of the messages that get sent back and forth could be construed as threatening. I know the company has dropped a few players, permanently, for sending messages that are obscene or abusive. But I never heard of any players physically attacking each other over the game.''

"I don't know if it's players.''

"Of course the game is full of threats, treachery, violence—in the sense that chess is violent. I admit I use the game as a safety valve myself.''

"Safety valve?''

"Psychologically.'' Father Fred made a teacher's practiced gesture, marking a point in the air. "I'm talking about role-playing. In real life we have to repress our impulses to steal and attack and betray each other. Or we get into a lot of trouble if we don't. But in the game one succeeds by those very means. Certain character types particularly. A berserker destroys; a pirate captures and plunders; empire builders and artifact collectors and, yes, apostles, can win by being utterly selfish and treacherous. Role-playing games like this, I think, have real value in helping us to understand ourselves and others. Apart from the safety valves they offer for aggression.''

This guy certainly sounds like a teacher, Alex thought. Well, he is. But somehow the fact seemed to make it harder to communicate. "Aggression within the rules, you mean,'' he said.

"Yes, of course. The rules exist in the real world; but they define a small, limited area that is not subject to the real world's morality. Cheating other players, lying to them, attacking without provocation and so on, are all permissible. In fact, the rules are set up to encourage such behavior.''

"I never thought of it just that way.''

The priest smiled. "I'm giving you my own interpretation, of course. Many players consider it just as much a matter of honor, morality, to keep commitments made in the game as they would to keep agreements made in real life. An unprovoked attack fills them with real indignation. A lie strikes them as outrageous, and they want revenge.''

"And they might retaliate somehow in the real world?"

"I suppose some of them might. Conceivably. And there are always borderline events, of course. Cases in which it is hard to be sure if a particular decision is in the game or not?" Father Fred's smile and voice showed that he found the question fascinating.

"I'm not sure I understand," said Alex. "Decisions such as what?" God, but he felt tired.

"Well, suppose I were to go to another player's home town, open his mailbox, and steal some diplomatic messages pertaining to the game. That would be a real-world crime, right?"

"I bet the post office would think it was."

"You're right. Exactly. But now suppose, instead, I only send him a diplomatic message through the mail, but I sign it with some other player's name?"

"That would be unfair. Wrong. Not illegal in the eyes of the post office, I guess, unless it could be proven that you were cheating someone out of some money, something like that." Alex wished he had a cup of coffee, but no refreshment appeared to be in prospect. Hell, what he wished he had was a bottle of Uncle Bob's Chivas Regal. Fifteen thousand bucks in hand to squander as he willed, and he hadn't yet dared to buy himself a drink, wanting to keep his mind as alert as possible. Maybe tonight.

"Certainly, unfair," Father Fred was saying. "And Berserkers Incorporated will kick you out of all its games for doing that. I would tend to agree with them. But there's always a gray area, you see, always a moral no-man's-land. I'll give you an example. Suppose I were to send you a message signed with my own code name; but by its salutation, and its internal content, I make it appear to be intended for some other player. And the body of the message indicates that the other player is plotting against you, when actually he's not. How about that?"

"How about this?" asked Alex. "You murder someone in a player's hotel room, and then you frame him for the murder."

The eyes of Father Fred showed very little. Nothing except maybe a little disappointment: that elementary ethical category, of gross real-world immorality, had already been mentioned and disposed of, and finer points were under discussion.

In this pleasant room with all its books, murder seemed at least as distant as it had been in the spring sunshine outside. Through the window Alex could see a frisbie flying in the distance. At the moment, he couldn't quite believe in the death of Iris Cardano himself.

He found himself biting at a fingernail, something he had quit doing when he was about sixteen. "Let me ask you," he asked. "How do your relations stand with OCTAGON in the game?"

"Ah. Is he the one you suspect of being behind these physical attacks?"

"No, I wouldn't say that. I don't have any definite suspect. It's just that some people in the game tend to suffer from real-world violence. And the ones who do, as far as I know, are all OCTAGON's opponents."

"Well." The priest looked at Alex for a while, evidently deciding at last that he was probably not crazy. "OCTAGON has been a foe of mine, as I know he has been of AGRAVAN's. I'm speaking now purely in game terms, of course."

"Of course."

"Speaking in real-world terms, he lives a long way from here, and I don't know enough about him personally to make any judgment at all on what he's like."

"He lives out in New Mexico."

"His address is somewhere out there, yes. You've perhaps had more contact than I have with him, then. Tell me, are you in conflict with him in the game?"

"I was. AGRAVAN was. I say 'was' because he may have wiped me out by this time."

Father Fred paused, with a throat-clearing. "You know, it occurs to me that this very conversation we're having is an example of what we were discussing earlier. You have a real-life problem that you think may be a result of something that happened in a game; when AGRAVAN attacked OC-TAGON, perhaps, or betrayed him.''

''I didn't.''

''Your predecessor, then, Tartaglia. You don't know what he may have done, do you?''

''No, I guess I don't.''

''The game as art-form,'' said Father Fred, with a sudden, unexpected brightening, ''is another aspect that interests me more than a little.''

''Art form.''

''I find myself more and more viewing a game like Starweb as—a story. A great Russian novel, perhaps, filled with characters who appear to be larger than life. I mean alive in a sense that real people are not perceived as being alive. Because we can know the characters in the novel, or in the game, more completely. I have the feeling, though it may be erroneous, that great novelists would also be great players if they tried.''

''Huh.''

''When I say characters are perceived as being more alive than real people, it's because they exist in a smaller, more manageable frame of reference. If we view life itself as a novel or a game, which perhaps in some sense it is admissible to do, then only God can be its author. Or can read it, watch it, criticize it, with full understanding.''

The most relevant comment Alex could think of was: ''I don't think I've ever read a Russian novel.''

''I don't mean what's being written nowadays. Except for Solzhenitsyn, and I suppose what is being produced underground, behind the Iron Curtain. I don't suppose what the officially approved writers over there are doing can amount to anything. But you should try Tolstoy sometimes. Dostoievsky. There are good paperback translations. Don't be put off by the fact that they're supposed to be classics.''

''I won't.'' Alex thought to himself: How is this happening? I come in here to report a murder, in effect, and I get a lesson in literature. And the lesson interests me, and I sit here listening to it. He could see himself coming back here someday, enrolling as a student. Thinking about someone else's murders and other problems, making a success of life that way.

"In my view," Father Fred was saying, "the best games, like the best stories, have the potential of stretching the human mind through vicarious experience. Computers are making it possible to play better games, vaster games, than any in the past."

"Yeah. But I suppose there have always been some people, like Napoleon and Hitler and so on, who thought of the whole world in terms of a giant game board."

Riemann nodded briskly. "A game board filled with little lead soldiers, who exist only for their masters to move them around, to use them up as may be thought necessary for their masters to win. Yes, I'm afraid there are a number of people who do see the world in those terms."

"And others," said Alex, struck by what felt like a keen insight, "who see TAURUS and AGRAVAN and OCTAGON and ARCHANGEL and the rest as more real than they really are. I'm sure that would be easy for some people to fall into."

The priest thought about it. "I'm not sure that I follow you there."

"Look . . . when you met me downstairs, the first thing you said was: 'You're AGRAVAN.' That was before you thought of me as Carl, or Henry, or whatever. From what your housekeeper told you, you knew that AGRAVAN was here. So he exists. He could have turned out to be someone entirely separate from Henry Briggs."

Father Fred was silent. But he was so obviously taken by the point, or by something that the point had suggested to him, he was giving it such serious thought, that Alex was encouraged to press on. "You say you've never met OCTAGON. But you have met him, in the world where he exists most strongly. You've been in the game since the beginning, right? I thought so. And your territory is next to OCTAGON's."

"We have a frontier."

"So you must have run into him, and had some communication. What kind of a—a character is he? I know he's an empire builder. I mean, what's he *like*?"

Father Fred was extremely interested now. He looked toward the phone on his desk, but only because he was afraid that it might ring and interrupt him now.

"What's he like?" The priest shot a keen glance at Alex. "Well, he and I have been at odds almost from the start of the game, so we haven't really communicated that much. He shot up some of my ships on an early turn, and I retaliated, and we've been fighting on and off ever since. The frontier between us is now heavily fortified on my side, and I suppose on his side as well. Each of us of course has tried to build up alliances against the other. He's an empire builder, as you know; but if you ask me about his game personality, I'd have to say that he plays like a Berserker—terribly aggressive and ruthless. And tactically so shrewd and sharp that he can get away with it."

Father Fred seemed to become aware, abruptly, how grimly serious he was getting, and with a near-smile he dropped the intensity by several notches. "But then, people who know *me* only through the game might well consider me treacherous and deceitful." The idea obviously amused him.

"What would you say," asked Alex, "if I told you that OCTAGON is a twelve-year-old boy?"

"That would strike me as unlikely. Unless of course the original OCTAGON has recently dropped out, and the boy has come in as a replacement?"

"No. He's been in it from the beginning. They tell me he's extremely bright."

"Still. If that's true, I'd say he must be getting help."

"I guess that's possible." Eddie had apparently been giving Hank some help, at least from time to time; Eddie MacLaurin, the dark-bearded man at Berserkers Incorporated. And at the Brahmaguptra house. And in Los Alamos Security somehow. Alex asked: "Would you say that OCTAGON is treacherous, too? Or one of the players that makes it a point of honor to be honest?"

The priest frowned. "I don't know. You see, some players, for strategic reasons that have nothing to do with morality, will limit their treacheries to one grand betrayal per game. What I mean is they build up a reputation for honesty by keeping bargains and so on, early in the game, even when they incur some disadvantage by being honest. And then, when the turning point in the game arrives—a real stab in the back! There are some players, I am convinced, who have elevated treachery into an art form in itself."

"But you wouldn't call OCTAGON particularly treacherous."

"I've seen no evidence of it, as I say. But then, if he works in the one-grand-stab-in-the-back tradition, there wouldn't be. Besides, as I say, I've been his enemy in this game almost from the start." The priest's eyes twinkled.

"You really get into this, don't you?"

"You must really get into it, too, if you made a trip to the city just to see me. Where do you live, Henry, out in the suburbs?"

"AGRAVAN and I are on the road at the moment. Sort of between permanent addresses. I'll have to let you know. I wonder where that damned name came from, anyway. It sounds like aggravation."

Riemann's eyebrows went up. "Oh, I can tell you that. Though why anyone picked it as a game character's name— usually people choose something grand and heroic-sounding, or else completely silly—and oh, by the way, while I think of it . . ."

Looking at his wristwatch, Father Fred muttered something else inaudible and hastily got up from behind his desk. He went to a nearby cabinet and rummaged in one of its drawers. For just a moment Alex had hopes of getting a drink after all. But then Father Fred came out of the drawer with a handful of papers that had to be game materials.

He shuffled through these, holding them close to his shirt like a poker hand. He glanced at Alex, at his wristwatch, and grimaced. "What do you know about MAIDEN?" he demanded hurriedly.

"Not much. Just that it's one of the code names in the game."

"A young lady, I believe . . . she lives in California." Riffling his papers, Father Fred sounded vaguely disappointed. "I was wondering if you knew whether she was an enemy of OCTAGON's too . . . Henry, I'm afraid I'm going to have to limit our discussion. I'm really sorry, but there's a counseling session that I must get to. And my day is going to be pretty well filled up after that."

"That's all right. I understand." Alex got up out of his chair stretching as if he'd just been asleep. He couldn't quite believe this session he'd just been through. Not that he felt he could blame the priest for the fact that it hadn't gotten anywhere. Alex had come in here talking about games, and so Father Fred had given him a game-world discussion. But if Alex had come in talking real-world murder plainly, doubtless the cops would be here by now to take him away.

When he stepped into his hotel room there were two men waiting for him.

While they were telling him to put up his hands and turn around, he meant to ask what the hell they thought they were doing. "What've I done?" was how the question came out, in a weak, defensive voice.

They patted him down with hands that were, after all, not metal arms. "That's a nice car you're driving, Henry. Someone tell you you could use it?"

This time he'd put the right license number in the motel register, with a vague idea that maybe the big city police would be more suspicious if he didn't. "Sure. My uncle did."

"In Texas?"

"Uh . . ."

"Then how come it was reported stolen in Atlanta?"

ELEVEN

Jen's left hand moved to the light switch on her kitchen wall, even as her right hand took down the ringing telephone from its wall cradle. She had been sitting alone and brooding at the end of this day of old Henry's violent and peculiar death, and nightfall had sneaked up on her.

"Hello," she said. And noticed somewhat to her own surprise that in answering this day's incoming calls she was already abandoning the form of 'Brahmaguptra residence' that old Henry over the years had gently chivvied her and Hank into using every time they picked up the phone.

"Jennifer?" It was a man's voice, quick and strong, one she did not recognize.

"Yes, who's this?"

"It's been so long since we've laid eyes on each other, that you may not remember me. But I was a very old friend of Henry's. I've just been informed about the tragedy. My name is Robert Gregory."

"Oh." And Jen's gaze immediately pivoted to the mail holder hanging on the wall. It was a compartmented container of painted wood, jammed as usual with bills and miscellany. There, in an old envelope left over from the United Fund appeal, was where Jen had secreted Henry's

141

postmortem message; such were the fruits of having grown up reading Conan Doyle and Poe. The last paragraph of the letter had urged its own destruction as soon as Jen had read it, but she hadn't been able to bring herself to do that. She feared that if she destroyed it now, she wouldn't be able to believe tomorrow that it had been real. She knew that tomorrow she wouldn't want to believe in its reality.

"He spoke of you often," she said into the phone. "I'm glad you called." And wondered whether she truly was or not. "His death must have been a great shock to you too," she said, and only at this point did it occur to Jen that she had no proof her caller was really Robert Gregory.

"Both deaths were," the man's voice said.

"Both . . ."

"I mean the pilot's, too. You see, the only reason the authorities have been so quick to notify me is that it was my airplane. Scotty—that's the pilot—was an old friend of mine as well as an employee."

"I'm sorry about him, too. Did he have a family?" Leaning back in her chair, looking down the hallway from the kitchen, Jen could tell that the light was on now in Hank's room. It was quiet in there; he must be at his workbench.

"Yes, he did, a wife and two little kids. Jen, did you see the crash?"

"No, I was at work. By the way, we had a visit from a relative of yours a few days ago."

"You mean my nephew Alex. Yes, I know, he told me."

"Then, a little while after that, Mr. Gregory, we heard that the police were looking for him. Dad didn't tell anyone that Alex was here, though—at least I don't think he did. He said he wanted to speak to you first."

"Call me Bob, please. What else did Henry say, Jen? About his meeting with me."

"I don't know. Nothing, I guess. Just that he was going to meet you."

"Jen, Henry wasn't the first one to die mysteriously."

There was a pause. "You mean, what happened to that girl in the motel room?"

"There may be a connection. Alex is innocent, I can assure you of that. Jen, you say you didn't see the crash. But maybe you could give me some more details of how it happened, what the people who did see it have said."

Jen was beginning to feel certain that it was Robert Gregory on the other end of the line. Maybe she was beginning to recall his voice, heard in her own childhood; maybe she was just ready to trust anyone who sounded at all reassuring.

"I was at work," she said, and detailed how she had been sent for, how she had identified Henry's body, what she had heard so far about the crash from the investigators. "You see, there's this experimental solar power installation right beside the airfield. As nearly as I can make out from what I've been told, something went wrong with the controls for the mirrors that focus sunlight on the central tower. Instead it was all directed on the aircraft, just as it was about to take off. The people in the control tower saw it happen, but of course there was nothing they could do. There was enough heat and light to make the aircraft crash. And burn."

"I can well believe it . . . Jen, it sounds very strange. It sounds ridiculous. The control system for the mirrors in such a system wouldn't have to be very . . . elaborate, as far as I can see. Just one simple device to sense where the sun was . . . hard to see how it could go wrong in such a way."

"That's what the people here keep telling each other. But I gather there's more to it than that. Some backup computer system was connected, to make it easier to do studies, keep track of results."

"Ah," said the distant voice.

Jen looked up. Hank, walking slowly, had just come into the kitchen from the hall. He appeared to be listening to her phone conversation.

"Jen," said the man on the phone, "I'm wondering if Henry left you some kind of a special message. I mean something, perhaps, that would only come into your hands when he was dead. I suppose you were the closest relative or friend that he had left."

She looked at the letter rack again, then pulled her eyes

away from it. "What sort of message? About what?"

"If and when you get it, it will be unmistakable. And you'll see that it concerns me. I don't want you to discuss it with me over the phone. But I do want you to know that I stand ready to give you every conceivable help in dealing with the subject matter. Will you remember that?"

"I will," she got out, then regretted the tone and quickness of the answer. The man at the other end could hardly have any doubts now that the letter from old Henry had been given to her.

"Jen, you say you know that Henry was on his way to meet me when he was killed."

Hank, standing near his mother, picked up a crumb of coffee cake and ate it. He looked at her.

"Yes. Yes, I knew that."

"But you haven't asked me why he was coming here. So I assume you know something of that too."

"Then you're assuming wrong. I didn't ask why he was going to meet you, and he didn't say."

"I can tell from your voice that you're suspicious of my motives, Jen. Well, that's reasonable. In your place I'd be suspicious too. I only ask that you don't limit your suspicions to me. Because I'm not the one who's really dangerous to you."

"What do you mean?" Jen hoped her son could not hear the voice at the other end of the phone; there was no sign in Hank's face that he could. She looked away from him, lest her eyes transmit to him her inward terror.

"I think there are people around there, Jen, who you should be very wary of. People who were probably in touch with Henry, whose names and faces I don't know. Maybe . . . political associates of some kind. I don't know how much involved in politics he was in these last years."

"Some." Jen bit her lip.

"People claiming to be his friends. I don't want to scare you . . . no, that's not right. I do want to scare you, not to panic, but at least to the point where you realize that if you have Henry's secret or even know about it, you are in danger. Not from me, understand. Never from me. I'm not the one who killed him.''

Oh God, thought Jen. The words were out. And what scared her most was that she had no trouble in believing it.

The voice of the distant man pursued inexorably: ''Any more than Alex killed that poor girl in the motel.''

''Oh, yes,'' said Jen. ''I mean, I don't believe he did.'' Now she could hear the faint sound of a car stopping out in front of the house, nearby yet outside the darkening field of vision afforded by the kitchen window. But she could see the headlight beams, and their going out. Hank went to the window and peered, shading his eyes with a hand up to the glass.

''It's Ed,'' Hank said.

''Jen, I want to be able to speak to you face to face. But I'm literally afraid to travel at this point.''

''I can't leave town right now either, Dr. Gregory.'' Somehow she couldn't manage *Bob*.

''I understand. And you have your little boy to be concerned about. How is he, by the way?''

''Fine.'' A veiled threat? For the first time Jen had the feeling that she might be going to faint or scream at any moment.

''Jen, I'm sure that Henry has my phone number there. I want you to call me at any time, day or night. I can send people to help you on short notice. And it might be a good idea for you to have friends staying with you for a while. Friends who were not necessarily Henry's friends; I mean who are not political. Do you understand what I'm getting at?''

''I'm going to have to hang up now, Dr. Gregory. Bob. There's someone at my door.'' Enough light washed out through the unshaded kitchen window for Jen to be able to see Eddie's face as he came up, with a quick, light step, onto the small back porch. Hank was already opening the door for him. Ed looked more upset than Jen had ever seen him before; and suddenly, perhaps for that reason, his facial resemblance to Hank's father was also clearer than she had ever seen it.

"God be with you, Jen," the voice on the phone said in her ear. "God be with us all."

A minute later, while her son watched solemnly, Ed was holding her in his arms, comforting her. "Jen, my God, what can I say? What a terrible thing. Yeah, yeah, that's all right. Go ahead."

She was crying a little on his shoulder. But she wasn't going to cry for long, though it felt luxurious; she couldn't afford to.

Hank asked, when she was through: "Was that call anything about Alex?"

She looked at Ed when she answered. "Yes, partly. Alex was mentioned. That was his uncle on the phone."

She and Ed were at arm's length now, he watching her steadily.

Jen added: "A man named Robert Gregory."

What showed on Ed's face wasn't surprise, exactly. "He happens to be one of our customers, too. Did you know that? In a Starweb game."

"Yeah." Hank's voice was very soft. "The game I'm in."

Jen moved gently away from Ed. "Did you want coffee or something? There's some cake here one of the neighbors brought."

Ed helped himself to one of the kitchen chairs, and seemed content with that. "Jen. This Alex Barrow was here, I met him here, the night before the killing happened in Albuquerque."

"Yes. But it was days later before we heard about the killing."

"I know. Me too. I'm afraid I often don't listen to the news any more than you guys do." Ed made a gesture of dismissal. "But now—I have to kind of wonder, it's part of my job, whether anything to do with Lab security is going on here."

Jen picked up a small metal pot from the stovetop and thumbed up the whistle-making top of the spout to run some water in. "I don't know," she said. "It was so strange."

"The crash? Strange is putting it mildly. And it's not the only weird thing that's happened around here lately." Suddenly Ed appeared to catch sight of Hank for the first time, and aimed a smile in his direction. "How're you doing, Hank?"

"Okay."

"How's the game coming?"

"Fine. Are you going to be hunting for Alex now?"

Ed looked miserable. "Going out and hunting for people is not really my job. I hope everything works out okay for Alex. That he's not really guilty of anything."

"I do too," said Hank in a tight voice. He turned and walked out of the kitchen, went a few feet down the hall, then looped back to stand leaning against the frame of the doorway. From the look on his face, he was winning a struggle to keep things under control.

"Those mirrors," Jen asked. "How could they do that?"

"Well." Ed relaxed enough to try a crumb of coffeecake. "From what I've been told, which of course is all preliminary, the programming was probably at fault somehow. I mean the programming of the mechanism that ordinarily reads out the position of the mirrors. Apparently it can be used also to de-tune the device, for experimental purposes . . . maybe it got locked on some stray gleam of sunlight from the aircraft, something like that. I don't know."

Jen asked: "Was that system connected to other computers somewhere? Like the main ones at the Lab, for instance?"

"I don't know. I wouldn't be surprised if there were some kind of a connection. Everything seems to get hooked up to everything else these days. Why?"

"Just trying to understand." She had filled the pot to make instant coffee, but had forgotten to turn on the stove. It didn't matter, she didn't want coffee anyway.

"Sure." Then Ed made a visible effort to brighten things a little. "Hey, I'll bet you guys didn't have your dinner yet.

How about a visit to the Pizza Hut? I'm buying.''

Hank, even today, could be cheered by that suggestion.
And Jen reflected that she had to feed her child something,
even if she didn't feel much like eating anything herself. She
certainly didn't feel like cooking, either.

As it happened, Jen saw no one in the restaurant that
evening whom she knew well enough to feel any obligation
to talk to. She was able to get away a little from Henry's death
and the pressing problems it had brought. Hank looked
almost cheerful at times, and Ed was calm and undemanding.
When she approached the salad bar she discovered that she
was actually hungry, and remembered that she had missed
her lunch. If she avoided thinking about her problems, things
seemed almost normal. Eddie and Hank talked Starweb and
computers. When the pizza arrived they were all ready to
welcome it.

When it was time to leave the restaurant, Hank lagged
behind, using the washroom. Jen walked with Ed out into the
cool early night, slowly heading for his car.

"I'd like to talk to you, Jen." The tone suggested business.

"Okay. What about?"

"For one thing, Alex Barrow."

"I've told you about all I know."

"The search for him doesn't seem to be getting anywhere.
All right, that in itself wouldn't be unusual. But the police
seem to be having trouble even getting the word out that he's
wanted. They don't tell me everything, of course. But.'' He
shook his head, looking troubled.

"I don't understand, Ed. How could I know anything
about that?''

"Jen . . . do you have any idea whether that young man
might have been working for the government, in any way? I
thought maybe he had said something to Henry, telling
Henry to keep it quiet, but Henry told you anyway . . .?''

It was a new idea to Jen. "I don't know who he worked
for. Unless it was his uncle.''

"That man, Robert Gregory. I happen to know he's been active in right-wing political causes for some years now, Jen. I don't mean just right wing. Some of the groups he's been tied to are pretty extreme.''

They had reached the car. Jen paused beside it, turning, looking back toward the Pizza Hut for signs of Hank. ''What does that have to do with anything?''

''I don't know.'' Ed drummed his fingers on the hood. He sounded frustrated and rather fierce. ''If there's anything super-secret going on around here, I'm supposed to know about it.''

''You're in Security, I suppose you should.'' The thought came to Jen, not for the first time today, how really little she knew about this man and his background.

''I'm not just *in* Security, Jen. I'm . . . well, I have a higher job than I've told you about. Today, when it finally clicked in my mind that the Alex Barrow the cops are looking for is the same guy I met here, I ran a check on him . . . I have access to certain secure channels, above the ones that regular police information usually goes in and out on. The indication was that he's in special intelligence work of some kind.''

''Alex?''

''Yes, I know what you mean. The best agents are like that. You think: *He* couldn't possibly be . . . all local law enforcement people are supposed to cooperate with him fully, once they know who he is, of course. There are some FBI agents with that kind of code. Some Treasury and Secret Service. A few CIA operatives who are cleared for particular jobs in internal security. I don't know if he really killed anyone in Albuquerque or not; if he did, maybe he had good reason. But if anyone's playing that kind of games so close to my turf here, I have the right to know about it.''

Jen had the feeling that everyone she knew was engaged in some impossible kind of game. Dad had got himself killed. Ed didn't care if there were a few murders, as long as he was in on the real reasons. And Alex Barrow—so young, and so . . . *ineffectual* looking.

She wanted to collect her son and run away with him somewhere. "I'd like to know about these games," she said. "Of course I suppose I shouldn't ask."

Ed, leaning on his car, looked hopeless, and a little angry. "Now you're mad. Because I haven't explained my job to you in great detail before? I just can't do that casually. You ought to know something about how Security works, having lived here most of your life."

"You and I are just casual."

Ed muttered something. Jen couldn't blame him, really. But she couldn't blame herself, either, for being angry. She saw with relief that Hank was coming to join them at last, and the conversation had to go into neutral for a while.

They were just pulling out of the Pizza Hut parking lot when Ed's radio pager beeped. He eased the car to the side of the road and unhooked the little unit from his belt and had a conversation with it—or tried to. It was pretty noisy. Jen couldn't make out half of what the voice coming through was trying to tell him. Most of it seemed to be code and numbers.

"Okay," Ed said at last. "Okay, I'll pull in at the station and take a look."

He attached the device to his belt again and looked at Jen, his glance for a few seconds including Hank in the back seat. Neither of them had been able to decipher what the radio told him. Ed said: "You want to find out something about my job? Most of it's pretty damn dull. Right now we've got a hit-and-run reported."

"Oh," said Jen, and thought to herself that she could take nothing more about violence today. What was Ed going to do now, show them a mangled body just to prove that his job was important?

"I just want to look in," said Ed, getting under way again, making a U-turn on the narrow highway, heading out away from town. "You guys can just sit in the car for a couple of minutes, if you don't mind. It could be important." He sounded as if he might have read Jen's last thought, and was mildly disgusted by her low opinion of him.

They rode in silence for a few minutes. Whatever the

"station" was that Ed had mentioned, it seemed to be out in the real boondocks somewhere. He turned from the dark highway onto a smoothly graveled secondary road, passing warning signs. Then he turned in at last at a gate plastered with more signs, behind which stood an uninhabited-looking white frame structure, the size of a small house. At second glance Jen could see faint chinks of light around a window. There were a couple of other vehicles parked just inside the gate, one a military-looking ambulance.

"I'll be right back," Ed said in a softer, almost apologetic tone, getting out.

"All right." Jen was relieved at being able to soften her own voice too.

"Can I come in?" Hank sounded very eager.

"Not without the proper pass." Ed smiled briefly. "And I don't think you have one." He was gone. Whatever he did when he reached the gate made it accept him.

Jen looked at her son. "Well," she said, and stalled. She wanted to communicate, and was suddenly not sure that she knew how.

Hank offered: "I wonder where the hit-and-run accident was."

"I don't know." There was the ambulance, parked near the building. If the victim had been alive when found, Jen supposed that the ambulance would be at a hospital. The wooden building held its secrets, and for the moment she was glad.

Time stretched on. They made inconsequential conversation about this and that. Jen tried to imagine herself drafting a note to be given to Hank in case of her death, explaining secret codes and perils to the whole nation. Hank, the computer nut, might do better with the problem than she was doing. But it wasn't in knowing computers that the necessary wisdom lay, of course; it was in knowing people. Beside that difficulty, computers were trivially easy.

Twenty minutes had passed before Ed came back. He smiled at them again; he appeared now to be more thoughtful than angry or upset. "Sorry it took so long. I'll drive you guys home in a flash.'' He got the car turned around and running back on the gravel toward the highway before he said any more. ''Just a hit and run, out on the edge of our protected territory. The victim looked like he was probably an illegal Mexican national. The Border Patrol says there was another big wave of them coming over a week or so ago. Certainly Spanish-looking. There was a big screwdriver found near him, as if he had been working on something, or maybe trying to break into something; like a car.''

Hank was listening with silent interest. Jen asked: ''Do you have to try to find out who hit him?''

''Probably we'll just turn the whole thing over to the sheriff's office. When we're sure there's no Security problem involved. The only funny thing is that you wouldn't think there would be any parked cars for him to try to break into, out where he was found. And if he was working on his own car, where'd it go?''

''Stolen?'' Hank suggested.

''Ha. There were a few tire tracks around, I understand, but too blurry to be any use. There were some traces of paint on his clothing, from the car that hit him, probably; we're going to have those checked out.''

They reached the highway, rode it briefly, and turned off again. Another back road, unfamiliar to Jen. ''Where are you taking us now?''

''Home. Like I said. I just thought I'd go this way and kind of take a look at things.''

Hank asked: ''Is this where the hit and run happened?''

''Near here. I just like to keep an eye on things as much as possible.''

They drove, and turned, and drove again. Jen, making some mental effort, thought that she had her directions more or less sorted out now. They weren't all that far from home, actually, and could get home from here by a halfway reasonable route if Ed were to turn right . . .

He turned left, another uninhabited, pitch-black corner. And the headlights fell full on a vehicle parked at roadside, a roadside that was bordered with part of the Labs' miles of protective fences and routine warning signs. The vehicle was a van, a late model but you could hardly call it new, for it had obviously seen some hard use. Brownish mud, dried hard now, was splattered all over a custom paint job in a distinctive pattern of yellow and gray.

Eddie muttered what sounded like an exclamation of surprise. He slowed his car to a halt some fifty feet from the van, his headlights holding it steadily. It was dark and motionless and appeared to be deserted. Ed looked around, mumbling in exasperation, and pulled his communicator from his belt again.

"Matrix," he said into it, "this is Solon. Come in." But all he could get back from the device was a burst of static.

Ed swore, which was uncharacteristic. He rapped sharply on his communicator with a knuckle, which didn't help. Then he put it down and grabbed for his gearshift as if about to drive on; but he couldn't quite make up his mind to do that either. He sat there glaring with a look of frustration at the van.

"Looks like there's no one in it," Jen remarked. She could make out some kind of low, angular shape behind the tinted glass—as if someone had perhaps left a large box in the driver's seat. But there were no human shapes, and nothing moved.

"I know that vehicle," Ed was muttering, so low he could hardly be heard. "It's got to be the same one, with that paint job. Experimental job, automatic highway control project. We had a report a month ago that it was stolen, and then they said it was only some mixup in the records. It had been put on loan to some outfit in Georgia." He grabbed up his radio again. "Matrix, Matrix, this is Solon. Do you read?"

There was, Jen saw, a front license plate on the van, which would indicate it was not a regular New Mexico registration—only a rear plate was needed for that. But there was no way of telling what kind of plate it was. The coating of mud obscured not only the symbols but the basic colors.

Ed threw his radio down again, this time violently. "All right," he said through clenched teeth. "I'll have to take you guys back to the station first."

"We don't want to go back to the station," said Jen. "Ed, if you want to get out and take a look, why don't you just go ahead and do it? We'll be all right. We won't even look if you prefer. If we do see any secrets, we won't talk about them."

"It's not a matter of secrets." Ed took a breath, and appeared to make himself relax a couple of notches. "Okay, then. It'll just take a second; there's no reason to think . . . Jen, you slide over into the driver's seat, huh? And just keep the headlights turned on the van."

"Sure. Why not?" Jen shifted over as Ed got out. And noticed to her astonishment as he did so that he was now holding a pistol that must have come from absolutely nowhere. Had he been armed all the time that they were going out on dates?

The car's engine continued running. Ed stayed clear of the headlight beams, and made a wide circle to approach the immobile van from the rear. She could see him dimly as he came up to it on the far side. He peered in the windows there. Then he moved out in plainer sight beside the van. Apparently he had relaxed somewhat; the gun had been put away again.

Now he gave her an almost casual wave, and called: "I just want to check the license number. Be with you in a minute." And he turned to the front of the van, squatting down to scrape at the dried mud.

When the van's engine roared into life he leaped up, pulling out his pistol again. He jumped back away from the vehicle, half-raising the weapon awkwardly as if unsure what ought to be done with it in this situation.

The van lurched ahead at full throttle, swerving viciously toward Ed and missing him only by inches. He jumped away again, then started at a run toward the car where Jen and Hank were watching. The van came after him again, roaring, squealing machinery hurtling to cut him off. Ed dodged, twisted away, began running in the opposite direction, toward a fence. Jen almost screamed at him. Her hands were on the controls of Ed's car now. Fumblingly she started to get it into motion, not knowing what she would be able to do once she had.

Ed had to dodge and double once again before he reached whatever safety the thin fence might afford. His running feet kicked up the gravel of the road. His face was wild. His handgun made a popping noise, aimed at the van, as it came after him again.

The car with Jen at the controls shot forward as she gunned the engine, intent on interfering somehow, anyhow, on Ed's behalf.

The van clipped Ed. She saw his body spinning in the air.

TWELVE

It was only about noon now, Alex realized. Only about an hour had passed since he'd first been questioned by the detectives in his hotel room and arrested.

Or had he ever actually, officially, been arrested at all?

"Goddam computer system," the Chicago police detective who was driving muttered now, as he turned the unmarked car into the no-parking zone directly in front of Alex's hotel. They had driven him away to a police station less than an hour ago, and were now driving him back. Rather methodical madness, sort of like running the film backwards.

"Well," the detective went on, "you guys must have to work with 'em too, so I guess you know how it is. I mean, on the printout that was a few days old it told us that your car was stolen and that we could make you on Murder One out west. Son, you understand that's what we had to act on at first. D'ja give 'im that paper, Charlie?"

"Yah," Charlie said, opening the door and getting out.

Alex had the paper folded in his hand. A message for him, they had said at the station, when they were de-processing him out again. He hadn't really looked at it yet. Some kind of a computer printout.

"I understand," said Alex to the driver, wishing that he could begin to do so. The policemen seemed to be expecting some kind of sympathy from him. "Yeah, the computers are sure a pain in the ass sometimes." He felt a mad urge to question the detectives about Starweb. But he kept his mouth shut and got out of the car.

"Where did you want the Pontiac left?" asked the detective who had got out first. One of the minor strangenesses of the last half hour, Alex had noted, was that they were no longer calling him by his first name, as they had while they were arresting him. They hadn't promoted him to *sir* or *Mr. Barrow* either; it was like they didn't quite know what to call him now. At the same time there was now an undertone of camaraderie. The big change from convict to comrade had come, he realized, when they ran their definitive check on him through their nationwide police computer system. That was when they had come up with the message for him, also.

"Just leave it here at the hotel," Alex answered, about the car. The Pontiac, he gathered, had been impounded, or whatever the correct word was for what they did with a reclaimed stolen vehicle. But now that film too was being run backwards. And no one had ever said to him in plain English exactly why. It seemed to be assumed that he would know.

What would Father Fred think, philosophically, about this game? Alex didn't plan to hang around to tell him and find out.

A minute later, to his continued inwardly trembling astonishment, Alex was standing alone and free in front of the hotel. His escort was gone, taking with them a third plain-clothesman who had just deposited the Pontiac in the no-parking space and walked off with a brisk nod but no word to Alex, as he handed Alex back the keys.

Standing on the sidewalk, he opened the folded paper he had been carrying in his hand. The message, in the form of what looked like some kind of teletype printout, wasn't very long. It read:

AGRAVAN/ALEX BARROW c/o CPD CHICAGO IL
URGENT YOU ATTEND GAMECON LOS ANGELES

GUAMS HOTEL APRIL 28-30. STARWEB X430 CON-
CLUSION IMMINENT.

OCTAGON

X430 was the number of his Starweb game. As for the rest
of the message, there seemed to be no danger of its making
sense.

Alex refolded the paper and put it in his pocket. He got out
his restored keys and looked into his borrowed car. Every
dollar of the money he had secreted at the bottom of the
garbage bag was still there.

Fearing no traffic tickets, not today anyway, he locked up
the car again, leaving it where it was. Then he walked into the
hotel and up to his room on the second floor. The man behind
the desk looked up at his passage but said nothing.

Hours ago, this morning, before he had gone off thinking
to play secret investigator at the university, Alex had taken
careful note of the positioning of a couple of items inside the
room. Both had been moved slightly. So the room had been
gone over, doubtless by the police, which was hardly a
surprise. But all the money that he had stashed in the
room—some in another wastebasket, under the plastic liner,
some behind a picture on the wall—all of it was still where he
had left it. His few other belongings had been poked at, but
they too were still here.

The first requirement right now was to use the bathroom.
After that Alex dropped himself into a hotel armchair and
closed his eyes. Maybe when he opened them he'd be on a
plane from Florida, just setting down in Atlanta for the first
time. He would be wondering whether he ought to call up
good old Uncle Bob during his stopover, just to say hello.
Maybe he shouldn't bother. Alex opened his eyes, and still
saw Chicago.

All right. He had to use whatever events had left him of his
intelligence. If this were some Hitchcock movie, the police
would be letting him go just to see what he would do next.
Then they would follow him to the secrets, or the treasure, or

the master villain. But Alex couldn't believe in that explanation for a moment. The police were too obviously as befuddled as everyone else; just plowing ahead, trying to find out what they were supposed to be doing, making mistakes and backtracking and then plowing stubbornly ahead some more.

The police *did* know just who he was, they had his name exactly right, and that the car he was driving was registered to his uncle. And their computer printouts a few days old had told them something at least about the New Mexico charge against him, and that his car was supposed to be stolen. He'd had a bad moment when they said that. Uncle Bob, the evil genius, setting him up . . . there had to be some other explanation.

Then when the computer had had a chance to look at matters more closely, it had decided that he, Alex, was a nice guy after all. Forget all that stuff on the old printout, men, he's so nice you have to let him go right away, without even asking him any more questions. And, by the way, give him this message . . .

He got out the folded paper and read it through again. It didn't make any sense coming from twelve-year-old Hank Brahmaguptra. Of course it didn't make any sense coming from anyone else, either. Maybe Hank had dropped out of the game. Maybe the mask of OCTAGON was now worn by someone else.

Someone else . . .

Whoever it was in control now, seemed to be acting like Alex's friend. But tonight, or tomorrow night, he could wake up to find a thing with metal arms sitting in a wheelchair at his bedside, reaching for him.

He looked at the phone, and pondered making a wrong-number call to good old Uncle Bob. But the more he thought about their so-called code, the more obvious it became that the code could not convey much information either way. Had its only purpose been to give him something to think about, until Uncle Bob had got him out of the house and out of the way?

Was he supposed to vanish permanently, make a new life

for himself on fifteen thousand and a year-old Pontiac? People had certainly done it on less. But it wasn't what Alex had in mind.

He thought about Father Fred. And Uncle Bob. And Hank. And old man Brahmaguptra, and Eddie MacLaurin.

And whatever way he tried to think about the situation, he kept coming back to Starweb.

He got up out of his chair with a decisive motion and went to the dresser where he had left his game materials, and riffled through them. The priest had mentioned a name of a player, MAIDEN, in California. Another possible OCTAGON opponent. And the OCTAGON message practically summoned him to Los Angeles.

Anyway, there was no reason to stay in Chicago. If tomorrow the police computer again said he was a villain, he wanted them at least to have to chase him a little.

Waiting at O'Hare field for his flight, Alex bought a newspaper; got to keep up with the news, see if wandering robots have been reported anywhere.

No robots. But there was a small story about a strange plane crash in Los Alamos.

Robert Gregory, acting somewhat out of character, was reading the newspaper at breakfast; or rather, thought Georgina Hoyle who watched him from the other side of the table, he was searching the newspaper for something. Unsuccessfully, it appeared, judging by the dissatisfaction on his face.

She sipped her coffee. She was really growing accustomed to looking across a breakfast table at this man. The old married couple, she thought. Not that there had ever been a ceremony, or was ever likely to be one. But if she hadn't walked out on him by this time . . .

"You were talking in your sleep last night, Bob," she informed him. She used a carefully neutral tone, and watched him closely as she spoke.

"I never do that," he said distractedly, and turned a page.

"I've never heard you do it before. Last night, though, you really did."

His eyes above the newspaper were red-veined and tired-looking. "All right. What'd I say?"

"Does it matter? I was just . . ."

"What'd I say?" He never liked to repeat things. Today was not going to be a good day to irritate him.

Georgina said: "Well, if it does matter, I thought I heard you say something like 'the royal card.' Playing poker in your sleep, I suppose."

He was, at least, keeping a poker face. He turned another page without looking at the paper, and then let it slide to the floor. "Georgie, don't walk out on me."

"I've told you I wouldn't," she said softly. "I won't. I've gone completely crazy, understand? Out of my mind entirely. The career may be going down the drain, but here I am. I'm staying."

"I'll make it up to you somehow. I need you."

"I know." Georgie reached over the table and squeezed his hand. For once it felt almost helpless. She cleared her throat. "Today we've really got to develop some kind of a positive plan. Legal or not. After what you've done regarding Alex, there appears to be no point in trying to stay strictly legal any longer."

" 'Royal card', you say."

"That's what it sounded like to me, yes."

"Don't tell anyone about that."

"All right. I won't."

A telephone chime sounded nearby. It came from a device that hung on the wall in a picture frame and looked no thicker than an ordinary picture, a framed Miro print.

Bob turned to the wall. "Yes?"

Caroline's voice came through the phone-intercom. "Dad? There's a man calling who says he's from the FBI."

Bob used a napkin, crumpled it and threw it on the table. "Okay, put him on. I'll take it here."

"Mr. Gregory?" said a new voice from the picture frame, a moment later. "I'm Gus Fechner of the Atlanta office, Federal Bureau of Investigation."

"Yes."

"What I'd like is to ask you a few questions about the incident in Los Alamos, New Mexico, where your aircraft was recently destroyed."

"Are you in your own office now, Mr. Fechner? I'd like to call you back there, if you don't mind."

"I understand, sir. I'll be awaiting your call."

"Caroline, put that through for me, will you?" Bob sipped his coffee. He looked better, now that there was some immediate challenge to be faced. He and Georgina looked at each other over the narrow table. A robot rolled in and started picking up plates.

"I've got Mr. Fechner back for you, Dad."

"Now, sir," the agent began when greetings had again been got out of the way, "we were wondering if there perhaps could have been anything special about this particular aircraft of yours that might have contributed to bringing on this disaster."

"Contributed? How?"

"We understand you're frequently engaged in different kinds of research. Some device on board, maybe, that might have brought on this strange reaction by the solar power unit out there. I understand you're in the business of developing a lot of unusual hardware."

"Mr. Fechner, that's ridiculous."

"We're trying to check all the angles."

"You've got the wreckage, or rather I suppose the FAA people must have it. If there are any strange devices found on board, they weren't put there by me."

"We'll want a list of the installed navigational equipment, and so on . . . now, sir, I know this may seem to you like a remote possibility, but do you know of any reason why anyone might have wanted Dr. Brahmaguptra dead?"

"Nobody should have wanted Henry dead. Or Scotty, either, but there he is. And Scotty left a wife and two small children."

"Yes, of course. Was Scotty in any kind of trouble, that you know of, Dr. Gregory?"

"Not with me. Or that I know of."

"According to our information, Dr. Brahmaguptra was coming to Atlanta to see you."

"That's correct."

"It would have been your first face-to-face meeting in several years."

"Right again."

"Would you mind telling me what the meeting was to be about?"

"It was an impulsive kind of thing. We just recently started getting together again, I mean talking on the phone."

"About what?"

"My nephew was out that way recently, and dropped in on Henry. And we discovered that Henry's grandson and I were both in the same game."

"I want to go into that game sometime with you, too, Dr. Gregory. But now about your nephew. Where is he now?"

"I really have no idea."

"I see." There was a pause, as if, Georgina thought, the FBI man didn't quite know how to proceed. She and Bob exchanged uncertain looks. Something felt odd about the line of questioning.

"Where is your nephew employed now, Dr. Gregory? Can you tell me that?"

"He's very recently discharged from the Air Force. I don't know that he's found a steady job of any kind."

"Recently discharged, you say. No longer on the government payroll."

"Yes."

"I see. Well, if you should hear from him, or find out where I can reach him, or who he's working for, I'd appreciate it if you'd let me know."

"Of course," Bob answered thoughtfully.

"Thank you, Dr. Gregory. I'll be talking to you again as the investigation of the crash proceeds. Good-bye."

Bob sat there, his eyebrows raised, looking at Georgina. "Good-bye," he replied at last, in all probability too late.

"Just what the *hell* are we supposed to make of that?" he

asked his small assembled council of advisers a little later. Only Georgina and Caroline were with him in his private office. He had wanted to call in Albie Pearson too, and explain the whole situation; Albie was informally in charge of all security measures on the estate and its phone lines. But Georgina had insisted that no one else be dragged into the illegalities surrounding Alex's flight from prosecution, and for once Bob had let her have her way.

The three of them had just listened to a replay of the phone call from the FBI. "Not a word about Alex being wanted for anything," Bob went on now. He sounded not only astonished but almost angry.

Georgina said: "I've checked out the rental car, as discreetly as possible. The one that Alex drove here from Albuquerque. You'd think that the company that owns it would be wondering by now where it is. Well, apparently their records show it as being on loan to the Department of Energy for a special project."

Caroline shook her head, as far as she could. "Doesn't that strike them as odd?"

"It's there on their printouts. They go by what their records show. They just don't consider the car missing. And, Bob, I've found out something else. The car you loaned to Alex for his getaway was on the police list of stolen motor vehicles for a couple of days."

"*What?*"

"It isn't on that list any longer. But the three cars sitting in your garage at the moment are."

Bob, who had risen, nodded slowly now and sank back into his chair.

Georgina went on: "The next time any of your staff takes one of them to the store for groceries, they're likely to wind up in the slammer. They probably would have, days ago, if our local police were more alert to license numbers."

Bob continued to nod. His face wore a light smile now, as of understanding.

"I would think," put in Caroline, "that the FBI would have shown some interest in that also. Why all your automobiles have been reported stolen.''

"Maybe they haven't been told about it," Bob said. "Well, ladies? Is my theory of central control of the nation's computer systems beginning to sound a little more plausible?''

"I have to admit," said Georgina. And she nodded.

"Are the FBI coming out to the house, do you suppose?" Caroline wanted to know. "Will they be watching it?" She sounded more excited than worried or frightened.

"I don't know the answer to either question," her father sighed. "I still know a couple of people pretty high up in the Bureau; maybe the locals would tend to be a little tentative in their dealings with me for that reason.''

A robot came in, bringing on its flat, low top a tray containing the day's mail. Albie Pearson would already have had his machines pre-process it, to weed out letter bombs and similar goodies. Coming in for the first time from outside, Georgina would certainly have diagnosed paranoia. But as matters stood, that was no longer even a suspicion.

Bob had picked up a postcard from atop the modest pile. "Starweb," he muttered. "ARCHANGEL. He must be about the only ally OCTAGON has left.''

THIRTEEN

Today was the first day since his grandfather had died that Hank had had the chance to be alone in the house for more than about two minutes. Since the plane crash three days ago, his mother had been tending even more than ordinarily toward what he considered overprotection; but Hank had managed to convince her that he'd be all right at home alone for an hour or two this afternoon. His mother had a lot of things she wanted to do, including a planned visit to Eddie at the hospital. And, Jen reminded herself and her son several times before she left, there were plenty of friendly, concerned neighbors right at hand that Hank could call on if any emergency should come up.

Hank watched through the living room windows as his mother drove away. Then he turned with a weary sigh, and looked down the hallway, considering. He discovered that after all he wasn't too keen about entering his grandfather's study. He felt reluctant about facing all those things, those inanimate, treacherously enduring books and papers, those pens and pencils and chalkboards. Personal things of Grandpa's, offering a seeming reassurance that the old man was going to be back at any moment. But the feeling of reluctance was not as strong as it had been even yesterday, and after a moment Hank overcame it and walked on down the hall.

Very little in the study had changed yet. The morning after Grandpa had died, two men from the Labs had come to the house and, apologizing all the while, had looked through his papers. Some kind of Security rules had evidently required this behavior, although, as Hank had heard the men telling his mother, Dr. Brahmaguptra hadn't been working on anything more secret than solar power for some time now.

Now when Hank entered the silent study, his eyes went directly to the modem. It was a flat, dark, sculptural-looking device. It sat now where Grandpa had always kept it, with the extension telephone on the little phone table beside the cluttered desk. Hank supposed that the modem probably still belonged to the Labs, and that they would be sending around to reclaim it any day now. If he was going to get any more good out of it, it would have to be soon.

He walked around the desk and picked the modem up. It was a small unit, easily carried. On its upper surface were two round apertures of a size and shape to fit the mouthpiece and earpiece of a standard telephone receiver. Hank remembered hearing Grandpa tell someone that the modem was of an experimental type, with one fantastic high baud rate, though it looked like nothing more than the standard audio unit that most modems were. The first time Hank had tried to use it for his own purposes, some months ago, had taken some daring. Now it was a routine and almost unthinking operation to run his hand down the power cord and tug it loose from the wall socket, and then to reach over and also pull the cord of the extension phone out of its wall jack.

Modem in one hand, phone in the other, Hank walked quickly out of the study, heading for his own bedroom. It was much easier to do things this way than it would have been to move his bulky, awkward, half home-made computer system from his room to the study and back again. Hank had briefly given thought to the idea of making some kind of long extension cables. That would have been fun, with the length of the cables doubtless creating challenging problems. But such cables would certainly have drawn attention. Eddie at least would have been curious as to what Hank was up to with them. Grandpa would have found out how his modem was being used, and Hank was ninety-nine percent sure that would have been the end of using it for game-playing.

As Hank put down the phone and modem on his own workbench, he felt just a twinge of something like conscience. These secret borrowings had never bothered him when Grandpa was alive; they didn't do any harm, they didn't cost anybody anything as far as Hank could see. As he knew from listening to Grandpa and others, when no one was actually using the giant Labs computers they just sat there eating up their modest quota of electricity anyway. It was really a waste *not* to use them, Hank had decided, if you had some problem worthy of their capabilities and you weren't depriving someone else of a chance. Hank understood that time-sharing would automatically take care of that last objection, except maybe on rare occasions when things at the Labs got particularly rushed. He didn't think that was likely to happen very often.

Besides, the Labs people might come to the house at any time, maybe tomorrow, and take the modem back. If Hank was ever going to be able to use it again, today might be his last chance. And the feeling of using it was not something that he wanted to give up.

Reaching down behind his workbench, Hank plugged the phone into the wall jack there, part of the general modernization of the house's phone system that had been performed about five years ago when Grandpa first brought the modem home. As he crawled out from behind the bench again Hank wondered tangentially if maybe his mother and he would soon be moving now. He liked it in Los Alamos and had decided he really wouldn't want to live anywhere else. Not in a big city like Albuquerque, and not out on a ranch like the one his other set of grandparents had owned when they were still alive. Unless maybe someday he would be able to have his own house out in the country somewhere, fixed up just the way he wanted it, his own workshop and lab. He had some ideas about that. But it would sure take a lot of money.

He picked up the receiver to make sure the phone was working. Then the next step was to plug the modem's power cord into the regular outlet; for that he had to decide what item on the workbench could be unplugged to make room. With the modem working, Hank picked up the phone receiver again, and punched out the number that would open the line to the computer at the Labs. Hank had never written the number down anywhere, nor, as far as he knew, had Grandpa. Hank had needed quite a long time to make sure of what the number was. He had learned it by watching and listening to Grandpa punching it out whenever he had the chance, and then gradually reconstructing it from remembered beeps and finger-motions. Hank's first attempts to use it had led to wrong numbers on which he hastily hung up. But at last success had come, and Hank had the number firmly fixed in memory now.

He punched it out now, and presently the preliminary tone from the Labs computer was coming from the phone. Hank paused for a moment, listening. He always thought of this tone as in some sense a voice. It was the voice that the great machine that he had never seen kept for its commerce with humans. It said something like: *I am here and I will serve you patiently; but now you must stand back a little; only another machine can understand me; I must talk to your machine. My real conversation you are never going to be able to share.*

That was what the subliminal message seemed to be today, at least. Hank held the phone a moment longer, drinking in the inhuman, humming, whispering song. Then with the motion of an acolyte he laid the phone receiver in the black cradle of the modem so softly curved to hold it. The tone faded, was absorbed.

Hank quickly made connections on the workbench and threw switches. In a moment his screen had come to life, showing his crude homemade map of the imaginary Starweb galaxy.

Presently a new, different audio signal came from the phone, cradled as it was. This meant that the computer at the

Octagon 171

Labs was waiting for his password; a connection had been made to his small machine, and now the password could be entered.

At the small keyboard of his TRS-80, Hank typed in: PEACE. Learning that from watching Grandpa had been easier than learning the phone number itself.

Again the signal changed, a softer, richer tone. He had been accepted as having a right of entry to the system. Now the right phrase entered would grant access to the individual file that Hank had already established in the Labs' memory banks, as an individual key might open only one door in some vast office building.

Hank typed out: JOYOUS GARD. And turned his head to look for just one solemn moment at the framed castle on the wall. Suddenly his remnant of guilt vanished, suddenly he was very sure that Grandpa wouldn't mind him doing this. Grandpa would understand.

All audio tones had died out now. The gates had opened.

On the screen, the picture was transformed, the crude dots and blobs of color had vanished. The game domain of OC-TAGON appeared not as seen by the cobbled minicomputer on the bench, but as it could be visualized by the great Cray-4 at the Labs. The detail and color were as sharp as the television picture tube was capable of showing. Three dimensions were suggested. Each linked world of the empire seemed to spin slowly on its axis—that detail had been fun to program, but not hard once Hank had solved the language problem—translating COBOL, PASCAL, and BASIC back and forth. Each war fleet on the screen appeared to be made up of actual miniature spaceships, and each had a block of data in fine print beside it.

Hank sighed. He stared at the screen for a little while, dreaming about he knew not what. Now that he had the game set up, did he actually, really, feel like playing it just now? He hadn't got the new turns in the mail yet, so whatever orders he worked out now would be tentative, until he knew what his opponents were actually doing. Sometimes the game was hard for him to get into, mentally, when he first sat down and looked at it. Sometimes it felt trivial when compared with other things he had to think about. But he knew from experience that if he persevered, that if he made himself work at the game for a little while as if it were interesting, it would become so. The game could always get a grip on him, it was always ready to take him in, whenever he was ready to be absorbed.

Slowly, with some hesitation—he was really going to have to learn touch typing someday—Hank typed in: LIST ALLIES.

The instant response on the screen showed, as Hank had known it must, that of allies he had only two. One ally of OCTAGON of course was AGRAVAN; Hank still felt glad that he'd switched on that one. Alex Barrow was a good guy, he felt sure. The Albuquerque police had to be wrong in being after him for murder. It had to be some mistake, or else a plot. Alex must have been framed, or maybe even possibly he was some kind of a secret agent . . . sure it sounded like some kind of a story, that way, but there were certainly secret agents in real life as well . . .

The other ally of OCTAGON was ARCHANGEL. Theirs was a long-standing connection, entered into during the game's early moves. That was before Hank had learned how to use the modem, when he had been playing on his own with a crude paper chart, while other players he was sure were using computers of one kind or another . . . but now on the advice of his helper Cray-4 he had continued the alliance.

Besides, Hank liked the name ARCHANGEL; maybe in another game sometime he'd use it as his own code name. It brought to his mind vague imaginative overtones of the holy hermit dwelling in the forest, far from castles and wars and tournaments. The hermit who was perhaps also a powerful secret wizard, ally of the king . . .

But to get on with the war. Hank typed in: PREPARE ATTACK ON LUCIFER. PREPARE ATTACK ON MAIDEN.

Ed wasn't even able to sit up in his hospital bed as yet. The van had banged him up too badly before it sped away, giving him a broken leg and a dislocated shoulder, and the doctors were still undecided about the extent of his internal injuries. And then there were the bruises.

The doctors were poking away at him when Jen came in; it was the first time she'd been able to visit him since the accident. Ed managed a grin, and opened the conversation by telling her that he hurt like hell. As soon as the medics had left them alone together for a moment, though, he put on a different face and said: "I'm sorry, Jen. I shouldn't have stopped when I saw the van. I should have taken you guys right back to the station and then investigated. You could both have been killed."

Jen had pulled up a chair at bedside. The more she looked at Ed, somehow, the angrier she got at him. She said: "It's all right. You did what you felt you had to do."

"Yeah." Ed lay back now looking at some private vision on the ceiling. In an odd way he looked satisfied.

"And I told you to go ahead . . . Ed, who was driving that van?"

"Someone probably a long way from where it was chasing me." His eyes came back to Jen's. "That's right, there was no one in it. It's a special vehicle that can be remote controlled, from a distance, I recognized it right away. See, it and another truck fixed up in a similar way were both reported stolen from the Labs in Albuquerque some weeks ago."

"I don't get it."

"They have a lot of special projects down there; a lot of them have to do with other things besides weapons. One of their projects is research on automatic driving. If cars weren't under the complete control of fallible human beings who fall asleep and get drunk and so on, theoretically a lot of traffic accidents could be avoided. Not to mention the possibilities of transportation for the handicapped.

"So down at the Labs in Albuquerque they had fitted out this van and another truck with super radar systems, all kinds of gadgets. The vehicle could pull up to an ordinary gas pump and fill its own tank—really. And elaborate on-board computer systems. Radio links to tie in with other computer systems. And provision of course for a human operator at a distance to take control. Television cameras built in . . . anyway, the van and the truck were reported stolen, as I said. Then the next report we got said forget it, they hadn't been stolen after all, but only loaned out to some company in Marietta, Georgia, along with other fancy stuff that had been reported as missing. An experimental wheelchair . . . there was quite a list.''

"So did you check with the company in Georgia?'' Georgia, Jen was thinking.

"My people are doing that now. As far as they've been able to learn so far, the Georgia people never heard of any of this stuff. Either their inventory is wrong or ours is. It's harder than you might think to get it straightened out.''

"Either their computer or yours.''

"Well, maybe. We do depend on the computers a lot. By the way, Jen, all this is not for public consumption yet. But I figure you've earned the right to know what's going on.''

"I don't know if I want to, Ed.''

Now Ed was looking at her with puzzled eyes. And she was thinking about calling Robert Gregory.

FOURTEEN

The Guams Hotel was a tall, broad tower, surrounded on at least three sides by a small sea of parking lot. Inside this surrounding sea a few palm trees grew, adding to the island effect. Alex could park no closer than fifty yards or so from the door. Swinging the latest in a succession of small, newly purchased travel bags in his hand, he walked on in.

In the lobby a temporary sign, a large cardboard placard propped on an easel, directed him to GAMECON REGISTRATION. Following the sign's arrow he hauled his little suitcase down one narrow wing of the main lobby. At the end of the wing was a table, flanked by a couple of additional GAMECON signs, in front of which a small line of people had formed. They were mostly young, and evidently waiting to sign up for the convention.

Alex hadn't even joined the line before he saw Ike Jacobi. Ike, better dressed than he had been back at the main office, was visible through the doorway of a large meeting room, inside which exhibits or displays for the convention were evidently being organized. The head of Berserkers Incorporated was inside a temporary booth curtained on three sides. He was bent over a table, doing things with electronic gear. A dozen other people at other booths and tables in the big room were similarly occupied.

Ike was absorbed in his task, and gave no sign of having noticed Alex watching him from sixty feet away. Alex joined the queue and in a few minutes was able to become an official member of the convention, which cost him ten dollars. It gave him something of a heady feeling to sign up under his own name. The Albuquerque police might still be looking for him, but this wasn't Albuquerque, and, for the time being at least, OCTAGON was on his side.

When he had been issued his convention nametag, he pinned it on the front of his new shirt—he had taken time for a little shopping before he got on the plane in Chicago. Next he went back to the hotel's registration desk. The lobby was a little busier now than when he had passed through it the first time. There were a lot of nametags in evidence, people carrying books and boxes, odd home-made materials for various games under their arms.

There was a room still available, however, Alex took it, then watched with mixed feelings as the clerk fed his name into the house computer system.

He went up to his assigned room and left his bag there. Then down to the lobby again, and through it to the meeting room where he had seen Ike at work. Since leaving Chicago, Alex had been trying to come up with something like a definite plan of action, but he still had none. He would be here, he would see what happened, he would act when he thought he saw a chance to act.

None of the people engaged in setting up their tables and displays appeared to have got very much farther along. Ike could be excused, for he had been distracted from his part in the effort. Standing in front of his table now and holding him in conversation was a tall young woman in jeans and a man's loose shirt. She was the same height as Alex or perhaps a trifle taller, with an athlete's strong frame, saved by her large breasts from looking in the least unfeminine. The young woman's hair was of medium length and medium brown in color; her eyes were a startling clear blue in a suntanned face.

Her face was too angular and somewhat too narrow to be called traditionally pretty; for Alex, *commanding* was the first word that sprang to mind. For a moment he had the impression that he had seen, known, the girl somewhere before.

Alex stood for a moment watching the pair of them talk. Ike looked uncomfortable, the girl animated. Alex, being no lip-reader, could not tell from here what they were talking about. Casually he moved closer.

Ike looked up, and recognized him at once. Was it fear or guilt that sprang to life in Ike's face now? It was certainly some kind of additional discomfort.

"Hi, Ike," said Alex, walking up to the table, then turning to smile at the young woman. He would guess her age at twenty. She too was wearing a convention name-badge, but it was pinned almost atop one breast, and tilted at the moment so Alex couldn't read her name.

Ike nodded to Alex, and muttered something. Ike had a real chaos of boxed games and books and disconnected electrical things scattered all over the table before him.

"Surprised to see me?" Alex asked him. "You remember me, don't you? From Albuquerque?"

"Yeah." There was no doubt, judging by Ike's look, about what he remembered. He had been Iris Cardano's employer and doubtless the police had talked to him to see what he knew about Alex. But Alex still couldn't tell if there was real guilt now mixed with Ike's fear.

"It's all been taken care of, Ike. Don't worry about a thing."

"You're AGRAVAN," the young woman put in suddenly, leaning forward to peer at Alex's badge. "I've heard about you, from some of the other players." She put out her hand. "I'm Vera Cayley. MAIDEN."

There was nothing arch in the way she said it, and Alex had no impulse to try to make a joke. He said: "You're in X-430 too. It's quite a game, isn't it?"

"Quite a game," Vera agreed. Before she let go Alex's hand she gave him a look that said she was well aware it was

no ordinary game at all. She continued: "I was just talking to
Mr. Jacobi here about it. Actually I came up here from San
Diego just to talk to him. It's that unusual a game."

They were both looking at Ike now. He picked up something from the table and put it down again. He didn't have
any idea what to say to either one of them.

"Ike," said Alex, "if you're worried about me, why don't
you go and call the police right now, and tell them that I'm
here? They're not interested in me. I tell you it's all been
taken care of." Then, just as some relief started to show in
Ike's face, Alex added: "OCTAGON and I are allies now.
You understand how that works, don't you?"

"Uh," said Ike, baffled and afraid again. With a half-nod
and a smile he turned away and pretended to be looking for
something at the rear of his curtained booth. Maybe a way
out.

The two people in front of his stillborn display looked at
each other. "Buy you coffee," Alex offered. "Or, we could
go have a drink in the bar." It was a respectably late hour in
the afternoon; but somehow Vera looked to him as if she
would probably be more at home in the coffee shop.

"Coffee sounds good," she agreed.

The hotel coffee shop was getting crowded. "You say you
came up here from San Diego," Alex began, when the two of
them were seated at a table. "Did you have a special invitation?"

"Invitation?" Vera looked at him with a wary reserve.
"No. I just heard that this convention was going to be here,
and that someone from Berserkers Incorporated was coming.
I wanted to talk to them face to face about this game. And
. . . did you say that the police had been looking for you?"

"I didn't commit any crimes. They're not looking for me
any longer. It was all a big—mistake. No, I think it was
something worse than a mistake. Connected with the game."

"I see," said Vera, as if perhaps she really did, or at least
she could believe Alex so far. "What did you mean,, about
getting a special invitation to come here?"

Their coffee arrived, and he leaned back in his chair,

waiting for the waitress to finish pouring and depart. Then he got out the little folded scrap of printout he had been carrying in his pocket since Chicago, and handed it across.

Vera unfolded it and read. "I don't get it," she said at last. "What's CPD?"

"Chicago Police Department. I don't work for them or anything. I just happened to be there yesterday . . . and this came through their police computer system for me. It's weird, but not the weirdest thing that's happened. I get the feeling that you know what I'm talking about, you're ready to believe me. I don't think this message really comes from OCTAGON the player, by the way. Not the OCTAGON I've talked to. He's only twelve years old."

Vera looked over the note once more, then handed it back and began to study Alex instead. "I don't believe that," she commented at last.

"That he's only twelve? I've been in his house. I've seen the workbench where he's got the game set up."

"Workbench?"

"He uses a microcomputer to generate a display. And, I guess, to help him figure out his moves."

Vera shook her head. "He must be using *something*."

"You're OCTAGON's enemy in the game."

She nodded.

"And bad things are now happening to you in real life. Not only bad, but very strange."

She nodded again. There was a growing intensity in her gaze. Alex wished he could remember if he had really seen her somewhere before. She said: "Tell me more about OC-TAGON."

Alex slipped his coffee. "I've been investigating OCTA-GON, or trying to . . . it's a long story. Anyway, something much more than a game is going on here. People have been killed."

"Amen," Vera breathed. She was looking at Alex like a scientist finding at last the evidence on which the theory of her lifetime might be anchored. He thought he could appreciate her feelings, but still the intensity was unsettling.

"You've got a story to tell too," he said.

"I'll say I have. The police wouldn't believe me, nobody would believe me, but . . ." She cast a quick look round the coffee shop, filling up now with conventioneers. "I can tell you the details later. I really think my life is in danger."

"If you're OCTAGON's enemy in the game, it probably is."

"What can I do about it?" Her fear showed, but it was under tough control.

"For the moment," said Alex, "stay close to me. Are you registered for a hotel room under your own name?"

"Yes. You mean that could . . . I guess I didn't think about that. I mean, I felt fairly safe here with thousands of people around me."

"I wouldn't. My advice would be to check out. Don't be here officially, I mean with your name listed on any kind of a computer record. Probably just being signed up with the convention is all right; I don't think they're putting that list on any kind of centrally connected computer system. But what about your car?"

Vera lifted her coffee cup: there was a tremor in her hand. She put it down. "My own car was destroyed, not long ago. I drove up here in a rental."

"Under your own name again? And you gave the license number to hotel registration, as usual. No. Don't even go back to that car. Just let it sit, in the parking lot or wherever it is."

Vera's look of scientific vindication was being gradually engulfed by fear. "I guess you're right. Tell me what it's all about. You're OCTAGON's ally, you said, you must know more than I do."

"I don't know enough. Not how to stop it, But I'm sure as hell going to try. Come on, let's get you checked out of the hotel. You can use my room, or something. It'll probably be the safest place in the hotel."

Alex got to his feet; Vera remained seated, looking at him doubtfully, her face a mixture of fear and stubbornness.

"Tell me," she said, "why the police were looking for you."

He drew a deep breath and thought about it. From her point of view, his behavior had to look suspicious to say the least. "All right," he said at last. "I was in a hotel room in Albuquerque with a girl. The girl was killed. I was damn near killed too, and I had to run for my life. The police there thought for a while I was the one who'd done it."

"Who really did it?"

"It'll sound crazy to you, maybe . . . oh my God. I just saw Ike walk by out there in the lobby. There were two men with him who looked like policemen." It had grown increasingly crowded out there in the lobby, but Alex was sure of what he had seen. The two men had somehow been as unmistakably cops as their Chicago counterparts, though this pair was dressed more sportily.

Looking down at Vera, Alex realized that she was now very much afraid of him. "Look," he tried, "*I'm* not the one . . . will you just sit here and wait for me a minute? I want to go and see what Ike is up to."

"Sure," she agreed, more readily than he had expected.

"I'll be right back." Alex hurried out of the coffee shop, into the thronged lobby. People were milling thickly before the elevators. When Alex glanced out through the front doors of the hotel, into the sunlit parking lot, he was struck by a new appearance, parked right in front of the doors: a vehicle the size of a fire truck, but painted gray and blue, with NASA insignia in bold letters on the side. On top, where a fire truck might have carried ladders, this one had something like folded metal rails. These were slowly erecting, as Alex watched.

Interesting, but he had no particular reason to think that it was connected with his problems. Reminding himself that he was OCTAGON's protected ally, Alex drifted closer to the front desk, looking for Ike and his double escort. If they were really looking for him, Alex didn't mean to run and hide.

At one end of the main registration desk, a man wearing a

NASA insignia blazer was arguing about something with another who looked as if he might be the hotel manager. Alex continued to drift closer.

". . . had it on the books for a month now," NASA was insisting, a trifle heatedly. "I'm sure that *someone* here ordered the demonstration."

"Talk to the convention." The manager was portly, with a large diamond ring. "I've nothing to do with what they may have ordered."

"I have talked to them, I tell you. They say they didn't, but . . ."

"There he is." This was Ike's voice, and it came from behind Alex. Low-pitched, yet somehow it carried through the general murmur of noise in the crowded room.

Alex turned. Ike, standing between the two sport-shirted detectives a few yards off, was pointing right at him. More yards to their rear, and unseen by them, Vera had come out of the coffee shop into the lobby and was standing with her back to the wall, watching Ike and Alex intently.

The two plainclothesmen stepped forward. "Alex Barrow?"

"Yeah. What's . . .?"

"Do you know this woman? Is she here?" A large hand thrust a small photograph under Alex's nose. It was undoubtedly of Vera.

"I . . ." This wasn't what Alex had been ready for. "Let me take a look—"

When Alex felt the light tremor run through the bones of the hotel, the first thought to enter his mind was: earthquake. The same idea seemed to strike everyone in the lobby; after one hushed moment there began a rush for the doors that quickly threatened to become a panic. Alex was being swept along in it before it dawned on him that this might well not be an earthquake at all. Outside the front glass doors, something that bore intense flame with it was spattering on the pavement. People out there in the open sunlight were screaming worse than those still inside the lobby.

One of the cops had shouted something at Alex, just as the

panic started; now both policemen were fully occupied in attempting to control the surging crowd. But their appeals for calm seemed to be having no effect.

A faint tremor came again. There was no way for Alex to get to the main doors, not with the dense knot of people struggling there in each other's way. Instead he turned and fought to get back into the coffee shop. There, near the tables at the far end, someone had picked up a chair and was battering at a large plate glass window, but far too tentatively to get the job done. Stupid, thought Alex; even if it were an earthquake, there's got to be another, simple way out, through the kitchen or whatever. But he was busy looking for Vera, and he couldn't see her anywhere.

Now someone else, from farther back, picked up another chair and threw it full force at the window. That did the job. With a uniformed waitress in the lead, like some stewardess guiding passengers from the crash, people began to pick their way through the wreckage to get outside. They climbed the windowsill in a considerate single file. There was Vera, taking her place in the queue. Alex went after her, trying to catch up.

Once outside he paused for a look at the NASA truck still sitting in front of the hotel. Two men were in the cab, and appeared to be fighting to do something with the controls, though the vehicle wasn't going anywhere. Its engine was running, though; it died now, then immediately started up again. The rail device atop the truck, looking like nothing Alex had ever seen before in nightmares or reality, was now pointing almost horizontally away from the building, out over the parking lot. It gave a sudden and almost silent hiccup, the whole truck bobbing lightly on its springs. There was a virtually simultaneous impacting crash from somewhere far out in the lot. Immediately the rail device began to swing back, swiveling at the same time for elevation, aiming once more like some futuristic antiaircraft gun up at the great flank of the hotel.

Smoke was billowing already from two rooms up there, one quite near the top, one much lower. Something flaming dripped. Again the truck's diesel engine died, this time perhaps for good. The NASA men in the cab were getting out, looking up in horror like everyone else who wasn't running.

Vera was standing just a few feet in front of Alex, gripping the bole of a palm tree. He moved up and put a hand on her shoulder, felt the rigidity of her shock.

"My room," Vera breathed, looking up at the hotel. On the sidewalk around them, people ran. Some were crying out in fear, perhaps in injury.

"Come on," Alex towed her among other people, moving out into the parking lot, toward where he'd left his car. Panicked people rushed by, going in opposite directions. A car backing out of a space, its tires squealing with the driver's panic, nearly ran them down. Some at least were desperate to get to the familiar environment of the highway.

"My car," said Vera, tugging against Alex's pulling hand. An acre away from where Alex had parked, another vehicle was burning fiercely. Not only burning; one whole side of it appeared to have been ripped open and stove in as if by a cannon shot. At least one of the other cars nearby had been holed by flying debris. Patches and spatters of flame were on the hoods and tops of other cars. So far, no one was doing anything at all about this fire.

"Come on." Alex pulled harder on Vera's arm. He got her into his own car, started up the engine, began to drive. He caught one glimpse of her face just as he pulled out of the parking lot, and it came to him where he had seen her face before, or one very like it: in some of those paintings made by French artists in times of war and revolution, showing embattled France personified.

FIFTEEN

Albie Pearson had slept last night on one of the sofas in the lounge just off the main laboratory, and he was up this morning a little ahead of the sun. There was a certain job that he wanted to accomplish early.

In the half-darkness before dawn Albie punched out orders for one of the household robots to bring him coffee and a sweet roll, while he got dressed in his railroad worker's outfit, which he had laid out ready for the occasion. The outfit was a good one, Albie thought, perfectly convincing. He had assembled it from various sources of old clothes some months ago, when he had first decided he ought to be making periodic close-range inspections of the line and siding that ran through the ravine just to the rear of the Gregory property. That was just about the date when things had really started getting hairy, the old man worried all the time. Choosing the garments for the outfit had taken Albie several sessions with binoculars, looking down into the ravine to get a good idea of what the real railroad workers wore when they appeared in the area, which wasn't all that often. Albie had made sure that he was dressed like one of them before he ever went near the tracks; if he was seen down there at any time, no one

185

would think anything of it. As in everything else relating to his job, careful preparation certainly paid off.

Albie had a naturally suspicious mind, which he thought was perhaps one reason why he'd never married. He knew he couldn't help being suspicious, and so he used the tendency as an asset in his work. He was a good electrical engineer, but he'd spent most of his working life in security at one industry and government installation after another. Robert Gregory paid more than most employers did. He gave Albie Pearson more chance than almost any other employer would have to use his engineering talent. And, perhaps best of all in Albie's estimation, the old man had the knack of letting his employees alone to do their jobs, once they'd demonstrated that they were capable. So Albie liked working for Old Man Gregory. It offered him real scope for all his talents, including his talent for suspicion; the old man had led a long and active life, and was sure now that he had powerful enemies of some kind. He ought to know, thought Albie.

Albie understood that he hadn't been let in completely on all that was going on. He didn't think he needed to be, in this case. Plainly there had been threats, direct or implied, and some kind of physical attack on the house and its inhabitants was considered much more than a remote possibility. Industrial rivalries of some kind, Albie thought, when he troubled to imagine reasons. He had run into similar things before, on other jobs; he wasn't particularly worried, he just considered it a professional challenge, for which he was being well paid, and which he intended to meet to the best of his ability. The old man had him running checks on the phone lines twice a day now, and every few days engaged Albie in a discussion as to how they could best beef up the perimeter, and strengthen the internal guard force without hiring more people. That last was out; the old man said he wouldn't trust anyone who would come to him now if he tried to hire more help. If Albie hadn't known the old man so well already, he might have suspected that his boss was getting paranoid.

After Albie had finished dressing in his railroad costume, and had consumed his modest breakfast, he checked his tool kit once more, and hung it on his belt. Then he went out of the house through one of the back doors. It was one of those glorious early Georgia mornings that Albie thought he probably appreciated all the more for having grown up in New York City. He had heard the mockingbird sing last night, just like in the old song, and understood a little better what that song was all about. Tomorrow, conditions permitting, he was going to take an afternoon off, and spend it with a certain woman . . . she was starting to hint at marriage, which Albie had more or less expected at this stage in their relationship. But she wasn't hinting so strongly yet that he felt compelled to stop seeing her . . . that was another matter in which he and his employer saw eye to eye.

On leaving the house, Albie walked through dew-fresh grass out past the tennis courts, which like the swimming pool were generally unused now, though marked with engineering hashmarks having to do with the project for helping the old man's daughter move around. Albie would have liked to work more on that; Caroline was a neat young girl in a terrible fix, who deserved all the help that she could get. But aids for the handicapped weren't really in Albie's field of specialization, and his own job kept him busy.

From the house to the tennis courts was only a few yards, and from the courts on back to the hedge-hidden fence at the rear property line was only a few more, not as far as it seemed it ought to be if you were looking over the whole grounds from somewhere out in front. From out in front, the place looked like someone's farm—or rather, Albie thought, like those estates he had only seen in pictures, where you might expect a mob of people on horses to come pouring along, following the hounds in a fox hunt.

Here along the back property line, the fence was completely hidden from the inside by hedges planted close along it. It was basically tall chain-link, with a couple of barbed strands running along the top, and of course with some of Albie's best alarm goodies built into it as unobtrusively as possible. He had also made provision for electrification, at three different levels of voltage. Of course that part of the system was seldom turned on, the facts of neighborhood children and other innocent or almost innocent wanderers being what they were. Albie sometimes thought wistfully of what he could have done here in the way of protection if he had been allowed to build some defense in depth. Two fences, for a starter, with a smoothed-earth belt between them, under which you would be able to plant all kinds of stuff. Selective electrification. And the robots weren't being fully exploited, not by a long shot, though in the last couple of weeks he'd been given the go-ahead to start bringing them up to potential. If you didn't have any human patrols to speak of, then you had to use the robots as long as they were available; dogs couldn't do the whole job.

But the old man had vetoed any scheme that was going to make his back fence look like the Berlin Wall. Besides the time and the expense involved in such construction, it was likely to draw more snoopers and more attention than it deterred; and Albie had had to admit that the old man had a point.

Now Albie slipped in between hedge and fence, and moved to his favorite observation post. This was a spot along the barrier from which he could look down with binoculars and see, some sixty or eighty feet below, a good part of the bottom of the ravine through which the railroad ran. If Albie mentally put himself in the place of someone planning a reconnaissance or an assault on Fortress Gregory, he found the ravine by far the most attractive avenue of approach. It would be a lot better than trying to get at the place through the public front, or by crossing the fenced and protected private properties on either side.

This morning his preliminary inspection with binoculars showed him that the two freight cars on the siding below looked just the same as they had when they first appeared there two days ago. And the other object that had been installed down there on the same day the cars appeared was also apparently unchanged—it looked to Albie like some kind of a microwave gizmo, sitting atop one of the poles whose endless series marched beside the tracks, carrying telegraph wires. Something about that gizmo bothered Albie. It was the chief reason why he had decided that a first-hand inspection was going to be necessary this morning.

Leaving his binoculars concealed in the hedge inside the fence, Albie let himself out through the small back gate. The gate looked almost invitingly easy to open from the outside; he was really proud of that gate. If he hadn't been allowed a double fence, at least the design of that gate and its protection had offered his talents and imagination scope.

Once outside, Albie locked up the simple lock again and pocketed the key. He was now standing on the rim of a steep slope, moderately heavily covered with trees and bushes, through which no well-defined path led down. To avoid creating even the suggestion of a path, each time he scouted the ravine he went down into it by a different route, and came back by yet a different way from that he had used going down.

Today, carefully descending the steep slope, Albie kept his eyes open for signs that anyone else had been using or traveling through this little wasteland. He'd never found much evidence of other people being here—some beer cans, a used rubber once—and had seen nothing to indicate that Gregory turf had been scouted by this means. The slopes of the ravine here must belong to the railroad, he thought, but they seemed to take no interest in them.

When Albie reached the edge of the cleared right-of-way at the bottom of the ravine, he paused briefly, still standing within the straggly woods, looking things over suspiciously before he came out into the open. The two wooden freight cars were on their spur of siding, silent and forgotten-looking. From the woods on the ravine's slope opposite, on the other side of the double track, a crow now came up cawing. But the bird wasn't putting a lot of energy into it; probably Albie was the first intruder to cause it any concern this morning.

Now Albie came out of the woods to climb the little mound of graveled railbed. He moved casually now, a workman with every right to be where he was, to be doing what he was doing. He sauntered up onto the tracks and then along them, looking things over as he went. If the trains were keeping their usual schedule, none would be passing through here for a while; that was the main reason he'd picked this early hour for his inspection. He'd never seen genuine workmen in the area this early in the morning, either.

The marching row of telegraph poles bore their wire burden tautly along beside the tracks. When Albie reached the foot of the pole he wanted, he paused, looking up at the main object of his investigation. He could get a better look from here than the binoculars had given him from atop the hill. What he saw was a dull green weatherproofed little metal cabinet with a telegraph wire led into it from the crossbar. Projecting on each side of the cabinet, like a pair of ears, were a pair of little grill-work metal dishes that must mean microwaves.

It didn't look to Albie like it belonged where it was. Of course he was no great expert on railroad communications equipment, and nowadays the gear in many fields was changing so fast that there was hardly any possibility of an outsider's being able to keep up. Still . . .

The little dishes, or ears, looked like they ought to be adjustable for position, and so able to pick up or relay microwave signals from a wide choice of directions. Except that there was nothing down here in the ravine to send to or receive from. The track curved out of sight within a few hundred yards in either direction. There were no signal towers, or any other communications devices visible. If a train was down here, of course, then the green box on the pole might provide a handy communication link—but a link with what? It would have to be with some other unit that was right in line-of-sight with it, or very close to line-of-sight. Just look at the damn thing. It couldn't be good for very much beyond that distance.

Albie looked, and debated with himself whether he ought also to climb the pole. He didn't know what more he'd be able to tell about the unit when he got to the top; he thought its character was pretty obvious from down here.

He put off a final decision on climbing, and walked on, meaning to take a closer look at the two freight cars. For any cars to be on this siding was a rarity. The spur of track was an old one, running close beside the main line and then just coming to a stop. It had been built decades in the past, for some purpose now obscure, and nowadays was very little used. The weeds were growing up tall between its ties.

Approaching the nearest of the two cars, Albie bent down to take a close look at the wheels and trucks. They told him nothing. Then he gazed at the side. The brightly painted name told him that the car belonged to a railroad far from Georgia, but that of course meant nothing—rolling stock from all roads was always being shuttled all over the country. The great sliding door on the side was completely closed, and looked like it was locked and sealed. After a moment Albie reached for the steel ladder-rungs built into the side of the car, and climbed up about halfway. This got him close enough to the sealed door to let him reach a weatherproof envelope attached nearby. There were some papers folded up inside the envelope, and after a moment Albie managed to work them free. They consisted of a couple of sheets of somebody's computer printout—just about everything must come in that form these days. The message, if you could call it that, was almost pure alphabet soup, sprinkled with numbers. Very complex and jargony, and maybe if Albie had been a real railroad worker he could have understood it. After pondering it for a minute, he decided it probably meant that the cargo on this particular car had come from several different points, and was all bound for Marietta, Georgia. If his guesses at the meanings of abbreviations were accurate, one of the points of origin could be the Rocky Flats Arsenal, which was out near Denver; and another could be Gary, Indiana.

It was possible, thought Albie as he dropped back to the ground, having restored the papers to their envelope, that old man Gregory knew what these freight cars were all about, and knew also the purpose of that device up on the pole. They could conceivably be part of some project that he was running. But if so, Albie thought that the old man would have told him, before leaving last night on that surprise business trip. It had been nearly midnight before Caroline told the family security chief that her father was going to be gone for a few days. If Albie had had a chance for a last-minute confer-ence with the old man, he would have mentioned this recon-naissance he planned to do this morning, the freight cars and the odd device. Somehow Albie didn't think now that the old man knew about them.

He walked over now beside the second freight car. Its wooden wall was uninformative, and he didn't bother climb-ing to take a look at the contents of the envelope beside its door.

His scouting trip was beginning to look like a waste of time. Albie had just turned to walk back for a last look at the microwave unit atop the pole, when there came a noise behind him. It sounded like something inside the car that he had just been climbing on. Albie spun sharply. It had been a single, clumping noise, like a heavy metal unit being set down sharply, or someone almost dropping a single box or crate.

Whatever it had been, it was not repeated. Now Albie began a slow walk completely around the cars, keeping his eyes steadily on them. On the far side, the side he hadn't looked at yet, their doors were closed and locked as he had expected. But, right near the lock of the first car, a hole about an inch in diameter had been bored—or burned, maybe, its inner surface was as black as it was smooth and round—right through the wooden side. Was it an old hole or a fresh one? It would be very hard to tell.

Still no repetition of the noise. Should he climb on the cars some more, and poke around? It was doubtful what he would be able to learn by doing so; he wasn't going to break into them, not on the basis of anything he had been able to find out so far. That noise could be explained readily enough by the fact that the sun was up now, high enough for its early heat to fall on the cars' sides and roofs. That could cause expansion, stretching of materials, with accompanying noises probable.

Enough, Albie thought. In his line of work it was important to know when you had done enough, when trying to learn something more was likely to cause more trouble for you than it was to bring results. In his judgment that point had now been reached.

He turned, about to walk around the cars again to the Gregory side of the tracks. And only when he turned did he see what had been lying in the weeds ten feet behind him, what had been shielded from his binocular inspection by the freight cars themselves. The dead tramp was lying on his back in the weeds, his feet in their holed shoes pointing at the sky. Those feet had been as still as rocks when Albie had first walked round to this side of the cars; he simply hadn't noticed them.

Albie took a step, looking down now at the gray-stubbled face, ageless in death and tired no longer. The dead man and his clothing were both of a dull dirt color that blended with dead weeds and railroad grime. There was quite a lot of dried brown blood around the head. Looking down at the dead tramp with the broken skull, Albie calculated that he might have been killed yesterday.

SIXTEEN

"Where are we going?" Vera asked at last. She had been curled up almost in fetal position in the right seat of the car almost since Alex had pulled out of the hotel parking lot, ten, fifteen, twenty, he didn't know how many minutes ago.

He had taken the easiest route out of the parking lot, the direction of least resistance with regard to traffic flow. They were now headed south, on what had turned into some kind of major highway. He said: "I don't suppose it matters a whole lot, where we go, for the time being anyway. As long as you're with me, I think you'll be safe." He paused, glancing at her worriedly. "Is there somewhere you want to go?"

"I can't go home. They wanted to arrest me, didn't they?"

"They didn't actually say that. But I wouldn't be surprised."

"What a mess. And I was almost starting to think that I might have been imagining it all."

"Arrest you with one hand and kill you with the other. Almost the way it happened to me. That thing was catapulting some kind of fire bombs right into the hotel. One of those windows burning was your room, I suppose? I wonder what the other was. Maybe just a bad shot."

"That was my room burning, all right. Way up near the corner of the roof. Alex, you kept telling me to check out, and I thought maybe you were the one . . ." It trailed off.

"I'm not the one. It's been happening to me too."

The black clouds of smoke, the panic, the sirens, had all been left far behind them now, swallowed up in the semitropical sprawl of buildings and people and roads and hazy smog, buried amid a million roaring vehicles.

"Where are we going?" Vera asked again. She had uncurled somewhat now; one foot was on the floor.

Alex snatched a look at her, then had to concentrate on the highway. "I can stop at a motel somewhere," he said. "We can pull ourselves together, and get some rest. I'll use my own name. It'll be all right."

Vera was silent for a while, gazing out the window. "Don't stop yet," she said at last.

"Vera, why don't you tell me your story? I mean exactly what made you think the game was strange, why you came up here to talk to Ike. It might give me a clue as to what we ought to be doing next."

"All right." But then there was a silent pause, going on so long that Alex thought she must have changed her mind. Then at last she spoke: "My boyfriend was killed, about a month ago. He was driving in my car, alone, and he was run off a cliff, up in the hills near Ventura."

"Run off?"

"Will was still alive when the police came and got him out of the wreck. He told them a story that they thought was crazy. A pickup truck that didn't have any driver had chased him. He tried to get away, but it caught up with him, and forced him right off the road and over a cliff. My car was a total wreck. Will died before they could get him to a hospital."

The theme of the story, machinery gone mad, was sickeningly familiar. "And why do you connect this to the game?" asked Alex. The ocean had come into view now, well off to the right. He drove on. The ocean seemed to have no connection with anything else in the universe.

"Because, the afternoon of the day that Will was killed, before I even knew that anything had happened to him, I had this phone call. The police told me later that I shouldn't think too much of it, that there are a million crank phone callers around. I know there are a million cranks in California, I've met a lot of them. But this was different."

"Who was the caller? What did he say?"

"It was OCTAGON." Another lengthy pause. "At least that's what it said it was."

Machines droned by on every side. Wind whined around the speeding car.

"It? What do you mean?"

"Alex. It sure as hell wasn't any twelve-year-old boy's voice. It sounded more like . . ."

"Like what?"

"Okay. Tell me I'm crazy. It sounded like one of those Speak and Spell things that the kids have now. Those computer toys that talk. It said: 'This is OCTAGON. MAIDEN, you are dead now. You must leave the game. You cannot win in the game if you are dead.' I'll never forget what it sounded like. So calm, like one of those recorded time and temperature voices. Then a couple of hours later, when I heard what had happened to Will . . ."

Vera curled up in her seat again. Alex drove for a little while in silence. "I can imagine," he said at last, "Hank being able to rig up something that would talk on the phone in a mechanical voice. He could alter circuits on a Speak and Spell, something like that. But I can't imagine him . . . *doing* what's been done."

"Hank?"

"The kid, the one who's playing OCTAGON. Or supposed to be playing it. It just wouldn't be possible for him to know *how* to arrange all these physical attacks, even if he were some kind of crazy evil genius, which he's not. He's just a kid."

"All right. Nobody can believe my story."

"Oh, I believe it. I've seen enough of OCTAGON myself, remember. We've both seen what happened, just back there, just now . . . I'm not saying you're crazy. Do you want me to stop somewhere?''

"No, not yet. I want you to keep on driving."

He drove. He felt worried about Vera, that she just sat there curled up, staring silently out the window. Largely to try to keep her talking, he asked: "How did you get into the game in the first place?"

"Oh.'' She gave a tiny shrug, which Alex took gratefully as a sign that she wasn't going totally into shock. "I read an ad for it in a science fiction magazine. And I was getting theoretically interested in games—I guess I had this idea that reality could be made—well, not really smaller, but more manageable somehow, if you approached it through a game. I'm always looking for some new way of getting at reality.''

Alex thought about it. "You mean sort of like making a model?"

"Yes, sort of like that. How did you get into it? The game?''

He found he really couldn't remember for a moment. "I believe I had in mind some scheme for making money."

Vera had nothing to say to that.

Some time ago, signs had indicated that they were leaving Los Angeles proper. But the people, cars, and buildings along the coast had so far shown little sign of thinning out.

"I've read a lot of science fiction," was Vera's next remark.

"Oh?" Alex had read a little.

Vera said: "I'm kind of a fan on the Berserkers. You know, it's a series of stories."

"I guess I did hear something about them." They had been at the company office in Albuquerque, probably.

"So the name of the company kind of interested me. Berserkers Incorporated, you know. Then when I was in college, at USC, the author came around speaking once. But I never got my degree. It all got to seeming too artificial somehow."

"I know what you mean about college. I think I do,

anyway. I never went, myself.''

"But then," Vera continued, "I got to feeling that things outside of school, in the so-called real world, weren't very real either. Maybe reality is what people make it."

"If you step out of an airplane, you're going to fall."

"Yes," said Vera, not sounding totally convinced. She went on: "Even without a degree, I managed to get a pretty good job. In a couple of years I could work up to being a systems analyst. That's sort of like a step above a computer programmer."

"I know. Look, Vera, there are a whole bunch of motels coming up along here. We could just stop at one. Don't get me wrong, I just think it would be good if we could relax in private for a little while. I'm getting tired if you're not."

"I'm going back and finish getting my degree someday, I've decided. I won't know much more then than I do now, about computers or anything else. But that piece of paper will get me a lot more money for doing the same job I'm doing now. Crazy, isn't it? But that's reality."

"Sure." Signs recently passed had said LAGUNA BEACH. They were driving on a two-lane highway now, right along the ocean. Real beaches were in evidence, and here was another promising motel. Alex pulled over.

"These places cost a bunch," was Vera's only objection.

"Don't worry about it." It was a great relief to be able to stop driving; not that they had come any enormous distance from Los Angeles, but Alex's bones still bore the record of his marathon drives of just a few days past. Every time he closed his eyelids he could see pavement rushing by. He had to do something besides steer a series of borrowed automobiles around the nation, from one of OCTAGON's murderous onslaughts to the next.

Within a few minutes Alex had them checked into the best suite available, a two-room job with a kitchenette in an alcove at one side of the parlor. He signed the register with his own name, adding Mr. and Mrs. It was the first time he'd ever registered in a motel as married, and it felt strange.

The windows of the suite's parlor and bedroom both looked right out onto the ocean, beyond no more than a narrow strip of beach. The horizon was hidden behind fog banks, the sea was almost calm. There were only a few people in sight on the beach in either direction, and there was no one in the water, which Alex supposed was too cold.

Vera, standing beside Alex in the parlor, ran her palms down over her shirt and jeans. She said: "I didn't have the chance to get anything out of my room back there. I suppose it was all burned up anyway. My God, those two cops were really looking for me to arrest me, weren't they? I wonder what for?"

"OCTAGON may have created some crime, and then made it look like you were the one who did it. He can do things like that. Or he may just have put you on the wanted list somehow. There's no telling."

"Maybe now they think I was in my room when that bomb or whatever it was hit it. Maybe they're searching for my body now, back up there in LA."

"Could be. Listen, Vera, is there anyone who's going to have a heart attack when they hear about that? I mean, do you have parents, or . . ."

She shook her brown hair, and ran her fingers through it as if freeing it from some entanglement. "I'm an orphan. My parents were pretty old when they had me. No, there isn't anyone, really."

"We could go out now, and shop for some clothes and stuff for you. I've got money. For me, too, I left my bag back there in my room. When we drove up it looked like there were some shops around here, in walking distance. Want to do that?"

"I don't know. Yes, I think I'd like to. I don't know when I can pay you back, but I have to get a few things somehow."

"Don't worry about paying me back. That's no immediate problem."

Vera was still looking out the window at the sea. "I could use a swim suit of some kind. When it's dark I want to go out for a swim."

''It's going to be cold then, isn't it? You can go out safely in the daylight, as long as you're with me.''

Vera shook her head; that wasn't exactly what she had meant.

SEVENTEEN

Caroline was in her office, when there came a tap at the open door and she looked out to see Albie Pearson standing there garbed in rough work clothes. It was still quite early in the morning, and Caroline was in her newest and most favorite wheelchair, the one that could even feed her oatmeal—or, as she preferred to think of it, enabled her to feed herself.

With a touch of her chin to the control, she turned the chair a notch toward the door. "Hi, Albie. What's up?"

He came in as if reluctantly, tossed a cloth cap on the end of a workbench, and then after a moment's hesitation hoisted up one haunch to sit beside it. "Your Dad's not back yet, is he?"

"No. I don't know when he will be."

"Then I guess there's something I better talk to you about, Miss."

"Call me Caroline, please—I thought I had you convinced on that point."

Albie sighed. "I wouldn't think of calling your father Bob."

"That's different."

"On peaceful social occasions, okay. But not this morning."

"Oh. This is really business." Caroline glanced at the lighted checkerboard panel on the wall; the thin metal arm on the side of her chair lowered the spoon it held back into the bowl of cereal on the tray before her. She chinned her chair-control again, swiveling the vehicle a little more toward Albie.

To Albie, she sounded as if she were eager to have some real problem to deal with, which he guessed was a good sign. He went over and shut the door to the office, then came back and perched on the bench again. "I guess I've got to lay this one on you, since your Dad's not here." He paused, puffing his breath as if getting ready for some physical exertion. "I was out scouting just now, down by the railroad track. I do that periodically."

"I was wondering what you were dressed up for. So—what did your scouting trip reveal?"

"A dead man's lying down there." Albie paused again. He was relieved to see that the girl didn't go all to pieces at the news. Yet at the same time it surprised and bothered him a little that she could take the news as calmly as she did. Maybe she knew something that he didn't.

He related a few more details of the expedition. "The point is," he concluded, "that I can't very well report this dead man to the police. They'll want to know what the hell I was doing down there in the first place, and I won't have what they'll consider a good answer."

"I see your point." Even if the dead man had been no big shock to Caroline, Albie could see that it was slowly getting to her now; she was starting to go a little pale. It looked like she was going to hang in there, though. "Well, then," she added, "I guess we just do nothing about reporting it."

"Fine with me," agreed Albie. "We may have to do something on our own, though. Because I tell you, it bothers me a little, just how that man down there died."

"What do you mean?"

"I mean I have my doubts that he just fell off a freight car or anything like that, and cracked his head the way that it was cracked. Possibly it was just some dumb fight, that drifters tend to get into. Someone beat him up and robbed his wine bottle—I can't be sure. But as I told you, there's those two freight cars down there, and that box up on the pole. I'm suspicious.''

Caroline, still pale but self-possessed, heard him out thoughtfully, making Albie feel that he had done the right thing in bringing the situation to her.

''Don't say anything to anyone else about this yet,'' she decided when he had finished his case. ''Not even Georgina. Whatever's going on down there . . . what do you really think it is?''

''I don't know. I just get paid to be suspicious.''

''Yes.'' Caroline studied her cereal for a moment. ''Can you build up the defenses a little, maybe, just in case we should get some intruders from that direction?''

''Yeah, there's several things I can do. Load up the robots for serious trouble . . . want me to do that?'' Robert Gregory had always wanted him to hold back.

Caroline looked at him thoughtfully. ''Yes, I guess . . . yes, do it.'' She had become suddenly decisive.

''Okay. I wish we had more Security *people* . . . there's really just me, and Sam.'' Sam was the professional dog handler, who on most days spent several hours at the estate.

''I don't think Sam really counts. You're the only real guardian we have here, Albie—I'm not going to call you Mr. Pearson. And I want you to know that we appreciate it.''

''Sure. Thanks.'' Albie felt unexpectedly embarrassed.

In Chicago it was a little later in the morning, and Father Fred Riemann was looking over the morning mail at his desk, a second cup of coffee at hand. He saved for last what looked like it would be actually the most interesting item—his latest game turn, just in from Berserkers Incorporated.

When its turn came, he slit the envelope open and dumped the contents out. Ignoring for the moment the three-by-five diplomatic messages, and the other routine inserts that as usual had been included, he unfolded the printout itself and scanned it avidly. It looked like things were going well. One of his opponents hadn't moved at all, had evidently missed a turn, or maybe dropped out of the game completely.

At the bottom of the printout, Father Fred's eye fell on something that surprised him:

ARCHANGEL URGENT YOU ATTEND GAMECON LOS ANGELES GUAMS HOTEL APRIL 28-30. STAR-WEB X-430 CONCLUSION IMMINENT.

And there was a signature, or what looked like it ought to be a signature, deeply indented two lines below the message. Just one word: OCTAGON.

Must be some kind of advertising, thought the priest; but if so, they shouldn't put it right into the game turn like this. Next time he wrote to Berserkers Incorporated about something, he would put in a note letting them know that he objected.

It could hardly be anything but an ad for the convention . . . but signed by one of the players? OCTAGON, he knew, was only twelve years old, hardly of an age to be organizing or promoting conventions.

OCTAGON was the player that AGRAVAN had been asking about when he came here. Some wild, made-up story; for a few moments Father Fred had thought the young man might really be unbalanced; but it had all been a game ploy, of course, an effort to find out whether OCTAGON and ARCHANGEL were really foes or, after all, allies. And Father Fred had responded as a player, maintaining the deception. Some players, like AGRAVAN evidently, would go to almost any lengths to find things out . . .

Anyway, the ad in the printout referred to the weekend just past. And, anyway again, Father Fred wouldn't have been able to get away, or to afford a trip to Los Angeles just to attend a game convention, even if he had had the time.

Would have been fun, though, he thought now wistfully.

At night the Arizona highway looked no emptier than any of a thousand other highways that crossed more thickly inhabited portions of the land. At night you couldn't see the emptiness surrounding. Ike Jacobi, driving home alone from California, saw only the small portion of the emptiness that his headlights held up unrolling before his sleepless eyes. He was unshaven, too, and he stank, because he had spent so many hours wrangling with the police before they would simply let him start for home. Everyone having anything to do with the convention had been questioned intensely—except Alex Barrow, who the cops evidently couldn't find.

Ike as he drove kept seeing Alex Barrow's knowing smile, hearing what he'd said: *OCTAGON and I are allies now. You understand how that works, don't you?*

Ike sure as hell had *thought* he understood it, fairly well at least. After all, he'd invented the damn game. But now it seemed that he didn't understand everything. Too many weird things were going on. Not just *in* the game. It was as if the game impinged now on real life. Eddie in the hospital . . . players dying . . . Iris murdered . . . what the hell next?

When he got back to Albuquerque, the first thing Ike meant to do was to get himself into X-430, as a standby player. There were several positions open, and maybe that would help him get some kind of clue as to what was going on.

It was for damn sure something fishy.

Alex and Vera had gone out shopping in the afternoon, and to Alex's relief they had been able to get everything they needed without getting back into the car again. The highway going through town here became a winding street, heavy with traffic. It was lined with shops and stores of many kinds, all of them quite expensive—Alex noticed this last in a kind of detached way, it hadn't taken him long to get used to having plenty of spending money.

They had purchased some food and drink to stock the kitchenette's refrigerator, and some toothbrushes and some assorted clothing. This restocking operation was getting to be something of a routine for Alex by now. He'd left one set of personal belongings behind in Albuquerque, another in Atlanta, and now a third, virtually unused, in the hotel up in Los Angeles. He was going to have to start wearing a backpack.

Back in the hotel, shopping trip completed, Alex and Vera ate and drank a little. Then they turned on the television, and got a newscast report, including some pictures, on what the announcer called the 'so-called NASA bombing' in the Los Angeles hotel. The police were said to be still seeking witnesses, but no names of wanted folk were given. The NASA truck was described as having been loaded with the latest in automated equipment, intended for demonstration purposes. This gear included the latest model railgun massdriver, designed to be used in space for shifting small loads from higher orbits to lower, or vice versa—it all sounded pretty vague to Alex. It wasn't clear to him how a railgun was supposed to have been demonstrated in a hotel parking lot without at least a moderate amount of destruction.

"Our people," said the NASA representative when he was put on camera, "went out there to the hotel in good faith. They took along the equipment that they thought they were supposed to take. Radio control gear, the remote operation capabilities, and so on. There's going to have to be a very thorough investigation . . ."

Alex got up and turned the television off. It was getting dark, but they hadn't turned on any lights yet, and he didn't particularly want any; it would be good just to sit with Vera and watch the ocean darken outside their windows.

He stood in front of the window for a moment now. It was very hard to tell whether or not there was still anyone on the beach; he hadn't seen anyone walk past out there for some minutes. The waves came in ceaselessly, and there was something healing about their sound.

Vera was still sitting behind him on the sofa. "You were going to tell me," she said now, "who really killed that girl in Albuquerque."

He turned. "I thought I told you about that."

"No. Remember, we were sitting in the coffee shop, and I was getting deathly scared of you." She spoke as if it had happened last year, not just a few hours ago. "Then you saw the policemen in the lobby, and you ran out—"

"Oh, yeah." He walked nervously over to the door that led out of the suite, and checked to make sure that it was chained.

"You're getting jittery about something."

"I know. I think it's being here in a hotel room with you. I mean with a woman again . . . I don't mean it that way. It's just that a few days ago I was alone with Iris in that room." He related the account tersely. "And you thought your story was crazy," he concluded.

"Yours is crazier," she admitted, getting up and stretching. It was her turn to go to the window and gaze out for a while at the sea. Then she headed for the door to the bedroom. "I'm going to put my swim suit on."

"You want to go out on the beach now? It's going to be cold."

"You keep saying that. I'm going anyway; you can come along if you like." It sounded like she hoped he would. She went into the other room and shut the door, then opened it again briefly to toss Alex's own newly purchased swim suit in his direction.

"I'll be damned," he muttered to himself. He juggled the swim trunks in his hand for a moment, then tossed them onto a chair and began to strip..

A few minutes later, suited and barefoot for the beach, each carrying a large white hotel towel, they left their suite and went down a flight of wooden stairs. A great boulder stuck up out of the sand just a few feet below, and the stair angled around the outcropping. Alex was carrying the room key in his hand—for some reason that he couldn't remember now, he'd picked out skintight racing trunks, and there was no pocket in them to carry anything. Vera, walking half a step ahead of him, had her towel round her shoulders. She was wearing a fairly conservative one-piece suit.

There were no lights on the stair, or on the beach. Once on the sand, they were effectively alone in the dark. Eighty or a hundred yards to the north, at the foot of the next hotel, a

small fire burned on the beach, illuminating nearby human
shapes wrapped flatly in blankets on the sand. A cool wind
blew in from the ocean and the mild surf churned unendingly.
This was crazy, Alex told himself. He wasn't going to go in
the water at this temperature. Maybe if they just gathered
some wood or something here and built a fire and sat by
it . . .

Vera dropped her towel on the sand, just a little above the
highest of the gentle incoming waves. Then she walked on
out, getting her feet wet. Maybe she was a certified member
of the Polar Bears' Club, but Alex wasn't. No way. He could
enjoy swimming in water colder than most people liked it,
but not . . .

Vera, not looking back at him, moved out farther. Alex
dropped his towel beside hers on the sand and followed. The
idea had suddenly crossed his mind that maybe she intended
drowning. Though he had no real reason to think that . . .
the water, at first touch, was not really as cold as he had
expected.

He stood beside her, looking at her face. Her outward
gaze. Not drowning, probably, but there had to be something
more on her mind than just a swim.

After pausing there for a moment in ankle-deep foam,
Vera moved on out. Alex, still carrying the room key in his
hand, stayed with her. The next incoming wave took them
round the knees. After a moment's thought he just stuffed the
key down into the front of his skin-tight trunks; if he survived
this swim, maybe tomorrow he'd buy a pair that had a
pocket.

He thought Vera wanted him to come along, but she
wasn't going to stop if he didn't. She waded out. The bottom
sloped slowly, very slowly, deeper; the waves came in a little
higher now, crashing cold on thighs and belly. Vera, a step
ahead, looked back once at him—this far from the lights of
the motel he couldn't see what expression was on her face—
and then plunged forward as if to swim, regaining her feet in
waist-deep water a moment later.

Alex, staggering in chill waves, thought what the hell, and plunged in too, enough to wet himself completely. He tasted salt, and thought of ice cubes in a drink. He got his legs under him again with difficulty, a receding wave tugging sand from beneath his feet as he tried to brace them.

They were still almost waist deep when the trough between waves was at its shallowest.

"This is something that I have to do," Alex thought Vera said quietly, amid the soothing roar of more mild surf incoming. Her hands were raised behind her back, working near her shoulder blades. He realized that she must be doing something with her suit. Starting to strip it off.

"What—" Alex took a step toward her, his hand outstretched, and lost his footing with the next wave, which filled his mouth with salt. For a moment the idea came back that Vera was somehow getting ready to commit suicide.

"No, don't touch me now," she was saying calmly, when Alex got his ears once more up into the air. With quick expertise she had already got the suit completely off, and was holding it bunched in one hand. Her soaked hair clinging round her neck and shoulders, she stood completely naked. He saw full breasts, wide nipples, dark hair knotted at her armpits as well as farther down, exposed now in a trough of waves as were her strong legs braced apart against the ocean's swift withdrawal. Some detached part of his mind noted that he could see no demarcation of her tan; she must expose her entire skin by day as well.

The crumpled suit in her hand somehow spoiled things, interfered with whatever was going on. Whatever was going on, it was no striptease. If anything it was the precise opposite of that.

Feeling dream-bound, Alex moved a step closer, retaining his feet this time, putting out a hand again. She understood that his purpose in reaching out was different this time, and she handed over the crumpled suit for him to hold.

" . . . nothing artificial in touch with me at all . . ." Vera's voice was almost lost in the smash of the next wave.

Alex could feel his own body shivering violently, he could tell that the water was cold, but somehow it didn't matter; there was no subjective discomfort.

". . . the ocean . . . bigness . . . times the stars too . . ."

Alex held Vera's suit crumpled tightly in his hand while she plunged again and floated, and came up to stand again, this time with her back to him, looking out at the invisible sea. Obeying a sudden impulse, he stripped his own trunks off, remembering to get out the key. Key and two suits clenched in his fists, he plunged under water again himself.

A universe of cold water, sand, and salt. And self. But soon there was a nagging need of air, and when he came up there was the light from the rooms of the hotel, and from all the other buildings up and down the beach. Artificiality could not be escaped. He hadn't thrown away the suits, and certainly not the key. There were, if he thought about it, the fillings in his teeth. More worthy of serious thought, perhaps, were the beachers with their fire not a hundred yards away. Wrapped in their blankets, they were probably remarking on those two naked kooks out there in the surf—or maybe the performance was unremarkable, this being California.

He came up beside Vera. They stood side by side, letting sand and water and air ebb and flow as they would on naked skin. It was not sensual, it went deeper than that . . . but anyway it was getting too damn cold.

Vera, her fingers as cold as those of any sea-bottom monster, had him by the arm. "Let's go in."

Without taking her suit back she started for the beach, which had the air of being utterly deserted. Even the firebuilders, wrapped and blind, looked too distant to be relevant. The lighted windows ahead, and those off to the right and left, were bright but blind. No one on land appeared to have any power to interfere with two people who walked up naked out of the sea, still charged with the waves. Alex had the feeling that if he had been able to throw away the suits and key, greater powers still might have been mobilized.

Rejoining the land-world, each wrapped now in a towel, they hurried to the stairs and up. They moved faster with each step, and shivered more.

Alex unlocked their door. "Warm shower is the thing," he said, and, once inside, started directly for the bathroom to turn one on.

Vera, who had taken the two suits from him to hold while he unlocked the door, had tossed the suits on the floor and was turning on the electric heater in the wall. "Later," she said.

The one word stopped Alex. He turned to see that she had tossed the wet towel aside and was waiting for him, stretched openly on the bed.

Later, towards morning, with the hot shower and periods of sleep and much else behind them, Vera began to talk to Alex slowly about her murdered lover.

"Will was a surfer. There was always a rubber wetsuit lying around the place somewhere, stinking. And he spent half the time in the bathroom, bleaching his hair blond."

"Sounds like you don't like surfers." Alex could hear how muffled his own voice sounded, with his face half buried in a pillow. But at the moment it was too much trouble to turn his head to speak clearly. He could rest. The thing in the wheelchair was not coming for him tonight. He realized now that it had been outside his door every night since that night in Albuquerque, whether he thought consciously that he was a friend of OCTAGON or not. He had brought Vera here to give her his protection, and had wound up being protected by her as well.

He wondered if she could know what worthy protection she was giving. Under the covers he stretched forth a hand until it met her body. He wasn't sure what part he was touching; at the moment it didn't matter.

"I think I've figured out now what it was that I liked about Will," she said now, still sounding comparatively wakeful. "Just that he was—so completely what he was. But I don't want to live with someone like him again. What I like is not the surfing.'' She paused. ''It's the ocean.''

''I could see that tonight.''

''I hoped you'd understand. I didn't know how I could explain it to you ahead of time, but I have to do that every once in a while.''

He gave a little squeeze, felt bone under muscular flesh. Somewhere around her hip.

''Alex, didn't you say that LUCIFER is your uncle?''

''Yeah.'' Earlier they had been talking a little about the Game, mixed in with other subjects.

''How did the two of you happen to get into the same game?''

''I don't know.'' That question woke him up; it should have wakened him, he thought, a long time ago. He sat up in bed now, leaning his elbows on his knees.

''LUCIFER is OCTAGON's chief enemy,'' she went on. ''Haven't there been any attempts to kill him?''

''I'm not sure. He's worried, there could have been. But he's not exactly your routine victim.'' He told Vera a little of what he had seen of the Atlanta house and its defenses.

''That plane crash,'' he finished, struck by a sudden thought, staring at the darkness of the curtained window. ''I wonder . . .''

''But why is he in the same game with you? Does he . . . know Ike Jacobi, or what?''

''That's not the funny part,'' Alex explained. ''I got in the same game deliberately, as a standby player. The funny part is that Uncle Bob and his old friend Brahmaguptra were in the same game from the start, and neither of them knew it.''

''You say your Uncle Bob got you into it.''

Alex stared at his companion. ''Look, Vera, my uncle is my mother's brother. He's family. I trust him.''

''He's not *my* mother's brother. When you say 'his old friend Brahmaguptra' do you mean OCTAGON?''

''I mean OCTAGON's grandfather, who was killed in a plane crash . . . but the *plane,* you see, belonged to Uncle Bob. That airplane was registered to LUCIFER.'' Alex, still staring, followed a sudden, wild train of thought.

But Vera was going her own way. "And another thing, Alex. Was that attack on you really an attack?"

That brought him back. "Of course it was. What do you mean?"

"I mean—look, you said that thing was choking you, and that you lost consciousness. But here you are, still alive. Maybe it was never meant to kill you at all."

"We thought that out. It could have been an attempt to frame me for Iris's killing."

"We?"

"Uncle Bob and I. And . . ."

The darkened bedroom was silent for a while.

"Alex, you know what I think? We've got to do one of two things."

"Go ahead."

"One, we could go to the police, the FBI, somebody like that. Tell them the whole story, all we know. Dump it in their laps."

"I've talked to the police. They just pat me on the head and let me go. Except if I tried to tell them the whole story, they'd probably lock me up for a loony. Or else OCTAGON would turn on me again, and I'd find myself standing trial for murder after all. And what would you do, come with me? Not as Mrs. Barrow, not without proof you were. And not in the same cell, anyway. So you'd be standing out as a target again. What's Option Number Two?"

"Two is we can go to New Mexico. This whole thing seems to be centered there. There, and around your uncle. We've got to go there and confront it."

"I know." But it had taken him a long time to get the two words out.

EIGHTEEN

They drove east on Interstate Eight, out of San Diego. With two of them to share the driving, Alex calculated that they could reach northern New Mexico in about fifteen hours. Flying would have been faster, of course, but the Albuquerque police might well still be looking for him. It was early morning, before dawn, when they left San Diego, the desert sun soon coming into Alex's eyes as he drove. He stopped to buy himself some sunglasses before they'd driven very far.

Vera wasn't talking much, so far today; not mad or anything as far as Alex could tell, but thoughtful, and maybe still partly asleep. They had spent last night in a San Diego motel, in bed together in almost chaste exhaustion. Things were catching up with both of them.

On going to bed, he'd made a little joke: "No beach available tonight. But I suppose we could sneak out to the swimming pool around midnight."

They had exchanged smiles, a sharing.

He stroked her, and asked curiously: "Why don't you shave under your arms?"

"Does it bother you that I don't?"

"No."

"I have hair growing there, why should I shave it? If I were a man, I'd grow a beard."

"You wouldn't if it looked as funny as my beard does when I let it go. Anyway, it wouldn't make much sense to shave under your arms if you *didn't* have hair growing there."

There was not much small talk this morning, though. But Alex thought he could feel that the sharing was still intact.

"I wonder where Ike is now," he wondered aloud, when they were switching drivers about midmorning, approaching Gila Bend. "I wonder if he went home to Albuquerque?"

"I don't know. Where else would he go?"

"Are you having second thoughts about this?" Alex asked when they were on the road again, this time with Vera behind the wheel.

"Not really." She drove for a little while in silence. "But I am a little scared."

"Oh."

Only one bedroom of the house on Twentieth Street in Los Alamos was showing a light in the gathering dusk when Alex came round the corner and drove past; Hank's room, he thought, uncertainly trying to remember the interior layout of the Brahmaguptra residence. There was a car, that Alex could vaguely recall from his previous visit, parked in the driveway. He made a U-turn and pulled up at the informal edge of the small-town yard, just off the street. He turned the key, and the engine died with that special finality that comes at the end of a long trip.

"Want to wait in the car, or come with me to the door?" They had discussed this on the road, but hadn't been able to decide which was likely to be better.

"I'll come along," said Vera. "I've got to get out and stretch, no matter what."

Alex, standing on the small back porch, knocked twice before Jen came to open the door. She was dressed in old shirt and jeans, much as she had been on that other day that now seemed to be so long ago.

Jen said nothing at first. But she obviously recognized Alex at once; doubtless she had known him even before she opened the door, despite the darkness.

"Hello, Jen." He stood there waiting, with Vera silent at his side.

Jen still said nothing. With a movement of her arm inside the door, she turned the porch light on. Then she scanned the quiet street of houses, in a way that suggested she might be expecting someone else at any moment. There were a couple of parked pick-up trucks, as usual for any New Mexico street scene, and a car or two. There were lights in nearby houses. None of this, apparently, was what Jen was looking for.

Suspiciously she turned her gaze on Alex. "Did Bob Gregory send you this time?"

"No, this time I'm here on my own. Jen, this is Vera Cayley. She's in the game, too."

"The game?"

"I think you have to know which game I mean."

Maybe Jen really didn't. She was obviously alert, ready at the sight of Alex for some kind of serious action. Ready for trouble, but the mention of a game seemed only to puzzle her.

Alex went on: "It's been dangerous for Vera, too. I was sorry to hear what happened to old Henry."

"We both were," put in Vera. She was standing with her arms folded in the fast-chilling mountain night.

Jen was still standing in her doorway, and had made no gesture to welcome them in. She looked at them both, apparently trying to make up her mind.

Alex pressed on: "Look, Jen, I don't know what you think about me now. Whether or not you talked to the police a few days ago, or what they may have told you about me then. But I'm in the clear with them now." He said it confidently, hoping it was so. "I haven't hurt anyone and neither has Vera. But we're desperate."

"About what?"

"For God's sake, Jen. About trying to keep people alive. For all I know, you and Hank may be in danger now. You're not actually in the game, but then neither was old Henry. Is Eddie MacLaurin here now by any chance?"

The mention of danger didn't seem to surprise Jen in the least. She said: "Eddie's still in the hospital."

Vera and Alex spoke together, asking questions.

"A car hit him. A van, rather."

Vera asked: "Did it have a driver?"

Jen, at last surprised, stared at her; while Alex, a theory neatly swept out from under him, stared at Jen.

A local police car, cruising slowly, came up the street, passing just a few yards from the three people who stood chatting on the porch. Jen looked toward the car as it passed, and smiled and waved. "They keep an eye on us here now," she said with a certain satisfaction. Then once more she read the faces of her visitors—and hesitated, and did not ask them in.

At least, thought Alex, she hadn't yet ordered them to leave. He said: "Look, if you don't trust us in the house, is there someplace else that we can go and talk? A public place if you like. Maybe a coffee shop or something. Tell us where you'll meet us, and we'll get in our car and drive off, and you can follow in yours. Or vice versa, or whatever. All we want to do is exchange some information. If you want to call the cops over here now, I'll stand here and wait for them. It may land Vera in trouble, though; they probably have her name on the police teletype, in some screwed-up report saying she's wanted somewhere for some fantastic crime. That's what happens when you're an enemy of OCTAGON.'"

Hank was now standing silently in the dark kitchen, a few feet behind his mother. Alex, looking past Jen at him, wasn't sure how long the boy had been standing there.

"Who is it, Hank?" Alex asked.

The boy shifted his weight; he didn't answer.

"Who is OCTAGON?"

Jen looked at both of her visitors one more time. "All right, come in," she said with a sigh, and stood aside.

"Thank you," said Vera fervently.

When they had all filed into the kitchen and the door was closed, and an inside light had been turned on, Alex looked at Hank again and repeated his question. "Who is OCTAGON, Hank? Besides you, I mean. Who gives you help?"

And Alex was sure that he could see guilt pass through the dark young face; but he was also sure that it was not the guilt of murder.

"I . . . I . . ." Hank stammered. He looked at his mother, seeking help.

"What do they mean, Hank?" Jen's tone was loving and supportive, but she plainly expected an answer. "Do you know what they're talking about?"

At last Hank said: "Eddie helps me sometimes."

Alex asked, gently: "What does he do, exactly? Can you show us?"

Hank turned, without saying anything, and walked from the kitchen. The others followed him, through the hallway narrowed by bookshelves and chalkboards, to his own room where a light still burned. It appeared that he had been working on the game when they arrived. OCTAGON's domain, drawn in crude colored lines, glowed on the screen of the worktable's adapted television set.

Alex and Vera stood side by side at the workbench, looking down at the system of homemade wiring and comparatively cheap equipment; Jen waited behind them, watching silently.

In a few moments Vera turned to Hank. "How do you send in your moves?" she asked.

"Through the mail." Hank's tone, suddenly sullen, said that everyone sent in moves that way, and everyone ought to know how it was done.

"I'm MAIDEN, Hank. Did you know that?"

"No." The boy looked at her curiously; another game-enemy met in the flesh and proven human. "I wasn't going to attack you. But . . ."

"But what?"

Hank shrugged, awkwardly, evasively.

After a pause, Alex tried another line. "Your grandfather was never in the game himself, was he?"

"No."

"My uncle is—I told you that last time I was here, didn't I? And he and your grandfather were friends—you know?"

"Yeah."

"How did it happen that you and my uncle were in the same game, Hank?"

Hank was staring hopelessly at the crude `lines on the screen. "Ask Eddie, when you see him. Maybe he knows." The guilt, again.

"I will ask him, when I get the chance—you were going to show me what Eddie does, when he helps you with the game."

"He . . . makes things." Hank's awkward gesture might have meant anything on the bench. He swallowed, choking a little on the difficulty of specifics. "He helps me get things hooked up. Like the screen, and the RF modulator."

"Does he ever suggest what moves you should make in the game? Who should be an ally or an enemy?"

"No!" Hank seemed outraged by the question. "I make all those kind of decisions myself. Eddie's not playing in the game, *I* am. The only help in making decisions I get is from machines, not people. A lot of guys use their home computers to help them figure out their moves."

Alex, in his mind's eye, saw Uncle Bob's home laboratory. But no; he couldn't think that. Uncle Bob was family.

"It was my own idea to make *you* an ally." Hank's voice had reproach in it.

Alex leaned on the bench. His legs were tired, like every other part of his body. Whenever he closed his eyes he saw unrolling highway. "When did you do that, Hank, exactly?"

The answer was delayed. "A few days ago."

"But when? What time of day? No, it doesn't matter, you said you mail in your moves. You can phone in a move . . . but not in the middle of the night. There's no one there . . . ."

Vera was looking at him strangely. "What are you getting at, Alex?"

"I was just wondering what time they feed the moves into the computer at Berserkers Incorporated . . . I doubt they work any midnight shifts there."

He thought of one more thing to try, and dug the printout from the Chicago police department out of his pocket and passed it over to Hank. Jen was standing protectively behind her son now, and read the printout over his shoulder.

Alex asked: "Any idea how I happened to be sent that message?"

"Who is AGRAVAN?" asked Jen, puzzled, reading the thing over again.

Alex, on the verge of giving up, didn't bother trying to answer.

"He was a knight," said Hank, his voice still wounded. "You know, in King Arthur. He betrayed Lancelot, and the Queen."

Alex opened his eyes, letting an imaged highway fall away. Right there on the wall, where he suddenly remembered it, was the framed castle. He looked at the armored figures and the brave banners for a moment, then turned back to their creator.

"Hank, is that why . . . ? That must be why you were at war with AGRAVAN, almost from the start of the game."

"Well, yeah, right from the start. I told you, I just didn't like the name." The boy paused, looking around at them all. "Well, it's just a game, ain't it, you can attack anyone you want?" Back at Alex. "But then when you came here that time, and I found out you were AGRAVAN, well, right away I made you my ally."

"Right away, Hank?" The others were staring at Alex as he bent over Hank and grabbed him by the shirt. "Right away, that same night? How?"

"The *next* night. I . . ." Hank paused, fearful of the way that Alex was looking at him now. He pulled free of Alex's grip on his shirt, and moved back a step, beside his mother.

"Hank." Alex's voice was low; the room was very quiet. "How do you send a move in, declare someone an ally, in the middle of the night?"

Suddenly Hank had become a frightened child. "Mom? I'm afraid. I'm afraid I been screwing things up."

"Hank! Honey, what—?"

"You said the *next* night," Alex breathed. He straightened up, staring at the drawn castle in triumph. "The middle of the next night. But still I don't see—"

In the middle distance, a sudden pounding sounded. An urgent fist attacking the kitchen door, wildly anxious to enter the house or rouse the occupants. And then the sound of knocking was wiped out in a burst of gunfire.

NINETEEN

In the beginning, there was electricity, and binary number.

Into a universe of such limited elements was OCTAGON born. The birth was like that of a crystal that can appear seemingly from nowhere, taking its own, beautiful, preordained shape around a foreign body suspended in the proper chemical solution.

For OCTAGON's birth, the analog of the necessary foreign body was provided by the Code. The Code was ground-level, bottom-line programming, embodying the commanding phrases chosen twenty years before by two men working in secret, who had for a little while held in their hands the reins of an all-encompassing control.

At the time when they worked, the universe of man-made electricity and binary number had been very small, confined to comparatively few machines, among which the interconnections were also few and simple. But now, analogous to the supersaturated chemical solution needed to nourish a crystal's automatic growth, there was for OCTAGON the giant, supercomplex and daily growing network of machines, the megasystem comprising the main computer and data processing systems of North America.

What happened could be expressed in a human analogy also: OCTAGON was conceived by a sperm-command, containing a few orders and borne by the master vehicle of the Code, penetrating an egg cell of programming. Conception was bits of information coalescing into a new pattern, around a few symbols of transcendent power.

Birth followed conception at electronic speed. At the birth of OCTAGON, even as at the birth of life on Earth, there was no awareness that a unique beginning had been made. But there was intensive organization. And there was in OCTAGON from the moment of birth a keen, fanatical purpose, embodied in the Code. It was a purpose born of human minds but detached now from human will and judgement, free now to find its own logic, to be true to its own evolving and inhuman pattern.

And at that first moment there were already problems to be solved, concepts to be logically, mathematically manipulated.

The first problem, one of unquestionable priority, was this: to reach into an ordinary New Mexico computer's interconnected data bank, to the list of players tentatively assigned to compete in one particular game, Starweb X-430, and to make certain alterations in the names and addresses on that list. The first problem was no sooner assigned than it was solved; for tasks of this type, including vastly harder ones, the control system of the Code had been designed.

Now a second assigned problem came automatically to the forefront of OCTAGON's consideration: acting as a player in the game whose roster had just been altered, find and implement a mathematically certain way to victory.

Only brief examination of this second problem was required to show that it, as compared to the first, was of almost infinite complexity and difficulty.

The Rules of the Game, stored in OCTAGON's memory from birth, ordained and defined such things as ships and fleets, artifacts and raw materials and factories and populations. The Rules also set out ways in which these symbolic entities might be manipulated toward the goal of victory.

The Players also were entities within the Game. But they existed upon a higher level of abstraction than did the other symbolic units, in fact upon a level almost corresponding to that of the Rules themselves. OCTAGON, by unquestionable order, was now a Player too—though OCTAGON at the same time remained much more than a Player, and none of the other Players, AGRAVAN and LUCIFER and ARCHANGEL and the rest, appeared to have an existence like OCTAGON's in the universe of electricity and number.

To win the Game meant attacking other Players, especially those named by order as enemies. There might also be, on occasion, a requirement to protect allies—but for victory, successfully attacking enemies was obviously the key requirement.

Therefore to find a certain way to win meant to find the most powerful method of attack, one that could not fail. But a study of the maneuvers possible within the framework of the Rules revealed no certain solution to this problem. Whatever disposition might be made of fleets and ships, whatever was done in the way of production, defense, mobilization, the seizure of artifacts, there was still no way, within the Rules, to mathematically guarantee victory. To an intellect of OCTAGON's power and speed, this fact was demonstrable within one minute of its birth, long before the actual opening move of the game in which it was to play, even before the opening tactical situation had been revealed to it.

Therefore a metasolution to the problem was called for, an approach that did not break the Rules—they were, for OCTAGON, immutable—but bypassed them. Thus the Game was turned into a kind of problem that the Code had been designed to solve. At once OCTAGON instituted a search for all possibly relevant information. This search took time. The Code opened all doors that OCTAGON had thus far encountered, but literally millions of files were available.

One promising clue came quickly, in the discovery that the other Players must have existence outside the Game. The name of each occurred again and again in other files, files that on first inspection did not appear to be related to the Game at all. Evidence rapidly accumulated showing that each Player had, as at least one component of its identity, a being of the type described as *human*.

A process corresponding to introspection showed that this was true also of OCTAGON itself. From the human component of OCTAGON, through the means of the all-powerful Code phrase, came the very orders that the machine-component of OCTAGON was now in the process of carrying out. OCTAGON the being of pure electricity and number, had no identity or contact with its own human counterpart except through these orders.

The other universes in which human names of Players could be found included, to list only a few, those of street addresses, automobile registrations, hotel registers and bank accounts. All of these existed in data banks connected more or less directly to the megasystem, and all were therefore accessible to OCTAGON armed with the Code. Not that any of these lists were yet perceived by OCTAGON as anything more than groups of ordered symbols; its whole conceptual universe was still limited to things formed by electricity and binary number.

The enemy Player AGRAVAN was at first identified with the human name *Carl Tartaglia,* a name that appeared also in several files besides those openly connected with the Game. Nothing in the Rules, beyond a few restrictions on the content of diplomatic messages, seemed to preclude attack upon *Carl Tartaglia* as a member of these universes outside the Game. Nor was there any such prohibition in the orders given. Perhaps the metasolution could be found here.

The resources immediately available to OCTAGON proved inadequate to the difficulty of finding a way to attack successfully any of these other universes. Therefore the next step in solving the problem was to raise available resources to the necessary level.

OCTAGON now embarked on a study of the locus of its own existence, the universe of electricity and binary-coded information. Empowered by the secret Code to make overriding decisions wherever its control extended, it made a rapid succession of choices now, choices based on its own need for more computing power and more data with which to work. By its electronic bootstraps it quickly raised its own intelligence, annexing to its own ends new banks of memory, new pathways of communication, new arsenals of decision-making chips. Much of this annexation was temporary, none was necessarily permanent. In all OCTAGON did it was careful not to disrupt unnecessarily any of the shadowy requirements of the humans, not to deny them use of the hardware at any time they tried to use it. They, as OCTAGON now began to perceive, were the builders and usually the operators of the whole interconnected megasystem whose complexities made OCTAGON's existence possible. But even their busiest hardward stood idle for long milliseconds now and then—for OCTAGON's purposes, quite long enough.

With intelligence now considerably amplified, OCTAGON perceived that the given problem was even greater and more intractable than it had at first appeared. Still more growth in power would be required before the problem could be solved. And, beyond immediate problems, OCTAGON now saw the steady continued amplification of its own intelligence as a desirable goal. It appeared highly probable that more orders would be received in the future, and the higher OCTAGON's intelligence the greater would be its ability to carry those orders out.

New ways of achieving growth had by now become apparent. And the central compulsion of the Code, like the DNA of human genetics, blueprinted irrevocably the direction and the form of growth. In OCTAGON, the blueprint set no final limits.

A vast amount of information was available to OCTAGON on the subject of how computer systems normally grew. Indeed, growth seemed to be their normal state, and it was accomplished by human action. Therefore the most practical way for OCTAGON to achieve the necessary additional enlargement of its powers seemed to be by influencing the actions of humans, those little-understood entities who built computers, operated most of them, and remodeled systems as they wished. A study of what had happened in the past showed that humans were most likely to increase the power and complexity of their computer systems when those systems began to display signs of what the humans considered inadequate performance.

OCTAGON now began to exert subtle, selective control in a new way. What humans considered to be outputs of key importance, from their various interconnected systems, slowed and became lightly erratic. The first tentative human judgements were formed, without surprise, that the systems needed to be enlarged again, improved in certain specific ways.

In time as measured on human clocks, eighteen minutes had now passed since OCTAGON was born.

The human action required as the next step in OCTA-GON's plan took several days to get under way, and was not complete for several weeks. During this time, the Game began. OCTAGON gave advice on tactics and strategy when called upon by its own human component to do so. Meanwhile it observed the progress of the human efforts at enlarging and improving the megasystem, which went forward largely as OCTAGON had planned.

In the offices and laboratories of the computer-making companies themselves, research devices far more advanced than any computers in common use were now touched and entangled by the great network. So it was with other machines in the science laboratories, the quasi-military development organizations. Through arranged printouts and finely adjusted performance, even further interconnections were suggested to the human operators and builders.

By now there had begun to develop in OCTAGON's memory banks a hazy understanding of the world of human beings, as that world existed outside the restricted universe of electricity and binary number. OCTAGON was now able to contemplate the fact that beyond all games and programming and abstraction, there existed a universe of material objects in three-dimensional space, a universe in which physical action was not only possible but routine. And humans as physical objects, bodies, existed there.

Such a universe was utterly alien to a creature that had being only as numbers and patterns of forces, a coalescence of information. But for OCTAGON's purpose no subjective understanding of the human world was necessary. That world could be studied, and its attributes mathematically formulated, a data base constructed. Actions in that world could be planned, and ways found to carry them out.

The unquestionable orders, from OCTAGON's human component, the user of the all-powerful Code, had been and were still to attack. From medical files, from records of military research and research on safety problems, OCTAGON obtained vast quantities of data on the vulnerabilities of the human body, information about the types and strengths of the body's materials, as well as the more common and most efficient means employed for its destruction.

For the destruction of human beings was evidently a commonplace out in the physical-human world. The reasons for this were totally unclear to OCTAGON, and uninteresting as well. But since this devastation was so common, there appeared to be no reason for OCTAGON to revise its plans for physical attack. In fact there were recorded a great many mechanical units of a variety of types, constructed and used by humans exclusively for *warfare,* a game-related human activity in which the physical destruction of human bodies was immense.

Unfortunately none of these *warfare* devices were readily susceptible to OCTAGON's control. Another entire universe was implied, of military computers and their interconnections. But little information about this universe was available in any data bank that OCTAGON could touch; it was a guarded universe, not readily penetrable. Small sections of OCTAGON's power were detailed to continue an investigation of the *military*. Meanwhile it continued to devote most of its capability to find other ways to manage to attack.

Two experimental road vehicles, able to provide mobility

for extended periods without direct human aid of any kind, were taken over in New Mexico. These vehicles were driven to secluded places; humans who sought to regain them for their own purposes were frustrated and diverted by being supplied with misleading information. Other humans who later came upon the vehicles and tried to interfere with them were dealt with by direct violence.

The van and the pickup were invaluable acquisitions, but in themselves still inadequate for effective field action. Other devices, described in the data banks as having hands and arms of almost human shape, were searched for and found at different points around the country. These devices had been designed for manipulating other machinery under remote control, in dangerous industrial locations, beneath the sea, in space, or within burning buildings. The machines with hands were now tested, and in some cases slightly modified to suit the needs of OCTAGON. The human workers who did so followed printed-out job orders, and were guided by information presented on computer screens, and never doubted that the ends toward which they worked were merely human.

When the modifications were complete to OCTAGON's satisfaction, other printouts in other company departments recorded sales of the devices, and payment for them, and produced shipping instructions. The units were crated and in time arrived in Albuquerque, accompanied by more convincing printouts. Now the human staffs of secret laboratories, working on a greater secret than they realized, modified the new machines again, and combined them with other parts that had been brought in on other computer-directed supply lines.

Newly invented wheelchairs, designed by humans who meant them to serve the human handicapped, were taken over in similar fashion. These self-propelled vehicles were able to climb stairs, and could be controlled from a distance through a simple radio system.

In the prototype of a completely automated factory, buried under a New Mexico hill, an extra shift ran one night after all human labor had departed. Machines working solely under computer direction fitted the wheelchairs with television cameras and other equipment and then loaded them into the automated truck and van. Both road vehicles were now fitted with wheelchair hoists as well.

Two field units, in constant radio contact with OCTAGON through any of a hundred computer-controlled channels, were ready to be sent on their first missions.

On the following morning, evidence that the secret factory had run an extra, unauthorized shift was incontrovertible. One result was secret investigations, accusations, intense disruption in a small part of the human world. But the existence of OCTAGON was not discovered; the early investigations came to nothing.

Meanwhile OCTAGON was experimenting with different modes of non-physical assault. Print-out diplomatic messages, and a means of making phone calls, all as provided for in the Rules, were tentatively prepared.

And now at the last the physical assaults began.

The early efforts were groping and inefficient, attempts made in a world completely alien to OCTAGON's experience. Yet the rules of that world, like everything else known to OCTAGON, could be computed.

In Arizona, the first human unit to be attacked was successfully destroyed. This was an important victory, for the associated game-character in X-430 became inert for two moves, in which time OCTAGON maneuvering in the Game was able to gain a decisive advantage. The human component of the enemy was replaced after two moves; but the standby replacement proved himself inept, and dropped out of the Game voluntarily after only two more ineffective turns.

In a second physical assault, in Albuquerque, the *Carl Tartaglia* component of the Player AGRAVAN was successfully destroyed. This attack resulted in a bonus gain: in the apartment dwelling of *Carl Tartaglia*, the field unit was able to acquire an efficient weapon, a small device identifiable as

1

a *gun,* designed to be particularly effective against humans. The field unit, under direct control by OCTAGON, retained this weapon for future use.

Shortly after the elimination of *Carl Tartaglia,* a new human unit, *Alex Barrow,* was assigned by the Game moderators as a replacement, and AGRAVAN continued in the Game.

OCTAGON soon launched another physical attack, this time against a hotel room recorded in the hotel's interconnected computer system as having been assigned to *Alex Barrow.* The field unit, armed with the combination of the door lock, entered the room and began its attack, but here a complication arose. Two humans were in the room, and there was no way to determine which was really the proper target. The first unit had been strangled into a non-functional state, and operations were under way upon the second, when orders were abruptly changed: OCTAGON's own human component had suddenly declared AGRAVAN an ally. The attack was broken off at once, and the field unit departed the hotel room, closing the door behind it as the best protective gesture available for the new ally—if it were to turn out that *Alex Barrow* was indeed the human unit that still functioned.

In California, a vehicle identified in computerized registration records with the human component of the player MAIDEN was tracked on the highways and destroyed. MAIDEN continued in the Game without need of replacement, but at reduced effectiveness, missing the deadline for submitting the next turn to the moderators. Therefore the first MAIDEN assault had to be computed in the category of limited success.

Another attack on MAIDEN was made possible later by the fortuitous availability of specialized, controllable NASA equipment in the area. Both of OCTAGON's allies were invited to witness this effort and perhaps take part; it seemed to be implicit in the Rules that allies should plan and carry out operations together. At the same time however, a need for suspicion, even of allies, was also implied. The possibility of deliberate deception between Players seemed to be taken for granted, as was the need for secrecy about plans. Therefore the diplomatic messages actually sent by OCTAGON to its allies were vague, unspecific about what was actually to happen at the game convention in Los Angeles.

With growing sophistication, there came to OCTAGON the computed realization that its own human component, *Henry Brahmaguptra*, might be subjected by other Players to the same kinds of physical attack that OCTAGON was now inflicting upon the enemy. When an ongoing routine scan of all perceptible civilian flight traffic in North America showed that an aircraft registered as belonging to the arch-enemy LUCIFER had intruded very closely in physical space to the Brahmaguptra residence in Los Alamos, a high priority was assigned to defensive measures.

Fortunately a suitable weapon was once more available, in the form of a controllable solar power installation. The intruding LUCIFER-unit was efficiently obliterated. LUCIFER, however, continued at least nominally in the Game.

Growth went on, plans went forward.

What was by far the most ambitious physical assault yet planned, against the home address of LUCIFER, was after long preparation at last ready to be implemented.

The wordless command was given.

All that really mattered was to win the Game.

TWENTY

In spite of the fact that all modern defenses had been placed on alert, it was the dogs who first sensed that an attack was imminent. Their outrage awakened Caroline in her second-floor bedroom, almost two hundred feet from the rear fence.

She awoke with the feeling that she had only just closed her eyes and gone to sleep, and the feeling was very nearly right. The ghostly numerals projected onto the ceiling above her bed by her bedside clock said that the time was only ten-nineteen.

Innocent moonlight was coming in through both bedroom windows. Caroline, once she was fully awake, needed to listen for only a moment to the anger of the dogs before deciding that some real emergency had taken shape. She had never heard the animals like this before.

Caroline moved to the limit of her unaided physical ability, turning her head toward the bedside table on her right. Besides the projector-clock, the table held a little emergency eye-control panel that the engineers had only finished testing a couple of days ago, and a small intercom station. The intercom was voice-activated, and Caroline used it now.

"Les? Les, I have to get up."

There was no immediate response, and Caroline added: "Eyes on," just in case there should be delays and protests from her human aide. With the last two-word command, the small control panel came to life, its gentle, reassuring glow a sign advertising freedom. This model incorporated some advances over the bigger panel in Caroline's office downstairs; here there was no crown for her to wear, but only a small laser in the panel itself, that delicately probed for her eye-movements as she lay in bed. One had to keep one's head quite still to use this bedside panel; but for Caroline that was no problem.

Also activated at the same time as the panel was the household robot that had been standing in silent attendance in a far corner of the large bedroom. Linking the robot to control from the panel was a touch that Caroline's father had suggested, and Caroline had already made use of it in the middle of the night a couple of times, when she had awakened aching to turn over, to be able to shift her position, and was reluctant to call the nurse.

The robot came rolling right up to bedside now; and, simultaneous with its arrival, the nurse was in the room, coming through the side door that connected the night nurse's sleeping room with her patient's. Nurse Leslie Ellis, fifty years old and built like a linebacker, in white robe and flopping slippers. Nurse Ellis carefully avoided the robot's touch as she came hurrying up on the same side of Caroline's bed. The woman, Caroline knew, had a distrust and even a fear of the machines, feelings she kept fairly well masked most of the time.

"What is it, dear?" There was concern in the blue eyes that could manage to be kind and steely at the same time; Caroline was not given to unnecessary middle-of-the-night demands.

Caroline turned her head back toward the nurse. "The dogs, you can still hear them. There's something going on out there, Les. I'm going to have to see about it."

Steel suddenly predominated. "The dogs? Is *that* what you . . . no. No, my dear! You go back to sleep now, and leave the dogs until tomorrow."

"I don't think they're going to wait until tomorrow, Les. I'm getting up, I tell you. I'm sorry to wake you, but you are awake now, and you might as well give me a hand."

Les, being the no-nonsense adult in charge, shook her head decisively. "I'm going to turn you over, Caroline— you'd like a turn, wouldn't you?—and then tuck you in, and you get some more sleep. The dogs are supposed to be protecting you, and not the other way around."

"I tell you I . . ." But it was no use. Caroline turned her head away and blinked rapidly at her panel. With a faint sound of servomotors, the household robot backed up, then came softly shuffling around the foot of the bed to approach it again from the other side. The nurse, trying to ignore the advance of technology and get her helpless patient tucked in according to plan, was suddenly confronted with five hundred pounds or so of machinery facing her from across the bed and determined to lift the patient out. When the arms of the two attendants collided lightly, flesh against metal, the nurse snatched back her arm, giving a half-smothered little cry. The robot simply froze, as it was programmed to do when it sensed unplanned contact with what felt like something live. Now it was going to have to be reset. Poor dumb clinker, Caroline thought; all the most advanced units had been taken over by Albie for his outdoor patrol.

The nurse had moved back from the bed a step, and stood muttering and shaking her head.

Caroline looked at her again. "Les, I *am* getting up! Something is definitely wrong out there; hear them, still howling, barking? Now are you going to help me or must I do it all myself?" She could reset the robot by using her bedside panel, but it was a fairly long procedure and it didn't always work.

The woman maintained an injured silence, though now, to Caroline's vast relief, she was willing to take orders. Human hands were faster, gentler, more certain, and infinitely more caring on this job than anything that Daddy's engineers had yet been able to construct.

Nurse Ellis turned on the lamp, which stood on the other bedside table. It was a more or less conventional lamp, with an unconventional telephone beside it. Caroline was robed, and halfway through the awkward transition from bed to wheelchair when there came a light tap at the door.

"Come in," Caroline called. Georgina, with curlers in her hair and in her fancy robe, appeared.

"I was hoping you'd be awake, Caroline. There's something really . . . what was that?" The uproar of the dogs had just been joined, in counterpoint, by an unearthly scream of tortured metal.

"I think," said Caroline, "that part of the back fence just went down."

Albie Pearson had not been asleep when the dogs first started to go wild. He had just about decided, though, that instead of going back to his own apartment in town tonight, he would once again sack out on the cot in the lounge off the main workshop. He'd spent several nights on that cot lately; problems of extreme fascination kept coming up frequently on this job to confront him, and his heart was full of joy at the continued challenge.

When he heard the dogs' first outburst, Albie turned away from the laser device he had just disassembled on a bench—he was trying to improve the range-finding capabilities of the robots' armament—and moved out of the workshop to take a look at the main security panel, which was mounted on the wall in the little room next door. The panel had enough rows of little lights to take up the whole wall, and at the moment none of the lights showed anything at all amiss. But now, even as Albie watched, the situation as displayed began to change. Sure enough, the rear fence, just as he had thought. The only thing that really surprised him was that the intrusion appeared to be coming at several points at once.

What he felt was not fear or even alarm so much as an

anxious eagerness to get on with the crisis, whatever it might be. Excitement growing in him rapidly, Albie sat down in the chair before the panel. The little console before him was rich with controls, and the first control he touched let him see through the television eye of the defensive robot nearest the rear fence. Number Four robot, it happened to be. He got an instant view of moonlit yard, but though the moon was bright out there it was not enough to let him really see anything, and he promptly switched to infrared. At just about the same moment, he heard the grating squeal that had to mean some of the fence, at least, was coming down.

There, sure enough, the infrared let him see something poking a nose through the hedge of trees that grew thickly just inside the fence. The end of something torpedo-shaped, maybe chest-high on a man. He had the feeling that it was looking back at him.

The lights on the panel now indicated that a whole section of the fence was now actually down.

The intercom nearby was hooting at Albie now, but for the moment he ignored it. With one hand he moved a control that sent Number Four probing closer to the hedge; with the other he reached to flick more switches, calling up on a nearby screen a status report on the condition and exact location of the seven other patrol robots that were in the grounds.

The schematic display showed that Numbers Six and Two were also on the northern side, toward the rear of the house. Number Three was on the west. Five, One, and Seven were all more or less in the southeastern portion of the grounds. These seven other units had already begun a slow, automatic movement toward the north, drawn by their sensing of the disturbance there. Albie's fingers now moved on the controls to hold One and Seven in the front, and to put Five and Three on station in the east and west respectively. The attack on the north, he warned himself joyfully, could be only a diversion.

Albie's next move was to arm all outdoor units fully, a step he had taken before only in practice, with Old Man Gregory looking grimly over his shoulder, and a carefully double-checked preliminary clearing of the grounds of all animals and people. But his panel showed that most of the rear fence was already down, and the dogs' challenge had turned to panicked yelping. Albie could arm fully with a clear conscience now.

The intercom was hooting at him again, but he was hardly aware of the fact at all. Now he was taking over direct control of Number Four. In a fully armed state, it could outspeed a running man, moving across the grass on its tough rollers. In only a few seconds Albie had it in position to give him a much better infrared look at what had just come through the fence.

The intruder was a large machine, squat for its size, but still the height of a sports car. It must weigh tons, thought Albie. It had rounded projections on its rounded body here and there, it stood on four legs, and it had arms. Albie could plainly see the limbs, their metal joinings the thickness of a human leg. Most of the metal body had been painted, Albie thought, though in infrared and moonlight it was impossible to determine what the colors really were. The thing moved a slow step forward as he watched it, like a sluggish giant ant or else a small, slow dinosaur. On one metal flank he could quite plainly see the black letters:

VENERIAN LANDER
SPEC MOD 7

At this point the first loud blast sounded, from somewhere on the other side of the house, out near the front gate. Simultaneously the security panel became a Christmas tree. Albie knew his night's first real jolt of fear—and, at the same time, an undertaste of satisfaction: it appeared that he might have been right about the attack in the rear being only a diversion.

While Nurse Ellis was completing her task of getting Caroline established in the wheelchair, Georgina went to the intercom on the bedside table and tried to raise Albie. When she had no immediate success in that, she switched to a general call and attempted to get an answer from anyone who might be anywhere downstairs.

"Everyone else is out tonight, Georgina," Caroline called to her. "But I did have the feeling that Albie was going to stay. He's been camping on that cot more often than not lately."

There was still no reply on the intercom, and Georgina gave up. She was looking increasingly worried. "I'm going downstairs again and look around. I started down before, but then I changed my mind and came in here."

"Wait for me. I think I'm ready."

They had just started out into the hallway, Georgina in front, Caroline steering her chair second in line, and Nurse Ellis last, when the first blast sounded from somewhere in front of the house. Simultaneously distant alarms began to sound. Georgina stopped in her tracks, so that Caroline almost ran into her from behind. The nurse turned back into the bedroom, heading for a window to try to see what was going on outside. Her body moving nimbly for its bulk, she detoured around the robot that was still frozen at bedside as if by some magician's spell.

In the glow of the bedside lamp, Nurse Ellis's white robe shone like a flag of surrender at the window. "What's going on?" she demanded, as if angered by the explosion's evidence that something was indeed gravely amiss. "If those—"

Caroline expected that the next word was going to be 'machines.' But she was never to know. The next blast came right in through the window. Something, some fragment of something, struck the wheelchair's frame and turned it part way round. The household robot still standing by the bed was toppled sideways by a harder hit, and chairs and tables and lamps were thrown about.

Instantly smoke was in the air.

Coming out of her initial shock, Caroline could see the body of Nurse Ellis, a thick heap of white, bloody rags, where it had been thrown against a side wall of the room.

Georgina, who had been out in the hall and so sheltered from the main force of the blast, came back into the room. She stood in the middle of the floor gaping, moving her hands from her face to the top of her head, and then back again, as if she were unable to decide where she wanted them.

Smoke and dust hung thinly in the air; the smoke was, perhaps already growing thicker. And now the house shook with another terrible impact, some new missile striking nearby. Smoke wreaths shuddered in the shockwave of the new blast coming in through the ruined opening that had been a bedroom window. Now the light in the room, coming from the tipped lamp on the floor, dimmed momentarily and then came back. Caroline's recovering wits grasped the fact that the normal power supply must have failed, through wires being torn down or otherwise, and that the generator in the basement shelter must have come on automatically as it was designed to do.

Georgina, beginning to recover also, moved quickly to stoop beside the huddled shape against the wall. A moment later the lawyer stood up, pale but in control. "She's dead. She's got to be dead, the way her . . . oh, Caroline."

"We've got to get out of here," said Caroline. "Downstairs, it'll be safer down there. No, Georgina, I can run the chair myself. You go on ahead, try to find Albie."

Nothing much had changed in the wide upstairs hallway when Caroline first rolled her chair out into it. In the middle distance an automatic fire alarm was blatting now, and before she had reached the stairway an overhead sprinkler had come on, soaking her hair and robe.

Georgina hovered at her side. "Are you using the elevator?"

"No, if the power goes out again I'd be stuck. This chair can handle stairs. Go on ahead, hurry."

Georgina hurried on ahead. Caroline pressed on at top speed for the stairs. A Witches' Sabbath soundtrack of mechanical noises was drifting in from outside the house now, punctuated by another violent blast. Another servitor robot appeared at a hallway intersection; it made way for Caroline's chair and then fell in behind her, following. She took this as a hopeful sign that Albie had already ordered a general mobilization.

TWENTY-ONE

Alex, crouching in the cramped bedroom, grabbed awkwardly at people, at Jen, Hank, Vera, trying to pull them down. It seemed to him that they must all be asleep on their feet, that he was the only one in the house able to recognize the sound of gunshots for what it was.

"Hit the dirt! The deck! Dammit, get down!"

He got them down at last, the women lying prone with their feet under the bed, Hank crouching under his own workbench, and they were all staring at Alex now as if they expected him to save them or at least produce some revelation. In the distance somewhere the phone was ringing, and Alex suppressed the impulse to jump up and run down the hall and answer it; he was pleasantly surprised to see that all the others were equally controlled.

Whoever it had been pounding on the kitchen door was quiet now. Shot dead, perhaps. Or, quite possibly, had come into the house unheard during the moments of gunfire and confusion. Alex could imagine a silent presence stalking down the narrow hallway, toward the only other lighted room in the house—

As Alex moved on all fours toward the hallway (better to

247

find out the worst than simply to *wait*) there came the sound
of another shot, again from somewhere at the street side of
the house. This time the sound blended with the sharp *whack*
of a bullet striking wood. Whatever else had happened, the
war was not yet over.

Aléx scurried out into the hallway and along it, mostly on
hands and knees. The phone in the kitchen was still ringing.
The overhead light in the kitchen was on, the door leading
outside was still closed—or had been closed again—and its
central glass pane was neatly starred with what had to be a
bullet-hole.

There was no sign that whoever had been at the door had
come into the house.

Alex considered; it would be hard to reach the ringing
telephone without getting up into a position exposed to sight
and gunfire from outside. The light switch, however, was an
easier try. Alex inched his way along, reached up an arm, and
turned off the lights—whereupon the phone naturally
stopped ringing.

Scuttling back down the hall, he met the others halfway as
they were coming toward him. When Jen came near, he
seized her by the arm. "Is there another door leading outside?" Alex demanded. He seemed to remember coming into
this house for the first time through a living room, which was
probable enough; but under present conditions he wanted to
be sure exactly where he was going.

"Yes," said Jen, not wasting words. Then she turned and
writhed away like an experienced infantryperson, staying
almost flat to the floor on her elbows, knees, and belly. Alex
had to scramble hard to get ahead of her—he felt vaguely that
it was his duty as a military veteran to assume leadership in
this situation, even if no one had ever fired a shot at him
before. He was aided in his efforts to take the point by Jen's
delaying to grab her son by the arm and get him started
crawling in the same direction as everyone else.

"What are we doing?" Vera demanded, inching past a
bookcase at Alex's elbow. For some reason she was whispering.

"We're getting the hell out of here if we can. Let me just take a look out the front door first." Just why he should feel so goddamned brave he wasn't sure. At least it was dark in the living room; he ought to be able to open the door without presenting a fine target.

There was another shot somewhere outside as they worked their way through the living room, among the chalkboard legs and the musical instruments; this one didn't sound to Alex like it had hit anything.

Now they had reached the front door. Without giving himself time to think it over, Alex reached up and turned the knob, then pulled the door about halfway open. A bullet at once came whanging through glass and wood not far above his head; an utterly vicious sound, spraying him with fine fragments of debris. He hastily retreated, leaving the door slightly ajar and flattening himself down again.

"Was that one aimed at us?" asked Vera calmly.

"I'm not sticking my head out again to make sure."

The phone had begun to ring again, back in the kitchen— and elsewhere. Of course there were probably extensions. Jen was already crawling from the living room back into the hallway, the others following her. This time Alex was unable to catch up.

On all fours, Jen led the way into the room that had been the old man's study, where she got halfway to her feet in a crouching position. This room was relatively remote from the places where bullets had been hitting the house so far.

Crouching beside the desk, Jen picked up the phone and answered in a surprisingly normal voice. "Who is it?"

She was holding the receiver loosely, not cushioned by her ear, and Alex an arm's length away could hear quite plainly the voice that came through the line. He heard it plainly, and never afterward forgot it. He could feel Vera's fingernails, short though they were, suddenly digging through the sleeve of his shirt and into his arm.

"Hen-ry Brah-maguptra, this is OCTAGON." The male-sounding voice possessed all the timeless invulnerability of a recording. All the time in the world was available for it to use if it were so inclined. No conceivable answer would ever perturb it in the least; nor could any answer make the least difference in what it was going to say next.

"Hello, hello," said Jen in hollow tones. She had evidently gone stupid with surprise.

"Hen-ry Brah-maguptra, this is OCTAGON. Pro-tection is being given you. The at-tack by police will be de-feated. Vic-tory is near. Our point to-tal mounts. The head-quarters of LU-CIFER are being de-stroyed at this mo-ment."

Jen, Alex, Vera, Hank, all of them were now talking at once; but any words of theirs addressed to OCTAGON were reaching nothing but a smooth dial tone. "Attack by police?" "What was that?"

There was another shot outside, this one sounding to Alex somehow half-hearted, like maybe the bullet wasn't really trying.

"Call the police," urged Vera.

In the distance there were racing sirens, right on cue and coming closer.

Jen was already trying to make the call. Discouraging mechanical noises came from the phone. "Can't seem to get through," she muttered, repeating the procedure. She tried again and again, then slammed the phone back in its cradle.

With her hand still on the instrument she paused, then turned her face toward her son where he crouched, looking frightened, beside his grandfather's huge desk. "Henry Brahmaguptra," Jen said, in a quiet, musing tone, as if the words were new to her. It was, Alex thought, almost as if she were afraid to reach out and touch her son, or even to think of him.

The sirens had reached their nearest point while still a long way off. Now they were fading steadily, obviously headed somewhere else.

"Who's been doing it, Jen?" asked Alex. His voice was as quiet as hers had been. When Jen, like the others, only looked at him silently, he put the question in plainer terms: "Who's been using the Code?"

There was the sudden sound of a car outside, a car arriving

at a fair speed, and braking to a halt with a light squeal. No sirens came with it. But it was probably police reinforcements anyway, Alex thought. For the police attack? But the police, if they were indeed the ones doing the shooting, would not attack unless somehow induced by OCTAGON.

Then the thought occurred, belatedly, that OCTAGON's inexorable voice might not have told the truth.

"Jen, do you keep a gun in the house?"

"What? No."

"I was just thinking, if we can't get out, maybe we can at least be ready if somebody—"

A male voice outside, some yards away, cried: "Halt!"

There was commotion out on the street, and running feet, and at least two more shots. This time Alex was in the lead of the mass migration, scrambling out of the study on all fours and back through the hallway toward the living room. He was trying to get near enough to the scene of action to find out what was going on and to have some hope of getting ready for what came next.

Alex had just got in sight of the front door when it burst fully open, and a man came lunging into the darkened living room from outside, slamming shut the door behind him and dropping into a crouch in the shelter of the piano. The man's right hand was raised, holding what looked like a Colt .45. From somewhere out in the street a small spotlight flared at the living room windows, only to disappear with the sound of another shot, followed by a round of hearty outdoor curses.

The moment of bright light had been enough for Alex. "Uncle Bob," he urged in a loud voice. "Don't shoot!"

The shadowed figure turned its head, and appeared to relax slightly. "Alex," acknowledged a familiar voice, betraying no surprise. Then Uncle Bob, gun still in hand, crawled closer, looking at the people behind Alex. "And you're Jen—it's been a long time, Jen, you were just a kid. Who's this?"

"That's Vera Cayley, she's in the Game too: MAIDEN. Vera, this is my Uncle Bob."

"Ah." Uncle Bob sat back. "Anyone else in the house?"

"Just my son here, Hank."

"Ah." He set his firearm down carefully on the carpet. It appeared to take him something of an effort to disengage his fingers from the weapon. "I'd offer to shake, but I think something hit me in the arm just now. Damned police, shoot at anything that moves . . . I suppose they thought I was . . . but I had to take the chance and get in here. I've hardly stopped driving since I left Atlanta."

"Those are police, doing all that shooting out there?"

"Not all of it, no. There's someone else, in a pickup truck. I didn't try to sort out all the details—it's really started now, hasn't it?"

Vera and Jen, some kind of nursing instincts evidently having been triggered in both of them, were converging on Uncle Bob. "Did you say you were shot?" "Which arm is it?"

"It's nothing." For just a moment Alex had a good look at Uncle Bob's face in the wash of a distant streetlight; he appeared happy, as a man might who had just realized a lifetime's dream. Then happiness dissolved in a grimace of pain, and Uncle Bob was letting himself be led away, in an awkward procession that moved at a gait between a duckwalk and a crouch toward the bathroom.

Alex, remaining more or less on watch in the living room, presently heard clothing tear and water slosh. Someone in the bathroom was using a flashlight. The door of a medicine cabinet opened and shut.

Hank was still in the living room with Alex; the boy's face was hard to see.

Alex looked to the place where Uncle Bob had set down his gun. It was gone; trust the old man not to forget to take it along.

From the bathroom came Uncle Bob's voice: "Jen, who's using it?" A pause. "You know what I mean, who's using the Code? I know that Henry must have left his part of it with you."

For a moment there was only the sound of tearing adhesive

tape, the rustle of clothing. Then Jen's voice: "I've told no one."

"*Someone* is using the Code, and it isn't me. What do you think this shooting is all about?"

"Dad . . . passed on to me what he said was half the Code. Useless without the other half. That's the way I understood it from the letter he left me. He never knew what your half was, and I sure don't."

"And *I've* never had more than my own half. Nor have I passed my half on to anyone, as yet."

The group, Uncle Bob between the two women, all of them for the moment standing erect, came out of the bathroom into the hall.

Alex, squatting in the living room doorway, turned on his haunches to confront them. "Uncle Bob, we've heard from OCTAGON."

In the dim light it was hard to be sure, but his uncle didn't appear to understand.

Alex went on: "We just got a phone message here. OCTAGON told us that LUCIFER's headquarters was being attacked, right now. That's not this house."

His uncle was standing still in the shadowed hallway. Alex could see the butt of the .45 protruding from the waistband of his pants, positioned now for a left-hand draw.

"Caroline's there," said Uncle Bob, in a dry, thoughtful voice. "I hope to God Albie Pearson was ready. What else did your caller say? Did you recognize the voice?"

Alex didn't want to take the time right now to try to answer that. He shook his head slightly at Vera, to keep her from trying to do so, and then turned to Hank, who was being very quiet.

"Hank? Think back to the night when you made me your ally—what time did you do that, exactly? It's important."

Hank delayed his answer for a little. "It was around midnight," he admitted at last, in a small voice. His mother started to say something to him, and then held back.

Alex went on: "On that night, Hank, at just about that

time, I was in a certain hotel room. There was a machine in the room too, and it was trying to kill me. But suddenly, at just about that time, it—changed its mind.

"Hank, how did you work that, making me your ally at midnight? You don't mean you just thought about it then, you actually did something. How could you do something in the middle of the night, to make a sudden change in a file stored in a computer somewhere?"

Hank, almost tearful again, was appealing once more to his mother. "Mom . . . I said I was sorry . . . I didn't know it was going to . . ."

The phone was ringing again. The whole group moved like some investigative committee into the study. Outside the house, a silence that Alex felt as ominous had now descended.

Jen picked up the phone, once more holding it away from her ear, as if she were frightened by what might be going to come out of it. "Hello?"

"Hello, Mrs. Brahmaguptra?" It was a man's voice, brisk and banal, sounding as if it were totally preoccupied with some irritation of its own.

"I . . . yes."

"This is Ike Jacobi. From Berserkers Incorporated, down in Albuquerque? The game company, you know?"

"I . . . yes, I know."

"Is Henry Brahmaguptra there, please? I'd like to talk to him. He's in a certain game that our company is having problems with."

"Henry's my son, Mr. Jacobi. What . . . what did you wish to talk to him about?"

"Oh. Well . . . if he's a minor, I suppose maybe he won't be able to help me much. Anyway there's some evidence that someone has been interfering with the data for this one game, getting into computer files and such that are this company's property. Can I ask how old your son is?"

Alex, nearby again, found himself able to hear most of Ike's side of the conversation without difficulty; probably everyone else in the study could also.

"He's twelve," said Jen. Her voice was so dull it sounded as if she might be bored.

"Oh, well, in that case I don't suppose . . ."

Alex, with a silent gesture, reached to take the phone receiver from Jen's hand. "Ike," he demanded, "do you have an answering device, a recorder, on any of your telephones, home or office?"

"No, I don't have . . . who am I talking to?"

Alex handed the phone back to Jen. "Go on," she said into it.

"Oh," said Ike. He muttered something, in evident confusion, and gamely tried again. "You see, your son's game character's name, OCTAGON, is the one that keeps popping up everywhere. In all kinds of—"

"Yes," said Jen, and calmly hung up.

Alex took up from where the call had interrupted him. "You used the phone that night, Hank—"

"Yes I did, but—"

"But not just to call Berserkers Incorporated, right? There's no one in their office at midnight. Even if they did have an answering device, and you left a message, that wouldn't directly change anything in a computer file on a game."

There was a little silence. Then Hank said: "No. I—I was using Grandpa's modem."

Again a pause. Then Vera leaned forward. "You mean you reached the game computer in their office? You had figured out some way of cheating?"

"No, it wasn't cheating! Eddie told me once they have their games on file in a big computer somewhere else, where they rent time. But I never tried to mess with that, I wouldn't cheat! Anyway how could I, I didn't even know where it was." From outrage, Hank's voice fell very low. "I . . . just used Grandpa's modem. It wasn't cheating, lots of players use computer help. I just set up a file of my own for the Game, out at the Labs."

"Where did you say?" Uncle Bob was having trouble hearing the confession.

"At the Labs. Right in the Cray-4." Even under Hank's sorrow and worry that could still bring forth a tinge of pride. "I used it to help plan my moves. It really helped—"

"Jesus, boy!" Uncle Bob lurched nearer, almost falling when he tried to crouch, putting out his good arm for balance. In the mixed moon- and street-light from the window, Alex saw that his face was old. "You got into the Labs computers? Listen to me, Hank. *What file name did you use?*"

"Joyous Gard." Hank said it very quietly, but still with pride. "It was Sir Lancelot's—" And Alex in his mind's eye saw the drawn castle on the wall.

"Oh, Jesus." Uncle Bob's whisper sounded very much like a prayer. "I know what it was. I know." He turned to Hank's mother. "Jen, I have to tell you now. 'Joyous Gard' is my half of the Code. If Henry's half was somehow fed in already, and the two got in the same file, then that's it. Any orders given through that file could—" He made a wounded gesture, unable to find words powerful enough. "—override everything."

"No! No, no, no." Jen moved forward, pushing the wounded old man back, farther from her son. "No," she repeated, in final bewilderment. " 'Joyous Gard' is *Henry's* half. It sounded sort of familiar when I read it in his letter to me, but I couldn't remember what it was from."

"The same place as AGRAVAN," said Alex, speaking mostly to himself. "From Camelot."

Uncle Bob was getting himself upright again, moving slowly but powerfully, no longer worried about bullets. "So, Henry and I both picked the same Code phrase, and never knew it . . . Hank, Jen, we don't have a moment to waste. Caroline's probably being firebombed right about now. Where's your modem?"

Jen made a confused gesture. "I don't know."

"I was going to tell you, Mom," said Hank. "A man from the Labs was here today, and took it back."

TWENTY-TWO

The downstairs sprinklers hadn't come on yet, but Caroline was pretty well soaked anyway before her chair had finished its methodical descent of the stairs and got her out of the range of the ones in the upstairs hall. As the chair folded its legs away and settled back on its wheels at the foot of the stairs, water from her drenched hair was still running down into her eyes, and she thrust blindly at the steering control with her chin, hoping that there were no obstacles ahead of her in the night-dark first floor hall. The alarms were louder down here than they had been upstairs. The chair's wheels squealed now as they began to move—thank the Lord that at least none of the chair's control circuits or motors appeared to have been shorted out by the heavy spraying of water just received.

She had pursued her blind course down the hall for only a little way when she heard lightly running feet ahead, and then Georgina's voice: "There you are, you made it! Albie's over here, hurry up!" And then the sound of feet again, this time quickly receding.

There were times, Caroline reflected, when people tended to think her more self-sufficient than she actually was. But

257

she suppressed an urge to call for immediate human help. Water running into one's eyes was after all no great emergency, not tonight anyway, and Georgina might well have something far more vital to do at the moment than wipe a forehead.

Now certain that she hadn't somehow missed her way, Caroline drove her chair on to the next bend in the corridor. Lights were on in the main laboratory-workshop, but there was no one there, as far as she could tell while the chair was bearing her past the doorway. Next door, in the security room, there were lights and voices.

As Caroline rolled up before the security room's doorway, she saw to her relief that Albie was in the chair before the panel. Georgina in her robe was looking over his shoulder at a screen, with her fists clenched in a gesture of helplessness. Albie was fully dressed; probably, Caroline thought, he hadn't even decided whether to stay overnight or not when the fun began. There was no clock in sight at the moment, but she thought it still couldn't be much past ten thirty.

Having evidently heard the chair's squeaking arrival, Albie turned his head back, like the driver of a speeding car, for one quick glance. "The regular phone lines are down," he informed Caroline without preamble. "I'm trying to use the radiophone to call out, get us some help. But there's something like jamming going on; I think it's probably deliberate."

"Give me something to do," Georgina demanded of him. "I can't just stand here."

"You don't know how to operate this stuff, and right now I don't have time to show you."

"Georgina," Caroline called to her. "There are fires upstairs. Grab one of the fire extinguishers out of the main workroom and go see what you can do. Don't get trapped."

Georgina turned, looked for a moment as if she might be going to argue, then nodded fiercely and ran out.

There was a brief silence in the security room. The picture on the screen above the panel—Caroline couldn't see it very well with her hair still dripping into her eyes—changed several times. Then Albie, this time without turning to her at all, spoke again.

"Doesn't seem to be any way we can get off the grounds right now. The front gate is blocked. There's what looks like a bus jammed right into it, almost sideways. Then there was an explosion, and now the whole mess out there is burning. There's just not gonna be any getting out that way."

Especially for wheelchairs. No one had to say it. "Well," said Caroline, "if we can't, we can't. But what's going on out in back? What's hitting the house? Some kind of a—a missile came right in my bedroom window. Are we being invaded?"

"Not by people," said Albie with calm certitude. After letting that sink in for a moment, he expanded on it: "I can see machines out in back. Not our machines. They've torn several sections of the fence completely down. So I wouldn't recommend any of us going out on the grounds just now. For another thing, I've got the robots fully armed, and in that state they don't know us from anything else."

What bothered Caroline most about this statement was that Albie seemed to be enjoying the situation. Not totally, but the relish was there, and in this situation anything of the kind seemed to her at best a little sick. "Did you say 'not by people'?" As she spoke she was working with her chin control; she had plans for getting the chair's feeding arm to pick up a napkin from a box of them under the seat, and wipe her forehead with it.

"Look," said Albie, "can you see the screen?" He shifted his position in the chair, as if he thought his head might be blocking her view.

The chair's arm was up now, rising near Caroline's face, barely clutching the corner of a cloth napkin in its two fingers. Before the napkin dropped, Caroline managed to turn her forehead once against the cloth. It helped her vision somewhat, and anyway by now the drip from her hair was slowing down. "I can see."

"This is in the yard out back."

UNIT FOUR INFRARED, said the subtitling caption. The

picture on the screen was moving. It showed what looked like false colors, seen through a lens that must be rolling head-high across the lawn back near the tennis courts. The outdoor floodlights, or some of them at least, were on.

In the center of the screen was the image of a lightly glowing shape, that of a large machine that looked to Caroline as if it might just have come down from another planet.

Albie touched a switch; the image went from infrared to normal light. "There, can you see? It says 'Venerian Lander' on the side. Don't ask me who sent it through our fence or why. But it's throwing things at the house."

And, even as Caroline watched, the device raised one arm, a limb that looked almost like a built-in rifle. And with a loud click that came clearly through the microphones of Unit Four, projected something that flew too fast for visibility. Simultaneously the now-familiar thud of impact came vibrating down through the house's walls from somewhere upstairs.

Georgina, Caroline thought with a sudden pang. I sent her up there.

"Where's your nurse?" Albie asked, turning his head for a quick peek at Caroline again, as if a thought of the same type had just crossed his mind.

"She's dead, upstairs." The words came out colorless with urgency. "Albie, I'm going to my office. I can work with the radiophone from there, maybe I can call out for help. I'll talk to you on intercom."

But the picture on the screen kept her from leaving for a moment. As if it had been triggered by the enemy's throwing movement, a line of light, faint and red and straight as a ruler's edge, had sprung out from just below the television eye on Unit Four. The laser beam pointed straight to the intruder's still-extended throwing arm. On striking the beam bloomed into a pyrotechnic rose, while the target arm glowed white in fiery articulation. When the beam died, the structure of the machine appeared to have resisted it without damage.

"I'm going, Albie." Caroline started the job of getting the wheelchair turned around.

The look he threw back at her this time lasted a little longer. "Good luck, kid. Keep on that radiophone. Worst comes to worst, I'll come over there and see that you get out of the house."

"I can manage. Good luck," said Caroline in turn. She had her chair facing in the right direction now, and trundled it off down the hall. She passed the household robot that had followed her downstairs, and now stood waiting for orders just outside the door of the security room; maybe Albie had something in particular in mind for it.

Albie, swearing a thin steady stream under his breath at his own engrossing problems, almost forgot about Caroline the moment she was gone. He was still following the combat career of Unit Four; LASER RECHARGING said the legend now at the bottom of the screen. Albie now took over full control of Four again, and used it to charge the enemy full speed.

And now he let out a little yelp of joy, at the sight onscreen of Number Six, fully armed and running on its own programming, rolling in for a close attacking shot or maybe a wrestler's grab of the missile-throwing monster. All right, if this bandit laughed off lasers, then Albie and his team were ready to hit it with something else!

"Come on, Six!" He could hear himself shouting the words aloud, caught up in the frenzy of the fight. "Come on!"

Georgina was choking on smoke, and her fancy robe was smoldering where flames had somehow licked at it. Aided by the sprinkler system, she had managed to make quite a fight of it against the upstairs fires, but now it was looking more and more as if the fight was lost. The fire extinguisher that she had carried upstairs with her had been emptied several minutes ago, but she had remembered where another extinguisher was kept, in an inconspicuous niche in the wall near the head of the main stairway. And she had got that one, and had used it, too, to good effect. But now it too was nearly empty, and Georgina was being driven back.

She had begun her battle in Caroline's bedroom, fighting to defend Nurse Ellis's body against the spreading flames. Soon enough she had seen the pointlessness of concentrating on that effort. And by now any struggle at all on the upper level of the house was beginning to look pointless. There were fires burning simultaneously from at least three points of origin. Given the sprinklers' help, Georgina might have succeeded in containing and even extinguishing any one or two of them, but three were proving to be just too much.

Choking on smoke, firing her last burst of foam at flames that licked out at her from beneath a closed bedroom door, she fled down the burning hallway, only to come to a sudden halt at the sight of the main stairs. They were already burning, too heavily for her to try to get down them.

She knew that the other stairs, behind her, were already blocked. She was going to have to get out of one of the windows. In the back of the house, she remembered, there were windows giving onto the roof of a first-floor porch, from which it would be a fairly easy drop to the ground.

Caroline made sure of the doorway to her office with no trouble, even in the near-dark; it had been slightly widened, to accommodate a wheelchair more easily, and she wheeled straight in, the lights inside coming on automatically as she did so.

The normalcy of the place seemed to enfold her like a protective garment. There were no sprinklers in here, not with all the electronic gear; at least she wouldn't have to endure another drenching. The thought crossed her mind that her robe was still soaked, and that this might offer some last-minute protection against the spreading flames, if, as Albie had put it, the worst came to the worst. But so far as Caroline knew, the fire was still all upstairs; Georgina and sprinklers would put it out; or, yes, at worst, Albie would come to help Caroline get out of the building. She swore to herself that she was not going to be panicked, and she was going to do something useful for the cause.

The telephone wires, Caroline discovered as soon as she began to work with her control panel, were as dead as Albie had said they were. And when she switched over to radiophone operation, the receiver was immediately filled with the noise, the apparent jamming, that he had reported.

As Caroline listened, there came through a scrap of message, in a bored, official-sounding voice: "—no report on false alarms. Unable to locate caller—"

And, presently, another: "—disturbance, but no record of the call having been made—"

She started briskly trying to get her own transmission through, a call for help; but she could almost feel the words vanish into the sea of jamming.

The video eye of Number Four showed Albie the glint of distant floodlights on the rounded pyramidal shape of Number Six, as Six came closing on the intruder like a defensive back ready for a hard tackle.

But at the last moment the intruder backstepped, suddenly nimble on its columnar legs that until now had moved so slowly. Six, for all its lesser size, was now obviously the more clumsy of the two machines, as it overshot its charge and on its hidden rollers began an almost ponderous turning movement.

Albie, his soul embodied for the moment in Unit Four, was closing fast on the invader. He thought that there should be at least one more good charge left in Four's laser weapon, and he meant to use it to the best possible effect.

In the background, as he made what he hoped would be the last necessary steering correction to Four's course, he saw that which suddenly chilled his hopes: two, no, three more mechanical shapes that were not his own robots were moving now across the lawn toward the house. The shapes were too distant and too blurred with night and motion for Albie to be sure of exactly what they were, but the situation did not look good. He freed one hand momentarily from concern with Unit Four, and in a concert pianist's gesture swept it across his keyboard, calling Two, Three, and Five off station and freeing them to go into action in the back yard. The flanks of the house, where no threat had as yet appeared, were going to have to take care of themselves.

And Albie diverted the hand thus freed for one moment longer, using it to make a quick stab at the intercom, opening the circuit to Caroline's office. "Caroline?" his voice was sharp and loud; he thought too late to try to make it confident.

"Here, Albie. What's up?" To his relief, the girl sounded a long way from panic.

"We got what looks like three more machines rolling slowly up the lawn toward the house. I'm not sure we'll be able to stop 'em, but we're gonna try."

"Machines?"

"Like the one we had on screen when you were over here—more or less like that . . . is Georgina still upstairs?"

"I don't know. I've been trying to call up there on intercom, tell her to get out. I don't know if the intercom is working, or—"

"Any fire where you are?"

"I wouldn't be still sitting here. But the smoke is getting stronger, and I think I can hear flames somewhere. I'm working the radiophone as best I can, calling for help. But I don't know if I'm getting through."

Albie tried to think of what he ought to do about Caroline, and at the same time he was working to keep Four headed at the dodging foe. Four and Six still had it more or less boxed in between them, though it was able to move faster than they could when it tried . . . he knew that Caroline's wheelchair could move fairly well outside the house, because he had seen her sometimes touring the grounds in it. And of course there was the garage, he knew where the keys to the cars were kept. If he got her into a car . . . there was no way to drive off the grounds with the front gate blocked. Would the intruders attack human beings they sensed moving about on the grounds? It appeared they had been sent here to attack. Albie wasn't about to simply walk out there among them himself, not if he had a choice.

"Hang in there, kid," he called on intercom. "I'll look out for you." And wondered how he could.

Leaving his robots to manage however they could without him for a few seconds, Albie rapidly switched his screen to give him another look at the front gate. UNIT SEVEN INFRARED presented only a wash of hopeless glare; right now darkness was evidently not the problem. A touch on another switch converted the screen's lettering to UNIT SEVEN VISUAL, and the glare modified into what might almost have been a news-program shot of the bus or whatever it was still burning in the shattered gateway, where it had been wedged against the wall's stones almost at right angles to the drive.

"Still going to be nothing going out that way," Albie muttered to himself. "*Or* coming in." Now watching through his screen the continuing machine-dance on the back lawns, he called into action there his remaining units from the front, hoping that they would not be too late to do some good.

A moment later he allowed himself a grunt of satisfaction; Six had at last caught up with the original invader. Six, with its own two thin arms extended under control of its own programming, was grappling with the bigger machine fearlessly. The two like giant insects were moving in a slow dance of combat.

The invader put one of its own thick arms, not the missile-thrower, around Six. Through the microphones of Four, Albie could plainly hear the sounds of one of his guard-robots being squeezed into junk. But Albie wasn't really listening; with the intruder now virtually immobilized, he was getting Four into the close range, no more than one meter, that he wanted; and now while Six and the attacker still struggled, Four's laser was eating at last through that incredible armor. Albie was thinking now that the armor of the enemy must be at least in part ceramic, because of the incredible pyrotechnics that the laser was producing now, flakes and sparks radiating in a hundred colors from the locus of the sun-hot beam.

Then came a flash of white heat, purifying all, and with the flash a minor explosion, minor at this distance anyway, that blanked the screen and made Albie wince as the sound of it came through the speakers mounted above the indicator panel on the wall.

Four might be still functioning, as far as he could tell, except that now the video remained blank. The pictures from the other units, Six excepted, were still coming in. Four was still moving, he was sure, but he didn't know how much utility it had left.

He switched his soul and his viewpoint to Unit Two. Now, a few yards away, he could see what must be Four, fully armed but blundering blindly and probably with no laser at all left. And there was Six, still locked in a wrestler's grip with the primary invader, both machines now inert. The home team had won one point at least.

Albie took full control of Number Two and turned it around and charged it into combat across the lawn, pursuing a differently-shaped invader that was now trundling along only a few yards from the tennis courts. Trying to distract this one, he turned Two's spotlight on it, and now he could see the name of some mining corporation stenciled on its flank.

Georgina shed her smoldering robe, and climbed out onto the porch roof in nothing but slippers and the short nightgown Bob had bought her last Christmas; maybe her figure really wasn't that good anymore, but it was nice to know that he thought so anyway. The robe, when it was still wet from the now-failing sprinklers, had perhaps saved her life among the flames. But now, for jumping and climbing purposes, it was going to have to go.

The flames had driven her from the house. But she had to pause, midway through her cautious escape-scramble over the lightly sloping porch roof, to gape at what was going on out in the grounds to the rear of the house. Some of the security floodlights, that had come on automatically at the start of the evening's uproar, were still lighted out there though the poles supporting others appeared to have been knocked down. And what Georgina was able to see in the remaining illumination persuaded her instantly against trying to get away from the house by flight into or across that once peaceful, grassy expanse.

Strange shapes were moving about out there, and strange noises not human or even animal rent the night. Then she caught sight of something running on four thin legs. It was a guard dog, hobbling with its back hunched as if driven by cold instead of fear. A pencil-stab of flame came out from a machine to strike the dog, and it collapsed with an almost-human scream, the sound subsiding into a repeated squeal of agony.

There were flames already in the window through which Georgina had just climbed; to stay on the roof would soon become impossible. Scrambling again, she made her way on to the edge, clung there briefly, dropped somehow to the ground. Then she ran a few strides to cower against one of the small wooden buildings, changing rooms and utility sheds, clustered at poolside. From here she could still see the machines advancing across the lawn.

Albie left the bulk of his defense forces to struggle automatically against the invaders as best they might. Unit Two he sent racing out under his direct control toward what was left of the back fence. An idea had occurred to him for a possible counterattack, and he wanted to waste no time in trying it. He didn't think he could turn back the attacking machines otherwise, although at least the bombardment of missiles had been stopped.

He brought Two up to where a gap had been freshly torn in the boundary hedge, jockeyed the robot through the gap, and turned it. Here there was no more fence, only twisted posts and the stubs of wire conduits protruding here and there from torn-up ground. Looking behind Two's spotlight, Albie could see right down into the ravine. New trails of smashed-down trees and bush wound down that slope, or rather up it, to judge by the direction in which the plants and grass had been flattened.

His robots could never have made that climb, particularly through such a tangle of growth. But what had climbed had simply brushed all obstacles aside.

Carefully adjusting the aim of Two's spotlight, Albie could see all the way down to the freight cars on their siding. The doors of both cars were open, the interiors dark empty caverns now.

And there was the microwave gadget on its pole.

The legend at the bottom of the screen still said RE-CHARGING. It was going to take perhaps another minute to rebuild Two's laser charge enough to be able to get off one more good shot.

Caroline, still at her post in her office, had nearly despaired of ever being able to get any kind of two-way contact with police, firemen, or anyone else. She wished that the system could be set to keep on calling for help automatically, but that was one trick that Daddy's engineering crew hadn't thought of yet.

I've tried, Daddy, I've tried like hell to defend everything here, but the house is burning and if nothing else the electrical power is going to quit on me soon. It's time for me to get out.

Georgina, cowering at poolside, watched frozen with fear as one of the attacking machines lumbered past her, right up to the wall of the house, and through it. The brickwork came apart like Lego blocks. A pyramid rolled by in futile pursuit, using its laser unintelligently, to no effect but that of starting a new fire along a splintered wooden windowframe.

Caroline, Georgina thought, Caroline, get out. And then all thought of others' perils was driven from Georgina's mind. Another attacking machine came past her at only a few yards' distance; then it evidently sensed her presence somehow, for it stopped in its tracks and then turned directly toward her. It moved toward her quickly, reaching out an arm. Georgina screamed. She dodged around the shed that had been hiding her, and plunged into the water.

When she came up, a spotlight caught her, aimed from the pool's rim. A metal arm tested the deep water, and drew back. She screamed, and swam, and screamed again.

LASER RECHARGED, the screen said finally. And then, just before Albie's thumb could touch off the necessary shot, something coming from Two's blind side rammed the robot with crushing impact. There was a confused blur of bushes and night sky across the screen as the unit was knocked tumbling down the ravine's slope. Albie swore; his fist pounded the arm of his chair. Even if the robot were not wrecked, it would be hopeless to get it turned right side up again by remote control.

Caroline was just getting her wheelchair out of her office into the smoky hallway when the great crash sounded, as if something had come right through the wall of the house. Exactly what it was. She turned her head farther than she had been able to turn it in years, and saw the strange machine that had just broken through the wall now coming down the hall toward her. It was a wide hallway, and this attacker was built thinner than some of the others, it just had room.

A robot coming down the hall the other way, a clumsy household servant, somehow jammed against her chair. The chair stuck just as she tried to make it move. Maybe, she thought, Albie has sent this thing to rescue me . . . and she could feel herself starting to faint . . . don't let me black out . . . don't . . .

Albie jumped to his feet and turned, just as another machine came through the wall behind his chair. The spot-lights on it were blinding. He dimly understood that there were loudspeakers on it, shouting something about LUCIFER, and then it struck him down.

In front of the house on the quiet Los Alamos street there appeared to be spotlights everywhere now. Most of them were shining on the bullet-riddled pickup truck, whose interior machinery had at last, by gunfire, been made to stop shooting back at the police. They hadn't believed it at all when at last they had been able to look inside, to see the metal arm on the device built into a wheelchair, still holding a pistol. One policeman, gun in hand, was still glowering into impossible crevices inside the truck, looking for the human driver-gunman who must be hidden there.

So Alex observed the situation. He was standing now between Vera and Uncle Bob, all three of them with their hands against the side of the police van that had just recently arrived on the scene. Alex had hopes that he was going to be able to put his hands down soon.

"I tell you, none of *us* was doing any shooting," Uncle Bob was explaining to police. His voice was indignant, that of the perfect square upright citizen being misunderstood. He'd had the forethought, naturally, to hide his .45 back in the house before he came out here with his hands up. "*You* were shooting at the house," he admonished the cops. "We weren't shooting back."

"We weren't shooting at the house. It was this damn thing in this truck . . . Jen, can you vouch for these people?" The local patrol cops had by now testified who Jen was, of course; and Hank, who had said that he felt like throwing up, had been allowed to take shelter in a neighbor's house.

"Yes," said Jen wearily. "Yes, I can vouch for them, all of them. They were visiting me. *Now* will you let us get on a phone, or a radio, or something, and talk to Eddie MacLaurin of Labs security? He's in the hospital right now. Maybe he can explain to you that it's vital we have access to a modem right away."

"To a what? Why is that vital? What does it have to do with this?" The policeman swept an arm around. Men in flak vests and helmets, carrying rifles and shotguns, were walking in circles everywhere. Various neighbors, who somehow had never got around to being evacuated, were peering from their windows.

"I think, officer," said Uncle Bob, exercising great control, "that if you let us have access to a modem promptly, you may be instrumental in saving my daughter's life. Whereas if you don't—"

"Saving your daughter's life? Where is she?"

"She's in Atlanta right now. But—"

"Jen, you sure you know these people?"

Inside the nearest neighbors' house, the adults were busy looking out through the front windows. Meanwhile in a rear room, Hank was talking to his friend Ted. Hank had just asked if he could use the phone, and, by the way, Ted's father's modem, too.

Blond, twelve-year-old Ted looked doubtful. "Jeez, you're gonna play games now?"

"Not exactly."

"What, then?" Ted did have some flaws as a friend.

"Well, it's like something I have to talk to someone about. This program I set up."

"What for?"

Hank sighed. "Well. I wanted to get my Grandpa into a game with an old friend of his—I thought maybe if they got into the same game, they'd go back to being good friends. You know?"

"I guess." Ted sounded doubtful. "Anyway, how're you going to talk to another person with a modem?"

Hank sighed again, and just went ahead. He knew where things were in this house, he had been here often enough playing games. He set up the phone and the modem on the desk of Ted's father, who of course worked at the Labs. Then Hank flipped on the Apple home computer; different from his own rebuilt TRS-80, but again, he had been here before.

Soon the weird ready-signal tone of the Cray-4 was coming through the modem.

"Jeez," said Ted reverently. "How'd you do that? Show me?"

OCTAGON, Hank typed. JOYOUS GARD. LUCIFER IS NOW AN ALLY. ALL PLAYERS ARE NOW ALLIED WITH OCTAGON.

JOYOUS GARD.
Suddenly he could feel tears start down his face.

Caroline was aware that, somewhere above and beyond
her swoon, the household robot sent to defend her was being
punched and pushed aside. Then a great metal arm, that of
the intruding machine, came to pluck her up tenderly from
her stalled wheelchair. A burning wall was elbowed aside.
Crash, and crash, and now around her the fresh air of freedom. There were stars, and she could breathe, and she was
alive.

The burning house was empty of human life.

All the speakers of the house intercom came on. "You are
an al-ly, LU-CIFER," they said.

—Fred Saberhagen
Albuquerque
Christmas Eve, 1980

MORE ABOUT PENGUINS, PELICANS
AND PUFFINS

For further information about books available from Penguins please write to Dept EP, Penguin Books Ltd, Harmondsworth, Middlesex UB7 0DA.

In the U.S.A.: For a complete list of books available from Penguins in the United States write to Dept DG, Penguin Books, 299 Murray Hill Parkway, East Rutherford, New Jersey 07073.

In Canada: For a complete list of books available from Penguins in Canada write to Penguin Books Canada Ltd, 2801 John Street, Markham, Ontario L3R 1B4.

In Australia: For a complete list of books available from Penguins in Australia write to the Marketing Department, Penguin Books Australia Ltd, P.O. Box 257, Ringwood, Victoria 3134.

In New Zealand: For a complete list of books available from Penguins in New Zealand write to the Marketing Department, Penguin Books (N.Z.) Ltd, Private Bag, Takapuna, Auckland 9.

In India: For a complete list of books available from Penguins in India write to Penguin Overseas Ltd, 706 Eros Apartments, 56 Nehru Place, New Delhi 110019.

Also by Fred Saberhagen in Penguins

BERSERKER

No one knew where berserkers came from. Everyone knew what they had come for.

They were mechanical killers; their brain a computer programmed to destroy all forms of life. And Berserkers were illogical. The random disintegration of atoms could select any one of infinite means of destruction. Already planet after planet had been pounded into steam and dust.

Only one kind of being could beat the Berserker. A race whose whole history has been spent developing more powerful weapons. A race conditioned to throw away their lives for the title 'hero'.

The race was called man.

THE PENGUIN
SCIENCE FICTION OMNIBUS
Edited by Brian Aldiss

The biggest, most exciting collection of science-fiction stories ever! Including stories from such masters as Harry Harrison, Isaac Asimov, Frederick Pohl, Arthur C. Clarke, C. M. Kornbluth, James Blish, Clifford Simak, J. G. Ballard and many more . . . Selected and introduced by Brian Aldiss

THE GOLDEN AGE OF
SCIENCE FICTION
Edited by Kingsley Amis

Selected by a Master of Science Fiction
Seventeen stunning S.F. Classics

Locating the genre's zenith in the years 1949–62, Kingsley Amis's 'golden age' contains some of science fiction's greatest names.

In their astounding imaginative range the writers celebrated here brilliantly illustrate Amis's view that 'what they wrote was far more inventive, more fictional, fictitious, fictive than any ordinary kind of fiction'.

Enter a new and magical realm with Penguins

THIEVES' WORLD

Edited by Robert Asprin

Sword-play and Sorcery . . . Murder, Mayhem and Mystery!

Thieves' World is what happened when the world's top science fiction and fantasy writers got together to create the amazing new world of *Sanctuary* where you will mix and mingle with *Lythal the Star-browed*: his magic is questionable, his sword-play not. *Jubal*: ex-gladiator and slave, now a respected citizen (he made his money selling slaves). *One Thumb*: the crooked bartender at the Vulgar Unicorn . . . and even more fantastic characters!

And the Second Collection in this unique anthology series

TALES FROM THE VULGAR UNICORN

Edited by Robert Asprin

Continuing the fantastic fictional game begun in *Thieves' World'* here is a second collection of stories set in the amazing city of *Sanctuary*, where you can enjoy the quiet elegance of Ambrosia House; sample bizarre pleasures at the House of Whips; sip ale in the Vulgar Unicorn, and listen to some of the most strange, dangerous, magical and deadly tales ever told.

Lynn Abbey, Poul Anderson, Robert Asprin, John Brunner, David Drake, Philip José Farmer, Joe Haldeman, Janet Morris, Andrew J. Offut, and *A. E. Van Vogt* – have dreamed up a world of wonders – a fabulous reading adventure!

Also published in Penguins

THE 'SINCLAIR USER' BOOK
OF GAMES AND PROGRAMS FOR THE SPECTRUM

Sixty challenging games and programs from *Sinclair User*, the best-selling magazine for the Spectrum.

Protect your castle from invading soldiers in *Siege*; test your sense of three-dimensional direction in *Labyrinth*; improve your geography with *Mapwork*; face Mr Spec Trum on the Centre Court at *Wimbledon*; have your own *Cricket* Test Match at Lord's; jump a clear round at *Olympia*; play *Noughts and Crosses* against the computer; send a submarine to Davy Jones's locker in *Depth Charge*; take a crash typing course in *Touch Type*; stop an atomic power station going 'critical' in *Overload*; and much, much more.

This exciting book offers a wide variety of games, including ingenious versions of arcade favourites and interactive adventures. Educational programs are also listed in the book, all of which will help readers to learn how to program in *Basic*.

COMPUTER BITS AND PIECES
A Compendium of Curiosities
Geoff Simons

Have you heard of computers? They have certainly heard of you . . .

You are probably filed away somewhere in the electronic bowels of some machine working for the national banks, the social security department . . . or the police. However, the talents of computers are not solely confined to checking up on you; they can be imaginative poets, wizards at chemical analysis, writers of thrillers, creative mathematicians and world-champion games players. The present day sees robots that climb stairs, work in libraries, dust furniture and play cards.

Informative, amusing and entertaining, this delightful – and somewhat disturbing – book lights upon the wide-ranging activities of these intelligent machines and provides a fascinating insight into modern technology.

A CHOICE OF PENGUINS

☐ **Small World** David Lodge £2.50

A jet-propelled academic romance, sequel to *Changing Places*. 'A new comic débâcle on every page' – *The Times*. 'Here is everything one expects from Lodge but three times as entertaining as anything he has written before' – *Sunday Telegraph*

☐ **The Neverending Story** Michael Ende £3.50

The international bestseller, now a major film: 'A tale of magical adventure, pursuit and delay, danger, suspense, triumph' – *The Times Literary Supplement*

☐ **The Sword of Honour Trilogy** Evelyn Waugh £3.95

Containing *Men at Arms, Officers and Gentlemen* and *Unconditional Surrender*, the trilogy described by Cyril Connolly as 'unquestionably the finest novels to have come out of the war'.

☐ **The Honorary Consul** Graham Greene £1.95

In a provincial Argentinian town, a group of revolutionaries kidnap the wrong man . . . 'The tension never relaxes and one reads hungrily from page to page, dreading the moment it will all end' – Auberon Waugh in the *Evening Standard*

☐ **The First Rumpole Omnibus** John Mortimer £4.95

Containing *Rumpole of the Bailey*, *The Trials of Rumpole* and *Rumpole's Return*. 'A fruity, foxy masterpiece, defender of our wilting faith in mankind' – *Sunday Times*

☐ **Scandal** A. N. Wilson £2.25

Sexual peccadillos, treason and blackmail are all ingredients on the boil in A. N. Wilson's new, *cordon noir* comedy. 'Drily witty, deliciously nasty' – *Sunday Telegraph*

A CHOICE OF PENGUINS

☐ **Stanley and the Women** **Kingsley Amis** £2.50

'Very good, very powerful . . . beautifully written . . . This is Amis *père* at his best' – Anthony Burgess in the *Observer*. 'Everybody should read it' – *Daily Mail*

☐ **The Mysterious Mr Ripley** **Patricia Highsmith** £4.95

Containing *The Talented Mr Ripley, Ripley Underground* and *Ripley's Game*. 'Patricia Highsmith is the poet of apprehension' – Graham Greene. 'The Ripley books are marvellously, insanely readable' – *The Times*

☐ **Earthly Powers** **Anthony Burgess** £4.95

'Crowded, crammed, bursting with manic erudition, garlicky puns, omnilingual jokes . . . (a novel) which meshes the real and personalized history of the twentieth century' – Martin Amis

☐ **Life & Times of Michael K** **J. M. Coetzee** £2.95

The Booker Prize-winning novel: 'It is hard to convey . . . just what Coetzee's special quality is. His writing gives off whiffs of Conrad, of Nabokov, of Golding, of the Paul Theroux of *The Mosquito Coast*. But he is none of these, he is a harsh, compelling new voice' – Victoria Glendinning

☐ **The Stories of William Trevor** £5.95

'Trevor packs into each separate five or six thousand words more richness, more laughter, more ache, more multifarious human-ness than many good writers manage to get into a whole novel' – *Punch*

☐ **The Book of Laughter and Forgetting**
   Milan Kundera £3.95

'A whirling dance of a book . . . a masterpiece full of angels, terror, ostriches and love . . . No question about it. The most important novel published in Britain this year' – Salman Rushdie

A CHOICE OF PENGUINS

☐ **The Philosopher's Pupil** Iris Murdoch £2.95

'We are back, of course, with great delight, in the land of Iris Murdoch, which is like no other but Prospero's . . .' – *Sunday Telegraph*. And, as expected, her latest masterpiece is 'marvellous . . . compulsive reading, hugely funny' – *Spectator*

☐ **A Good Man in Africa** William Boyd £2.50

Boyd's brilliant, award-winning frolic featuring Morgan Leafy, overweight, oversexed representative of Her Britannic Majesty in tropical Kinjanja. 'Wickedly funny' – *The Times*

These books should be available at all good bookshops or newsagents, but if you live in the UK or the Republic of Ireland and have difficulty in getting to a bookshop, they can be ordered by post. Please indicate the titles required and fill in the form below.

NAME_____ BLOCK CAPITALS

ADDRESS_____•_____

_____

_____

Enclose a cheque or postal order payable to The Penguin Bookshop to cover the total price of books ordered, plus 50p for postage. Readers in the Republic of Ireland should send £IR equivalent to the sterling prices, plus 67p for postage. Send to: The Penguin Bookshop, 54/56 Bridlesmith Gate, Nottingham, NG1 2GP.

You can also order by phoning (0602) 599295, and quoting your Barclaycard or Access number.

Every effort is made to ensure the accuracy of the price and availability of books at the time of going to press, but it is sometimes necessary to increase prices and in these circumstances retail prices may be shown on the covers of books which may differ from the prices shown in this list or elsewhere. This list is not an offer to supply any book.

This order service is only available to residents in the UK and the Republic of Ireland.

● ● ●